KISS OF DEATH

SICARIUS SECURITY BOOK 1

SUSAN HARRIS

sicarius
security

ISBN: **978-1-63422-423-9** (paperback)
ISBN: **978-1-63422-422-2** (e-book)
Cover Design by: Marya Heidel
Typography by: Gem Promotions
Editing by: Chris Kridler

DEDICATION

This book is dedicated to my parents,
who to my knowledge, have never tried to kill me.

And my brother,
who pushed me out of a moving car when I was a child,
and still denies it to this day!

FOREWORD

Memento mori
"Remember that you have to die."
Malakai Cavanagh

Illegitimi non carborundum
"Don't let the bastards get you down."
Keeva Cross

CHAPTER ONE

Malakai

SOMEONE WAS GOING TO DIE SOON AND PAINFULLY SO.

Malakai Cavanagh's face gave none of his murderous intentions away as he regarded the other members of the council of elders. They had been debating the issue for hours now and were no closer to an amicable conclusion. Each member might have an equal vote; however, the different species, some of whom had been at war with certain clans since the dawn of time itself.

"The shifters are complaining that the security contract should have gone to them rather than the vampires."

Malakai regarded Duncan, alpha of the shifter clans, with an incline of his head. "Sicarius Security won the bid fair and square. This was not a power play. Had your people made it clear that you were also in for the contract, we would have backed off. We filed the necessary paperwork with the council. As far as we were aware, we were the only Inferna in the running."

"Malakai is right," the high elder stated, and Malakai leaned back in his chair. "His lawyer filed the paperwork as per the rules and announced their intention to bid. The shifters did not. Perhaps you need to teach the pups to follow the rules rather than focusing on trying to get a one-up on the vampires."

Duncan growled softly but refrained from saying another word because he knew that his people had been underhanded in their attempts to win the security contract for their respective companies. The very reason the company that Malakai ran with members of his Kiss excelled was that they always covered their bases. His night-blooded brother, Ezekiel, was a stickler for having everything just right, and Malakai loved him for it.

The contract that they had secured was to test the security for a number of military facilities and see if they could be bypassed. It was worth millions to Sicarius and would mean they would need to hire some new employees who could work during the day.

Having a vampire burning to death in the sun would be a sure-fire way to make the little humans aware that the Inferna existed right on their doorstep and would definitely be frowned upon.

The Inferna was the name given to the supernatural community. Whether you were vampire, shifter, witch, fae or anything in between, you were a member of the Inferna. That meant obeying a strict number of rules enforced by the Elders, himself included.

Vampires were allowed only one sanctioned kill a month, though it was generally preferred that feeding related kills didn't happen. Shifters would only hunt on pack lands and animals owned by themselves. Violence against another clan was forbidden unless under the rarest of circumstances, and even then, all disputes had to be brought before the Elders.

This was how peace had reigned for so long, because most of the Inferna were predators who looked like every other human in the world and if let off the leash, humans would die. It was just the way of their kind.

The meeting wrapped up shortly, and they were dismissed, Duncan storming off to bark orders into his phone. Malakai buttoned up his suit and donned his shades, striding out of the Elder chambers and heading for the underground car park. He unlocked his beloved Aston Martin DB9 and slid into the black leather seats. Of all the cars he owned, this was his favourite because it was a present from the members of his Kiss. They had bought this for him, customized with everything he always wanted, and given it to him as a gift.

Malakai spoke into the car's Bluetooth as he fired up the engine and steered his way out of the car park and into the night.

"Jasmine's house of delinquents, how may I direct your call?"

Malakai chuckled, rolling his eyes as he said, "Jazz, you gotta stop answering the phone like that. What if I was a client?"

"Give me some credit, Kai. I knew it was you."

Of course she did. Even if there hadn't been caller ID on the phone, Jasmine had a gift for seeing the future. The only member of the Kiss that he was related to by blood, his sister had been a powerful seer when she was human, even more so since becoming a vampire. That secret of premonition was well guarded between the senior members of Sicarius Security because there were collectors out there that would love to lock someone like Jazz in a cage.

It was what they had done to their other brother before he died.

Shaking away memories of the past, Malakai flicked on his signal and headed for the ramp that would take him deep into Cork's city and the apartment complex that not only was their business base but also their family quarters. "I've put an ad on the Inferna web looking for candidates. We need recruits for this new project, Jazz. Can you work with Dylan to set up the interviews?"

"You know I'm not your PA, right? Maybe you should add that to the jobs you're hiring for and let me get back to doing what I do best."

There was no bite in his sister's tone, yet Malakai knew that Jasmine was right. Business was picking up, and he needed someone to manage him and his time. At the moment, he, Jasmine, Ezekiel and Dylan were running things and trying to juggle too many responsibilities. And Jazz was right; they had another job that required a fair amount of their time.

When they had first decided to build up Sicarius Security, it was to be a legitimate front for their activities. But under the world's number one security consultancy agency, the members of his Kiss were cold-blooded assassins. They travelled the world and rid the Inferna community of those whose actions could lead to humans discovering that every single day the chances of them standing beside an Inferna was likely.

So he and his family took contracts on such creatures: the murderous, the sadists, those who would harm women and children. They stalked and studied their prey before making a kill to ensure that the person who petitioned the contract was being truthful. Sometimes, they even took a kill pro bono, for his entire Kiss took pleasure in taking the life of any fucking animal who harmed little children.

Malakai had been twenty-five when vampires had stormed his village and raped and murdered entire families. He and Dylan had managed to hide Jasmine, who had been barely fifteen at the time, from the onslaught. Being the Celtic warriors they had been, they fought back even as other members of their clan were being slaughtered. The vampires decided that they needed fighters just like them, so Malakai and Dylan were spared and had been changed.

Bloodlust had consumed them in the first few years, and Malakai had pushed Jasmine from his mind. He was an emotionless monster until he was strong enough to break away and went in search of Jasmine, if only to know she was still alive.

But it was his sister that had found him a decade later, no longer the sweet, innocent teen. Jasmine had shown up dressed as a warrior with a bloody sword, now the same age as he had been when he was turned, and demanded that Malakai make her a vampire. He and Dylan had argued for days about her request, but when her eyes flashed white, her tone advising that it was her destiny to be a vampire, they had known there was little choice.

Jasmine's visions were never wrong.

"Stop thinking of the past, my brother. We are exactly where we are meant to be."

Malakai blew out a breath, knowing that Jasmine was right. Switching lanes, he edged the car into traffic, not unusual for early evening as the nightclubs opened. Glancing at the clock and knowing full well that they had spent all the hours they could to secure the lucrative contract, he asked Jasmine to check on the one vampire they all worried about.

Ezekiel Collins was what TV shows like *The Vampire Diaries* called a ripper, a vampire who could not handle his thirst for blood. A young man when he was changed, Zeke was a novice priest about to take his vows when the monastery was attacked, and because of his build and his strength, they cursed him, as Zeke liked to say, and he became a demon.

It was Zeke who had awoken from the change and slain all his fellow priests. He could not sate the hunger. Even when he had sought out his family, they, so deeply religious themselves, had tried to exorcise the demons from him, and the vampire still bore the scars and burns. Most he now punctuated with tattoos.

"I knocked a while ago and asked if he wanted to join us for dinner before I headed for my shift at the club, but he shooed me away. He was playing with the cross again. I could smell the burnt flesh."

Noting the worry in her tone as Jasmine answered his silent question, Malakai murmured that he would talk to him before he disconnected the call and headed to the company's underground private car park.

Sicarius Security had been built near the Port of Cork, Malakai and the consortium having purchased a vast amount of land to have access to the city but also be private enough not to attract too much attention. The building had speciality glass that kept the sun at bay from the ground all the way up including the top six floors, which were his and his family's living quarters. Each member had a floor to themselves, with a communal dining area, gym and entertainment space separating the business from the personal floors. The bold Sicarius Security logo was embossed on the glass doors as you entered the building, a sleek black background and an S that Dylan had designed himself.

Parking the Aston Martin next to Jasmine's yellow Mini Cooper, Malakai locked the car before he headed to the elevator and pressed for the tenth floor. He hummed along to the soft rock playing in the elevator. Unbuttoning his jacket, Malakai loosened his tie and popped open the top button. Closing his eyes, Malakai leaned his head against the glass until the doors pinged just before they opened.

His sister was standing on the other side, a warm smile on her face as she swept her golden hair off her face and into a high ponytail. Apart from the little hint of fang when Jazz grinned at him, his sister could pass for any twenty something, fresh out of college. Sometimes, Jasmine seemed like the most human of them all, and maybe that was why she liked working at their other venture so much.

Sicarius Security had their hands in a lot of businesses worldwide, but in Cork they owned and ran a bar and nightclub called Dante's. By day, they served food and drink in the downstairs bar, and by night, upstairs became one of the city's most sought after venues that had humans queuing to get in. Humans and supernatural mingled here, the former having no clue that the Inferna community danced side by side with them. Sicarius was well known in the Inferna community, and any who dared to breach the rules and cause harm to a human was met with swift consequences, entirely sanctioned by the council.

And whilst recreational fun was encouraged, there had not been any Inferna stupid enough to draw the attention of any of Malakai's vampires or security staff.

Jasmine loved it there, and even though tonight had been Zeke's turn to take a shift, they regularly swapped shifts with each other, so as his sister wore a tee with the club's name embossed across the chest, another of Dylan's designs, his artist impression of a firepit where they had decided to be more than mere merchantries, a tight pair of leggings and killer heels that made her just as tall as his six feet, it appeared that Jazz was covering for Zeke … again.

When they had been human, no one would have believed that they were blood-related. Jasmine had sunny hair with blue eyes and the same disposition. Malakai had dark chestnut hair with brown eyes. In their clan, it has been common for the wives of the families to sleep with the chieftain, so in truth they were half-siblings, but Jasmine not only had to deal with Malakai's protective nature but that of her other half-brother as well.

"Gotta run, Kai. Dylan is trying to get Zeke out of his library, but I think Dylan is going to end up with a concussion before the sun rises. I mean, the testosterone is—"

Jazz broke off mid-sentence as her eyes rolled back in her head and shifted from blue to complete white. "Death's kiss comes for you. Flames seeking to burn the Primus. It is the beginning. Beware."

Jasmine staggered, and Malakai grabbed her arm to stop her from falling. Her hands were trembling as her eyes closed, and when they reopened, Malakai was looking into her pale blue eyes once more.

"Any idea what that was about?"

"It's not like these visions come with an instruction guide."

Malakai called out for Dylan, who strode out of Zeke's safe haven. His best friend was grinning even as he wiped blood from the corner of his mouth, his blond hair pulled back in a ponytail. He raised his brows. Dylan's own eyes were the same pale blue as Jasmine's with just a hint of green. They shared the same father and were easily mistaken as twins.

"Take Jasmine's shift at Dante's tonight."

"Kai." Jazz sighed hard, and he knew she was about to argue with him. "I'm fine. I've worked before and after having visions. I'm sure you can persuade Dylan to come with me so he can get his slut on."

"I resent that perfectly good assumption, little sister."

Malakai held Jasmine's gaze for a minute and then said, "Any sign that you are unwell, and you tell Dylan. No arguments."

"Yes, Optimus Primus," Jazz retorted with a salute as she dragged Dylan into the elevator before the doors closed. If Jazz was joking, then she was fine, even if he did worry. Yet Malakai would indeed heed the warning given to him by Jasmine. They all would.

Striding into the kitchen, he pulled a beer from the fridge as he called Zeke's name. Even though the vampire was in his library, Malakai knew that Zeke would not ignore his call. The door to the library opened a moment later, and Zeke came across the room before stopping to rest his hip on the counter with his arms folded across his chest.

Ezekiel Collins was scary to look at, and Dylan once remarked that had he been successful and been ordained a priest, he would have scared the bejesus out of any congregation.

Zeke stood at nearly seven feet, and his face looked mean. A scar in the shape of a small cross marred his lip. His eyes were so dark they were almost pitch black. His skin was pale, deathly so, and the tattoos that wrapped around his neck made him look like a serial killer, which was accurate as well as a contradiction to the mild-mannered man he could be.

Contrary to some TV shows, while vampires were in a sense dead, after ingesting blood, their hearts could beat, air could fill their lungs, and sometimes, they could even take a piss. But once the blood left their system, they returned to the undead version just like Zeke. Once blood ran through your veins, every part of your anatomy worked. Sadly for his kind, though, it did not mean there would be any little vampires running around.

"You need to feed."

It was a statement that held a slight command that had Zeke shifting his weight. Malakai might not be the vampire that made Zeke, but he had been the first vampire strong enough to influence the cravings and have Zeke see clearly.

"I'm fine," came Zeke's grunted response.

Malakai lifted his brows at Zeke's gruff tone as he opened the fridge for another beer and held a second out to Zeke. The vampire shook his head until Malakai forced the bottle into his hands. He needed Zeke to be relaxed if he was going to have this argument with him again. Zeke had earned the name of "The Monk" by the Inferna assassin community because of his clean living, so to speak.

"You are pale as death, my brother. I can get Jazz to pick up a human and bring him home … we can't have you on a hair trigger for violence when I'm interviewing for assistants."

"I'm fine," the man grunted, but there was no conviction in his tone.

Malakai broke his beer bottle on the counter and slit his wrist. Zeke's eyes went molten silver as he surged forward and took the vein offered to him by his Primus, his leader. Then after three pulls at the vein, Zeke jerked back and stalked away from Malakai.

With Malakai being Zeke's Primus, the power in his blood would help keep Zeke alive, but unless Zeke fed from a living, breathing human, Malakai's blood, which included the blood of the human he drank from last night, was far too diluted to sustain Zeke. It also did not appeal to the monster that lurked inside Zeke, the only reason the other vampire was able to stop himself.

"That little taste will do nothing to sate the hunger, Ezekiel. And you cannot spend your time hiding away in that library of yours. This may not be the life you have chosen, but it is the one you are living."

Zeke said nothing as he headed back into the library, ignoring Malakai's words as he closed the door with an audible click that told Malakai that the conversation was over. Malakai strode to the glass window and watched the city lights twinkle and blaze with the heartbeats that walked through it.

They were all worried about Zeke. While Sicarius Security took out those who might be reckless enough to expose the Inferna to the human world, all three of them were aware that Zeke posed one of the most credible threats to the fragile peace accords. He, Dylan, and especially Jasmine worked hard to try and humanize Zeke as best they could. Malakai forced him to attend meetings where legal advice was needed, even though he was almost as good as Zeke. Dylan forced Zeke to go to every single superhero movie with him. Jasmine played the weak girl routine and had Zeke do everything from change her tyres to helping her with her shopping. They all worked hard to try and get Zeke to live his life. But his blooded brother had so many demons, had killed so many people because of bloodlust, that they all feared he would never be normal.

They sated his monster by sending him after the vilest of creatures. Those who defiled children. It was only after nights where he had bathed in blood that Zeke emerged from his self-imposed exile and they all saw who Zeke could be.

It was quite possible that a permanent solution to Zeke

would have to be voted on soon, and that was not something that Malakai wanted to worry about right now.

His thoughts drifted back to Jasmine's vision. Tensions had been brewing within the supernatural community; however, Malakai didn't think any of the other species would be so stupid as to try and take out the Primus of the vampires. He ruled all vampires in Ireland and even had some in Europe.

Some thought it wrong that he was not only Primus but CEO of Sicarius Security. Some felt that the vampires had too much of a strong hold within Cork and even Ireland. While vampires were made, most supernatural creatures were born, and some clans had dwindling numbers.

If the vampires wanted to rule, all they needed to do was change thousands of humans and they would have an army. The Inferna seemed to want to ignore the fact that Malakai had changed but a few humans in all the centuries he had been immortal and those were extreme circumstances.

But if death was lurking and it was coming for him, Malakai would be ready. Sometimes the Inferna community saw his expensive suits and calm demeanour and forgot that he was a lethal assassin, a Sicarius who liked to kill as much as the next vampire.

Should death come calling, he would answer the door with a smile on his lips and murder in his eyes.

CHAPTER TWO

Keeva

"WHERE THE HELL ARE YOU OFF TO DRESSED LIKE A NUN?"

Keeva Cross grinned at her roommate's outraged face while she teased the succubus, and Scarlett glanced down at her ensemble with a frown. "It's a job interview, Keeva, not a party. This is how I always dress."

Now that was a hella true statement. Scarlett, despite her species, tended to dress very conventionally, and while her kin might make their livings wearing little or no clothing, Scarlett couldn't even walk through a lingerie shop without being scandalized. She wouldn't even venture out shopping unless Keeva was with her. Not that Keeva had as many colour options to go with red hair and freckles …

Jumping up from their well-worn couch, Keeva reached out and popped two buttons on the blouse. "Not that you are like any normal succubus and go to parties. Who did you say the interview was with?"

Scarlett buttoned up one button, her fingers hesitating on the second one before she dropped her hands to her hips. "It's for a personal assistant job to Malakai Cavanagh at Sicarius Security."

Keeva whistled as she sank back down on the couch, tossing her Irish red hair off her shoulders. "Scar, that's a seriously big deal. You are perfect for the job."

Scarlett flashed her a grateful smile that made Keeva curse the members of Scarlett's Seduction. The Seduction—a group of succubi and incubi—had been so critical of Scarlett and her "affliction" that the young woman had been forced to go it alone and fend for herself, having only minimal contact with her own species.

Succubi were overtly confident in their sexuality, training that way from their teens. Nothing at all phased them. They worked as anything from strippers to high-end escorts that brought in thousands of euros a night for an hour or two. Not that many men complained about spending a night with a sex demon. And then there was the anomaly of Scarlett.

Keeva had met Scarlett in a club one night as her friend tried to feed off the sexual energy from the club-goers with a blush on her face to rival the colour of her own hair and tears in her eyes. Seems ludicrous, right? A succubus who gets embarrassed by sex. Keeva had instantly felt a kinship with the girl because she knew all too well what it was like to be ousted by your own family.

Scarlett slipped her feet into her heels and twirled when asked to do so. Keeva gave her an expression showing she approved. Her roommate was absolutely gorgeous, even if she didn't think so. With curves that Keeva envied, Scarlett had ample cleavage and an hourglass figure that had men and women panting after her. Onyx-black hair was straight and cut at her shoulders, but now she wore it up in a very respectable bun.

Scarlett had big wide eyes the colour of the ocean, lips that seemed to be in a constant pout, and her skin was that creamy sort of porcelain that looked like she had bathed in milk for days. Keeva knew in a room where they both stood, eyes would go to Scarlett first, even if the succubus had little confidence.

Dressed now in an A-line skirt that kissed her knees, a crisp blue blouse that brightened her eyes and a blazer that all screamed *I'm respectable,* her friend chewed on her bottom lip.

"Keep biting your lip like that, and maybe one of the bloodsuckers will decide to take a bite out of you. Oh, maybe you'll get to live out your fantasy about being bent over a desk and being royally f—"

"Keeva!" Scarlett let loose a shocked exclamation as her cheeks reddened.

"Hey, I'm just saying. You look good, girlfriend. You got this."

With a little humph, Scarlett collected her purse and asked Keeva what her plans were for the evening.

"I've gotta go see Angus about a gig."

Scarlett froze, halting with her hand on the front door of their little apartment. She made to speak, but Keeva held up her hand.

"It's okay. I can see the finish line, and once I'm done, you and me are gonna go on a nice beach holiday where we can have sun, sea, sand and … sangria. And you can pay since you are going to be rolling in the money once you get your new job."

Scarlett waved at her with a roll of her eyes, and then she was gone, leaving Keeva alone in the apartment. It wasn't much, but it was theirs. Keeva had purchased the apartment after a big payout for a side job, and it meant she could finally move out of the housing complex that all banshees resided in.

The apartment was a small two-bedroom with an open-plan kitchen and living area. There had been times when Keeva hated living here all alone, but when Scarlett moved in, Keeva finally knew what it was like to have a friend, a sister.

Checking her watch, Keeva got up and grabbed her camo print jacket and threw it over her battered Nirvana tee. Dressed in black jeans and sleek black trainers, Keeva smirked as she considered what Angus would do if she walked in dressed like Scarlett.

Grabbing the keys to her ten-year-old Volkswagen Golf, Keeva considered taking a weapon with her to the banshee headquarters, then decided against it because, well, she already was a weapon.

After she had locked up the apartment and jogged down the steps to the car park, Keeva unlocked her car and prayed that the thing started. It took three attempts to get it going. Keeva blessed herself as the car edged out of the car park and into traffic. She drove the short distance tapping her fingers along to the music.

Angus McFergus—the leader of their Scream, the name for a group of banshees—was as pretentious as his name sounded and considered Keeva the bane of his existence. And perhaps she was, considering that Keeva was the reason why his only daughter was dead.

Keeva was born a banshee or Bean Sidhe, a breed of supernatural creatures known to predict death and, once predicted, helped to usher the spirits of the dead to the realm of the dead. Back in the old days, banshees only predicted the deaths of certain families, but marriage with other clans meant that their range had expanded more and more.

A lucrative business, was death. You would be amazed at how many immortal creatures sat and thought about their death. It would appear that the higher up you were on the immortal food chain, the more you contemplated your own demise. It must be nice, however, to sit on your gold-encrusted chairs and stare at your priceless tasteless artefacts and know today was not your day to die.

Mythology, as it had about so many supernatural creatures, had some of its facts wrong. A banshee didn't have to scream or wail to predict a death. Their ancestors were dramatic fools who created the misconception of the legend, and now, every time Keeva introduced herself as a banshee, they asked her to scream.

Usually, it was Keeva that made other people scream.

Keeva's mother had been human as far as Keeva knew, had not known what to do with a supernatural child, and had handed her over to Angus to be reared. Then her mother had been killed by the Elders in order to maintain the order and balance of the Inferna. Keeva's father had also been killed for telling her mother about the Inferna and his name erased from all records. She didn't even know their names. The origins of her gift were unknown. Keeva had grown up with Angus's daughter, Clodagh, a very powerful banshee who had already been signed to a contract to marry and predict deaths for a Russian corporation.

Angus thought Keeva a dud, a banshee with no powers of prediction. It wasn't until she was fifteen and she killed Clodagh that Angus realized what a monster she was.

Sneaking out of the country estate where Angus lived, Keeva and Clodagh raced through the forest until they could see the ocean that they could hear from the estate. It was their favourite place to disappear to, imagining that one day a ship would come and take them away from their lives and they would ride the waves and be pirates.

They had been walking along the cliffside when Keeva heard the ground move and Clodagh let loose a scream of terror. Keeva raced forward as Clodagh disappeared from view. Screaming her name, Keeva crawled to the edge as Clodagh gripped the grassy embankment for dear life.

Keeva reached out as her adrenaline spiked, power coursing through her as she lost control of the power that she and Clodagh had kept hidden for years.

"Keeva! Help me!"

Keeva reached for her best friend, then snatched her hand back as Clodagh's eyes widened.

"Keeva, save me," Clodagh begged, and Keeva had to at least try.

Keeva reached out and grabbed her friend by the wrists, using all of her strength to drag her up over the cliff even as her power seeped from her fingers and Clodagh jerked, screaming at the agony ripping her apart, even when Keeva yanked her hands away.

Clodagh's body spasmed as she seized, foam in her mouth as her eyes clashed with Keeva's, and then she simply stilled. Angus wailed as he came up to where they were, taking his daughter in his arms.

Keeva cried, her silver tears staining her face. She held out her hands as one of the banshees tried to drag her away. Keeva slipped in the grass, and her fingers grazed the man's arm. His screams of pain rang out as he dropped to the ground dead a second later.

No one tried to touch her again after that.

Blinking away the memories, ones that were decades old, Keeva spotted a free space and yanked the wheel hard to fit her little car in before anyone else tried to take it. Glancing up at the nondescript building that stated the company was an analytics company, Keeva squared her shoulders, crossed the road and marched inside.

In order to know exactly what the banshee's headquarters was like, you had to think of a call centre with hundreds of employees. The moment Keeva put in the code and entered the ground floor building, she could hear all the chatter and the noise from the main contact centre where clients would call in and price plans. Some could only afford the basic, like house insurance or health insurance. It was as easy as signing up on a new mobile phone plan.

These ones would have an initial phone consultation and then an experienced predicter would go to their place of work or home and give a prediction. Banshees were never wrong in their prediction of death.

Those who oozed money bypassed the initial call centre monotony. They were assigned the best of the best, and that banshee only dealt with their client exclusively. It was like portfolio management. In a way, Keeva was happy to have avoided this kind of work because she would have been bored to death—pun intended.

Keeva walked down the hallway, conscious that people avoided her gaze and glanced at the floor, careful not to come within touching distance. Keeva might have been in her sixth decade, appearing as if she were in her twenties, had managed to learn some semblance of control over her death touch, however, if she lost control, let her guard down, the chances were she would get complacent and her touch would kill.

It had happened once, when she had fallen in love in her twenties, and after lots of heavy petting on both their parts, Keeva thought she could risk sex with him, but the moment she let go, Keeva had grabbed his arms and Craig had died.

She knew never to risk it again. Sex became just one of those things she did in order to sate her body's needs. She never got to touch.

Striding right past the secretary and into Angus's office, Keeva stood just shy of his desk as he ended his phone call and looked at Keeva with open contempt. She didn't blame him, really. After all, her actions had killed his daughter.

Angus McFergus was older than dirt, at least that's how he always appeared to Keeva, with a mean streak even if he looked like a man in his fifth decade instead of the couple of hundred years he was. When he discovered what Keeva could do, he blamed the small number of human genes in her for the fact that Keeva didn't predict death, she dealt it.

Angus was a shrewd businessman, and instead of condemning her to death, having locked her in darkness for two years, he offered her a bargain, as if he were offering a plea deal. One hundred years of servitude to kill those Angus told her to, with the ability to knock years off depending on the mark. A month later, she had killed her first mark intentionally.

Over the years, Keeva learned how to fight, to defend herself without having to touch someone. She was the banshee assassin or Death, as the Inferna liked to call her on official records. She meditated, she studied hard, and now, she didn't need her touch to kill someone.

In the time Keeva had spent as Angus's pet assassin, with every kill she had shaved five years off her sentence. Keeva was proud that she was down to twenty years now, which meant four more kills and she was done. Angus thought because he kept her fairly poor financially that he could persuade her to continue working jobs for him and whoever gave him the contracts.

But she had been doing side jobs for decades, careful to hide her money away until Keeva was free of Angus and the rest of the banshees. That money had dwindled once she had bought the apartment and paid the bills, but once she could take jobs at her discretion, she could earn enough to keep her and Scarlett safe. There was a reason why she was drawn to Scarlett; she was an outcast, just like Keeva.

"Ms. Cross."

"Angus."

Angus ran a hand through his silver hair before he smirked at her. "I have an offer for you that I think will please you."

"Cut the bull and the hard sell, Angus. Just give it to me straight."

Angus paused and took his time, knowing that every minute Keeva spent in his company, it made her skin itch. He also knew that she wanted him dead, had told him so on many an occasion, but she was powerless to strike at him while she was a prisoner at his mercy.

Angus made her wait for another five long minutes before he leaned forward in his chair and said, "How would you like to shave the last twenty years off your sentence with one kill?"

Eyes widening in surprise, Keeva didn't even try to hide her eagerness, which only caused Angus to smirk even more. If she killed one more mark, then she could be free? She would never have to see this prick's face again, unless the day came when she would come for him.

But the offer seemed too good to be true, and if Keeva had

learned anything in her long years, if it looked like it was too good to be true, it usually was.

"Who's the mark?" Keeva asked, letting her suspicion flow with her words.

Angus leaned back in his chair. "That matters not. All you need is the location of the mark. The client wants the identity to remain a close-guarded secret. All you need to do is kill him. And once you show me proof of death, you walk away. It's as simple as that."

The way Angus was saying it was enough to send blood rushing to her head, but nothing was ever as simple as it sounded. He pushed a file toward her, and when she hesitated to take it, Angus got up and walked around her, careful not to touch her even though he knew she had learned to control her touch of death. His fingers tugged on one of her curls as Keeva tried not to shudder at the intention in his eyes.

"It is such a pity that you are cursed with such a touch, because I would very much like to fuck you."

Keeva stepped around him as she remarked with a feral grin, "Hard pass. I'd rather go fuck a cactus. At least it would be less of a prick than you are."

Angus snarled, storming back to his desk and shoving the folder toward her. "Kill the mark and then we never have to see each other again. I never have to look into the eyes of the monster who killed my little girl."

Keeva grabbed the file, holding her tongue from blurting out that he wasn't so worried about what had happened with Clodagh while he was leering at her moments ago. Spinning on her heels, Keeva yanked the door to Angus's office open, left it so as she vacated the asshole's office and headed out of the drone of banshee life.

Checking both ways before she crossed the road, slipping into her car, Keeva opened the file. There was no picture, just a description of the mark and location. Her pulse raced as she read through the one-page document and then thumped her head against the headrest.

Her mark would be residing in the penthouse suite of one of the most secure buildings in the world: Sicarius Security, the very place Scarlett was interviewing for a job. She had come across some of the security measures that had Sicarius Security as the number one security consultancy in the world. They were damn near impossible to infiltrate, and now Keeva was expected to venture right into the home of the Inferna assassins of choice?

Keeva grinned as she closed the file. By gods, she loved a challenge, and this was definitely going to be a challenge. If Scarlett got the job, Keeva wouldn't dare use her friend's contact to gain access. No—this was going to be a dawn drop-in, and before whoever she was meant to kill realized it, she would already have dealt him his death.

If this was to be her final job for Angus, then at least it would be an interesting one. Then, she could take any job she liked and earn some serious money, because it was not like Keeva had any other skills like Scarlett's that would allow her to be a functioning member of society. One of the places she had considered applying for a job was with Sicarius Security. What was it Alanis sang, *isn't it ironic?*

Keeva made the sign of the cross as she put the key in the ignition and the car spluttered to life. Heading home for a quick shower and to get dressed properly, Keeva wanted to get this over with quickly and quietly.

And, if she played her cards right, Keeva would be home and planning on celebrating Scarlett's new job and her new freedom.

Piece of cake, right?

CHAPTER THREE

Malakai

SITTING IN HIS OFFICE, MALAKAI GLANCED DOWN AT THE STACK of applicants that Jazz had handed him and sifted through them, separating out who he considered might be a good fit. Then he handed back the pile to Jazz for her to work her magic on. Jazz might not be able to see all the futures, but she got these feelings about people that made Malakai value her opinion.

Malakai watched in amusement as Jazz pretended to flip through the pages and then cut his choices in half and handed him back three or four sheets with a grin. There came a rap of knuckles on the door, to which Malakai called out for them to enter.

The Inferna who walked in was not what Malakai had been expecting when he read through her application to be his personal assistant. It was a requirement on the application that each applicant had to declare their species, and the woman standing in front of him with a coy smile was not what he was used to when dealing with succubi. To be honest, he had almost dismissed her application because he wasn't at all interested in a personal assistant who just wanted to fuck his brains out.

Malakai stood, extending his hand to shake hers, and when she looked at him with those big blue eyes, he noted the slight look of panic in her expression.

"Ms. Russell, please have a seat."

Scarlett Russell took the seat that was offered to her and spent a few minutes making sure she was seated with poise and posture. Any other succubus would have at least flashed her panties at him, that is, if they were wearing any. Malakai knew he was attractive, so she should have been sending out some serious pheromones to reel him in, but this little succubus was trying very hard to be professional.

Malakai liked her already.

"Ms. Russell, tell me a little about yourself."

Malakai only half listened as Scarlett began to list her experience and her qualifications. They knew all of that already, knew that she was the most qualified of the bunch. He liked how Scarlett divided her attention and eye contact between himself and Jazz. They had done an extensive background check on her to ensure she was not a plant; however, by all accounts, Scarlett didn't seem to have much contact with her Seduction, lived a mundane life that seemed to have her home by ten at night.

"I'm very perceptive when it comes to knowing whether someone is paying attention to me or droning me out."

Malakai smiled at the arctic bite in her tone, took a quick glance at Jazz to see his sister beaming at Scarlett.

"My apologies. As you can tell, my mind often wanders to other things, and that is why my sister has decided I need an assistant. I appreciate that part of the job may require you to slap sense into me at times."

A flush coloured Scarlett's cheek as she ducked her eyes. This woman could be tough as nails or as shy as a schoolgirl. It was rather endearing and surprising, though Malakai had thought nothing could surprise him anymore.

"Can you start Monday?" Jazz queried, her expression eager, hungry even, as Malakai quirked his brows.

"Do I get a say in this?" Malakai teased as Jazz dismissed him with a wave of her hand.

"Oh puh-lease, you chose her before she walked in the door. Scarlett will fit in quite nicely at Sicarius. She is meant to be here."

An outsider would have missed the change in tone, yet Malakai knew his sister, so he stopped teasing and said to Scarlett, "As you are aware by the job posting, I work nights but may need you to work some early evenings. Come by on Monday at around five and we can have breakfast and discuss things in detail."

They exchanged a few more pleasantries. His new PA was beaming as she made to leave; her left hand was on the door as she gave them a happy wave with her free hand. That was until the moment she opened the door and came face to face, well, face to chest with Ezekiel.

Malakai rose to his feet a second later. A hand on his arm halted him as Jazz shook her head, her eyes all-knowing. Malakai simply took his seat, ready to react if needed. As Primus, a single command would halt Zeke long enough to take him down.

"I'm so sorry. I didn't see you there."

Zeke glanced down at the woman and blinked, a frown curling his lips as he regarded Scarlett. Malakai watched in amusement as the succubus ran her eyes over Zeke, taking in his stature, his stocky build and the tattoos, and then went cherry tomato red all the way up to her ears.

Jazz beside him was struggling not to laugh as Zeke simply stepped aside and studied Scarlett as she thanked him with a warm smile, even though Malakai got the sense that she was terrified of the vampire. But something else had caught his attention. It was the first time in over a hundred years that Malakai noted something in Zeke's eyes other than sadness and disgust: interest.

His dark eyes followed her as she walked down the hall and disappeared out the door. Then Zeke shook his head, glanced at them for a second as Jazz grinned at him. Zeke grunted and left without even stating what he had come in for.

Malakai turned to Jazz. "What just happened? What is she?"

"Redemption, dear brother, redemption. And the possibility that we won't all lose a piece of our souls if we have to kill him. Only time will tell."

Now that the PA position was filled, he set aside those applications and asked Jazz to dismiss the rest of the candidates. As Jazz did just that, he scanned through the applications for new guards. The top one would be Malakai's top pick, yet he was suspicious that a werewolf would contemplate signing up to the vampire-run company, as many shifters had a blatant dislike for one another.

And some vampires really disliked shifters.

The office door slammed shut so hard, the glass rattled. "Really, Kai? You snuck a fleabag in under my nose?"

"You know the candidate can hear you, Jazz."

"I don't give a rat's ass what he can or cannot hear. You know how I feel about dogs."

Malakai was well aware that Jasmine detested shifters, especially werewolves. About three decades ago, Jasmine had gone on a mission and come home in foul humour, locking herself in her room for days until she emerged one day as if she had not been in a depression for days.

When Dylan managed to pry a sliver of information from her, Jazz had simply muttered, "I fucking hate the smell of dogs," and that was it, never to be spoken about again. Until now.

"He is the ideal candidate. Read his resume, Jazz. We need someone like him to do the day jobs, and he has only worked contract work for human companies. He was never employed with any Inferna company." Malakai lowered his tone. "I might not have your powers, Jazz, but this one feels right. Give him a chance."

Jazz pursed her lips as if she were to argue. Instead she

flung open the door and, much to Malakai's amusement, called out, "Fido, come."

There were snickers of amusement from the remaining candidates as Jazz bounced round and took her chair again, her expression less than happy. The werewolf in question strode in, his eyes darting to Jazz before he turned and held out his hand to Malakai.

Almost as tall as Malakai, the wolf had shoulder-length hair in a deep chestnut brown. His face was also scruffy, in the less clean-shaven way shifters liked to wear. Intelligence shone in his brown eyes, and Malakai knew he could handle himself. Dressed in black combat pants, army-issued boots and a snug, black, long-sleeved T-shirt, this wolf screamed lethal.

"Roman Lowe, sir. Nice to meet you."

His handshake was firm, steady, and Malakai couldn't help but chuckle when Roman grinned at Jazz. "I'd offer you my hand, ma'am. However, I'd hate to leave the dog smell on your skin."

Jazz shot him a look that promised hours of torture as Roman took a seat.

"I see from your resume that you served in the US army?"

Roman grinned as he immediately came out with an American accent. "Yes, sir, two tours in Afghanistan." He switched back to his Irish accent. "Then I worked for a number of private security companies escorting diplomats in wartime countries."

"What disciplines are you efficient in?"

"Sniper for long-range targets, can wield multiple weapons including guns and blades. I know a few languages fluently, can speak a handful well enough to get by. I also took an advance survival course with a member of the SEAL team and can swim for lengthy periods."

"Well," Jazz drawled as Malakai braced himself for Jazz to

speak. "That won't do at all. We'd never get the smell of wet dog out of the office."

Without skipping a beat, Roman answered, "I'll make sure to shower and dry myself off in one of those dryers the groomers use before daring to step foot in the office."

Jazz clamped her mouth shut as Roman turned back to Malakai with a smile. "I know you must be wondering why or even how a shifter did two tours and why I haven't signed up to work for Alpha Security."

Malakai leaned forward in his chair as he regarded the other Inferna. "The thought had crossed my mind."

"I have not lived as part of the pack for over fifty years. I would not work for a pack-related company, and while I have no grievances with the pack, I do what I want. My loyalty is to my employer, so I assure you that I am not a spy."

Not sensing any lies in his words, Malakai continued, "I assume the only days you have issues with working, day or night, are around the full moon?"

"Kai, Fido could still work. We just need to get him a collar and a leash."

Malakai shot his sister a horrified look and went to apologize when he noticed the wolf ginning. "Darling, I would gladly wear a collar and leash if that's what you're into."

This made Malakai let loose a deep laugh as Jazz sat back with a hiss at the innuendo. She folded her arms across her chest and ground her teeth together.

"In regards to the full moon, that won't be an issue for me, sir."

Now that piqued Malakai's curiosity. "And why is that?"

The werewolf's jaw ticked, the first indication that he was self-conscious about what he was about to say. "I can't shift. I am a werewolf who does not turn. For some unknown reason to all the doctors and scientists I called on, I am unable to change from man to wolf."

Roman waited as if he expected either disgust or pity.

Malakai gave him none of those. Gathering up the paper-work, Malakai asked him, "Does that affect your work?"

"Not at all, sir. I merely have a lot of motherfuckers to prove wrong."

Oh, Malakai really liked this guy. It sounded exactly like something Dylan would say.

"We would like you to start work as soon as possible, Roman. I think we can have you work the door a few nights with Dylan, another of the partners. I think you guys would get on well, and he can show you the ropes."

"Thank you, sir."

Malakai made to rise when he heard Jazz speak. "I still have a few questions."

"Shoot," Roman said as he settled into his chair with a grin.

"Are you microchipped? All dogs in Ireland are required to wear a chip for tracking from their owners."

"I have the chip number at home on my official papers from the vet's. I'll bring it with me Saturday."

"When was the last time you were treated for fleas?"

Malakai watched the exchange as Roman's grin widened with every question Jazz threw at him.

"I'm up to date with all my inoculations, including kennel cough."

When it was obvious that Roman would not be baited, Jazz got to her feet and flicked her blond hair over her shoulders as she sauntered from the room. Malakai shook hands with Roman, and the wolf left. Malakai advised the other candidates to leave and that all open positions had been filled.

He made his way up to the main communal area to find Jasmine banging cupboards in the kitchen. Malakai leaned on the back of the couch, folding his arms across his chest.

"Jazz, it's not like you'll have to work with him. I'll keep you on different shifts at the club."

Jazz slammed a cupboard shut so hard the door came off the hinges at the exact moment that Dylan emerged from the elevator.

"Hey, little sister, what's upset you so much that you are murdering the furniture?"

Jazz pointed at Malakai. "Ask him."

Dylan leaned against the couch as he held back a smirk. "You hired the wolf?"

Jazz spun round to face them, the cupboard door still in her hand. "You knew? You knew and didn't warn me?"

"And miss the chance to get something past Jasmine the all-knowing? Not a bloody chance I was telling you."

Jazz snarled and flung the cupboard door at Dylan, who caught it with a hearty chuckle of laughter. Then their sister gave them the finger and left them standing there laughing.

"She's not going to talk to us for a month," Malakai said with a sigh.

"Kai, you know Jazz," Dylan mused as he set the cupboard door down on the countertop. "She will be pissed at us for a couple of hours and then it will be as if nothing had happened. She give the new guy shit?"

"If by shit you mean did she call him Fido, ask him if he was microchipped, then yeah, but he just grinned and gave as good as he got."

Dylan ran a hand through his blond locks. "I like the dude already."

"He starts with you on Saturday."

Malakai scrubbed a hand down his face and yawned. He hadn't slept in around three days, and the sun would soon begin to rise. Dylan clapped him on the back and pushed him toward the elevator.

"Get some rest, big brother. You look like you need it. I'm gonna go bug Zeke and see what's gotten him all riled up."

Malakai kept his lips pressed together in a smile as he held back that little snippet of information to himself. He was still worried enough to issue Scarlett with a warning on Monday to not be alone with Zeke. It would protect them both.

Stripping off his jacket and shirt as he exited the lift and flinging them off to the side, he instantly relaxed the moment he was alone. His penthouse apartment had been tailored to his taste, all open spaces and all about just being Kai, not having to be Primus or boss or sir.

The space was open-planned, no walls apart from the closest and bathroom, with a bed that faced the window to overlook the city. He had a small kitchenette area in case he wanted to dine by himself, not that he had much chance with his family. Off to the side was a bathroom with a shower big enough to fit the entire management team, as Dylan liked to jest.

Jazz had demanded that he have a huge walk-in closet built when they purchased this building, and he did, the wardrobe lined with suits and a few casual clothes.

Slipping off his shoes and stripping, Malakai lay down on the bed in just a pair of boxers, kicking off the covers as the night felt warm and felt himself succumb to tiredness.

Awareness prickled at his senses as he felt the whisper of a presence in his room. The moment the intruder was within his grasp, Malakai moved lightning fast and pinned the intruder onto the bed. He wasn't expecting to have an assassin come for him in his own house, nor was he expecting the lush press of a female body beneath him. Her features were obscured by a hood, her runner's body clad in black.

His fangs elongated as Malakai snarled, "Who sent you?"

"Bite me, bloodsucker." Then Malakai found himself on his back, the assassin having managed to reverse their positions, the women's legs pressing into his sides.

"Not that I'm opposed to having a woman on top, but you are heading down a dangerous path here, little assassin," Malakai warned.

An amused look in her cat green eyes, her soft lips

twitched as if she tried not to smile. "You're kinda pretty. It's almost a shame to kill you."

Malakai froze as the woman grinned and placed the palms of her hands on his chest. Her smile slowly faded as she pressed harder against his chest as if she were expecting something to happen.

She jerked back and scrambled off the bed, causing her hood to fall, revealing a mass of flame-red hair and a dusting of freckles on her face. She was breath-taking, and his body stirred, his throat burning with the need to taste her.

Her eyes widened as she glanced at her hands like something was wrong.

"What's the matter, little assassin?" Malakai teased as he carefully edged off the bed in order to grab for her once again.

The petite little redhead's pulse quickened, the predator in him becoming hyper aware as hunger and lust raged through him. Her cat eyes darted down to the bulge in his boxers, and she licked her lips.

Then, as if common sense prevailed, she flashed him a haughty smirk. "I guess today is not your day to die, vampire. I'll see you again."

Bracing her knees, the assassin jumped upward, swinging up into the air vent that led to the roof. Malakai heard her boots on the roof and then nothing, as if she simply had disappeared. Stalking into his wardrobe, he pulled on a tee and a pair of loose pants before he pressed the com on the wall in his room so that he could speak to the other floors.

"Security breach in the penthouse. Someone just got bloody close enough to put hands on me in my own goddamn bed. Rise and shine, you bastards. Let's find out how an assassin managed to slip inside the most secure building in the world to try and fucking kill me."

CHAPTER FOUR

Keeva

KEEVA WATCHED AS THE LIGHTS FLICKERED ON IN THE TOP FLOORS of Sicarius Security as Malakai Cavanagh stepped out onto the balcony, his dark eyes scanning his surroundings. Standing there in track pants and a snug tee, Keeva couldn't get the tingly sensations that were coursing through her body to leave. Panic fluttered in her chest as his gaze seemed to stop where she was hidden on a roof across the river, and it stayed latched onto the spot until a hulking man stepped out onto the balcony, his expression grim as he ordered Malakai inside.

That did not stop the vampire from glancing over his shoulder as he strode inside, giving Keeva a nice ole view of his ass. What the hell was wrong with her? Her powers weren't working, and she was sat dangerously close to her mark, drool all but dripping from the corners of her mouth.

But that wasn't right, was it? Keeva could feel her powers inside her veins, but the moment she had put her palms on Malakai's smooth, well-sculpted chest, zip, nada, zilch.

Wiping the sweat from her palms, Keeva glanced down to see a small contingent of black-clad men head across the bridge and toward the building where she waited. Keeva had lost the element of surprise, and now she would have to be more direct in her attempts. Malakai Cavanagh might be panty-melting gorgeous, but she would take him out without blinking in order to gain her freedom.

Keeva took off with a run and jumped to the next building, continuing the pattern until she was halfway across town. She jumped and rolled, landing in a side alley in a crouch, heading out into the quiet morning as sunlight began to slip through the grey clouds. Keeva instantly relaxed, knowing that she had the day before she had to worry about vampires showing up at her door and dragging her off to some black site.

Reaching her apartment complex, Keeva jogged up the stairs, dropping her hood before she stepped inside to have Scarlett waiting for her, chewing on her bottom lip, a mug of coffee in her hands. She was dressed in pink Care Bears pyjamas that tugged Keeva's lips into a smile.

"Honey, I'm home," Keeva said in greeting, trying to keep her tone light.

"I was worried."

Scarlett's tone was clipped, but Keeva knew Scarlett wasn't angry with her. When they had first become friends, Keeva had sat down and been honest with Scarlett about her "job." To be fair, the succubus hadn't recoiled in horror; she had simply nodded, made Keeva a cup of tea and asked that Keeva text her after a job to let her know that she was all good.

This morning, Keeva had been too shocked to remember, and Scarlett had worried. It was nice to have someone worried for her.

"I'm sorry, Scar, but something went wonky with my powers and I totally forgot to text you."

Scarlett lips formed the shape of an O as she set her mug down on the coffee table in front of her. "Define wonky?"

"Well, I was straddling my absolutely gorgeous mark, and my hands were on his chest, and nothing happened." Well, something had happened, but that was a story for another day.

Hands waving in a little jazz-hands motion, Scarlett said, "No death?"

"Nope, just a pissed-off vampire considering how I managed to get inside the most secure building in the world."

Keeva watched as realization dawned on Scarlett's face. "Oh my God, Keeva. Please don't tell me you just tried to assassinate my new boss!"

"You got the job! That's great. I knew you would nail it."

Scarlett looked at her with an exasperated expression. "Well, I might not have a job if you kill my boss before I start on Monday."

Keeva grinned, flicked the switch on the kettle as she walked into the small kitchen. "Malakai Cavanagh is just one small part of Sicarius Security. I'm sure the other owners will keep you employed. He has to die, Scarlett."

"What bullshit did Angus offer you to get you to take out not only the Primus of the vampires but an elder?"

With a small sigh, Keeva turned to face Scarlett as she waited for the kettle to boil. "Freedom. The last twenty years gone from my sentence. No leash, no chains, no blood-bound oath to keep me in line. I could be my own person, and all I have to do is kill Malakai."

Scarlett said nothing as she rose, nudged me with her hip and fixed me a mug of coffee. Handing it to me, Scarlett offered me a friendly smile. "Can we hold off on the assassination until I've at least had my first day? I have to at least start the job before I have to go on the lam with my bestie because she murdered my boss."

"I hear Mexico is nice this time of year," Keeva joked as Scarlett rolled her eyes.

"Once it has a non-extradition order in place, we good to go. We need some new clothes though."

Laughing at the mischief in Scarlett's tone, Keeva shrugged her shoulders as she kicked off her shoes. "I don't think the vampires give a damn about extradition countries, babe. But definitely on getting you some skimpy bikinis."

They went their separate ways then, both tired for

different reasons, and Keeva left the bedroom door slightly open so she could hear if anyone decided to try and gain access to their apartment. Keeva changed and sat with her legs on her bed in an old tee that came down to her knees. Reaching under the bed, she lifted her laptop and began to do some research.

The first attempt to research Malakai Cavanagh brought her to a variety of human-based articles on the CEO and Sicarius Security company. Awards for achievements, innovation and services to the military. In every single article there was a picture of the vampire in question dressed in a thousand-dollar suit and a very human-looking smile.

But every time Keeva saw that smiling picture, all she could think about was those wicked fangs that had been close enough to pierce her skin. Keeva shivered and tried some of the Inferna dark sites to search for information, but all she found was some explicit fan fiction that she stored away to read to Scarlett so that for the little time she worked for Malakai, all the succubus would think about would be of her boss and some nymph's orgy.

Not that Keeva was thinking about him naked or anything.

Shutting the laptop, Keeva rubbed her temples and decided to call one of her assassin buddies. Mac was a vampire, so he might have some information that she could use. She'd known Mac for years, only seen him once or twice, and neither of them had seen the other's face. But his information has always been solid.

Dialling the number she had for him, Keeva waited until she heard him say, "Death, it's been a minute."

Keeva rolled her eyes at the nickname given to her by the Inferna. "You been missing me, hun?"

A throaty laugh came down the phone. "Life is always a little more exciting when Death herself is calling me. What you need, sweetheart?"

"Give me all you got on Malakai Cavanagh."

The phone line went deathly silent, and Keeva wondered if she had made a mistake calling Mac until she heard the other Inferna swear. "That's not a contract you want to be taking."

"I don't have a choice, Mac."

That caused the other assassin to swear again. "This a contract you are being forced to do?"

"You know it is. Only a sadistic bitch would try and take out the vampire Primus for fun." Keeva took a chance and added, "Remember how we talked about getting out of the obligations and taking the jobs we wanted? I do this and I'm free. Please, Mac, just tell me what you know."

Mac was quiet for a minute, and Keeva contemplated hanging up, but then Mac sighed, the sound of resignation. "Malakai Cavanagh is a killer in an Armani suit. Don't let the good looks fool you, Death. He is vicious, smart, calculating and won't go easy. His partners in Sicarius would die for him and he for them, so if you come for him, be prepared to take on them as well."

"You sound like you're a fanboy, Mac."

"I just appreciate the fact that Malakai earned his reputation by getting his own hands dirty. He fights his own battles. This might be the one mark you can't hit, Death. No chance you'd leave it go?"

Keeva shook her head, even though Mac couldn't see her. "He's seen my face. Even if my freedom wasn't on the line, I can't let him live now he's seen my face. Can't risk him finding out who I am and coming after the people I care for."

Mac said nothing for a couple of heartbeats then. "Come meet me, Death. Tonight, Dante's. The place will be crawling with humans, and I can try and talk you out of this."

"You asking me out on a date, Mac?" Keeva teased, amused when she heard him grunt.

"You already have enough vampires to deal with, sweetheart. I'm just trying to be a friend."

"Is that what we are, Mac, friends?"

Mac snorted in response. "As much as assassins can be friends, Death. I've always liked you. Would hate to miss out on all this witty banter if you got dead. I'll see you tonight."

Mac ended the call, and Keeva lay her head back on the pillow and closed her eyes, utterly exhausted.

Keeva was back in the apartment of Malakai Cavanagh, dressed head to toe in black, her arms folded across her chest as Malakai lounged in a chair, his eyes on the sun as it rose in the sky. A beer bottle hung from two fingers at his side, making him seem normal, human even.

For a couple of heartbeats, Keeva wondered if she was dreaming as she waved a hand in front of his face, and then his hand snapped out and caught her wrist. The skin where his fingers touched felt like it burned, and Keeva snatched her hand back.

The bastard's lips curved into a smug smirk. "Who sent you to kill me, little red?"

"I'd tell you, but then I'd have to kill you."

The vampire laughed as if he found her threats amusing. "How did you get inside the building undetected?"

Keeva snorted. "A girl's gotta have some secrets."

"I could use someone like you."

Keeva lifted her brows at the innuendo in his words, and when Malakai smiled then, her stomach fluttered and her pulse raced.

Malakai rose, stalking toward her as Keeva retreated a step or two, her back hitting the glass window as Malakai crowded her. She flattened her hands on the window because they were useless against him. He leaned in so that she could smell the beer on his breath as well as the crisp scent on his skin, like a stormy night.

His fingers twirled a curl of her hair around his fingers and gave a tug. Keeva swatted away his hand as Malakai leaned in, his nose to her neck, and inhaled. Heat flooded through her body, and she clenched her thighs together to try and hide her arousal.

Malakai stepped back, the smug grin still on his face. "Are you sure you wouldn't rather fuck me than kill me?"

And Keeva was seriously considering taking him up on that very suggestion when it dawned on her that this was a dream and she could wake herself up.

"What is your name, little red assassin?" The vampire all but purred in her ear.

Keeva pushed him away hard, knowing that the well-built vampire could have stayed rooted to the spot if he wanted to, but he moved.

"My name is Death," she said with a wink. "See you soon."

Then Keeva bolted to the right, hitting the glass with her shoulder, and the glass shattered as she dove for freedom.

Keeva woke with a start, sweat drenching her skin as she checked her body for wounds. Dragging her hair off her face, Keeva was surprised that it was already the afternoon. She could hear Scarlett humming along to the radio as she pottered about the kitchen.

Legs a little unsteady, Keeva made her way out to the little kitchen area, taking the coffee that Scarlett handed her. "Bad dreams?"

Keeva glanced at Scarlett, who blushed a little as she sat down on a chair and hugged her knees to her chest.

"Sadistic erotic kind of dreams about the vampire I'm going to kill. Maybe I need therapy," Keeva jested as she sipped her coffee. Hell, it wasn't much of a jest, considering her life.

"Maybe we should go, Keeva. Maybe we should pack up what little we have and start over."

"Scarlett," Keeva began, feeling her friend's sorrow as if it were her own. "You know that I can't. I tried that once at the very start, and it was a year before I saw the sun again. There is no running from what I did. I just need to complete this last job, and then we are home free."

"But freedom is no good to you if you're dead, Keeva."

"Isn't death a form of freedom in itself?"

Scarlett was quiet for a long time, her blue eyes sad as she continued to drink her coffee. Glancing at her watch, Keeva grinned at her friend.

"So, Miss Scarlett, what wicked plans have you for this evening?"

Scarlett rolled her eyes at Keeva, leaving Keeva to tap her temple. "I have an idea. I have to meet a contact tonight, and I think you and I need a night out. Cocktails, dancing and lots of humans to feed off of. You're going to get all dressed up, and we can pretend for one night that you and me are just Keeva and Scarlett."

"I don't know, Keeva," Scarlett began to argue, but Keeva could sense the fact that Scarlett needed to feed, and considering her friend hadn't had any sexual contact in like forever, the girl had to be starving.

"C'mon, Scarlett. Let's go let our hair down, dance our feet off and get blind-ass drunk. We'll go to Dante's; the music is always good, and we will have fun. You remember what fun is, right? Something that doesn't involve you curled up on the couch on a Saturday night with a romance novel with a cover of some dude who forgot to put on his shirt."

For a minute, Scarlett looked like she was going to try and find an excuse to cry off like she usually did, but then resolve flashed in her mind and her expression turned stern. "I'm in."

Keeva made a fist and pulled her arm down with a gleeful yes. "No granny outfits tonight, Scarlett. Tonight, you are not respectful, chaste Scarlett Russell, who is afraid of getting laid because she wants an epic romance. Tonight, you are hot as hell Scarlett Russell, who leaves men and women panting after her. Dress accordingly."

Keeva dragged Scarlett into her bedroom and began riffling through Scarlett's wardrobe. She pulled out a bodycon dress in the same black as Scarlett's hair, with a panel of lace cupping the breasts and running down the front. The skirt would come to Scarlett's knees, yet with her friend's long legs, it would look classy. Straps would give the illusion that her breasts would be secure. Keeva yanked a pair of red heels from the bottom of the wardrobe.

Scarlett ran a hand over the dress and then nodded with that coy little smile of hers as Keeva left her to go get ready. Scarlett might have magic hair that was dry in seconds, but Keeva's mane of red curls had its own personality and mind. There was no taming it in an hour.

Keeva showered, ran some product through her hair with her fingers and applied a little dark eyeshadow and a strawberry-flavoured lipstick. Slipping on some lace boy shorts in green and a matching strapless bra, Keeva shifted through her own clothes to find something a little less like her normal grunge attire and something that could keep up with sultry Scarlett.

"Wear the emerald-green dress," Scarlett said from the doorway as she fidgeted with the hem of her dress, which looked like it was painted on Scarlett's curves. Her lips were painted the same colour as her shoes and little clutch bag.

"Damn, girl. I could go naked and no one would be looking at me. That dress on you is criminal."

Her big blue eyes widened as doubt crept in, so Keeva took the emerald dress from the hanger and slipped it on. The dress fit her like a second skin, but Keeva didn't have the killer curves that Scarlett had. Scarlett laughed as Keeva grabbed a pair of combat boots, slipped her feet in and then tied a little skull pendant around her neck to match the earrings already in her ears.

Winking at Scarlett, Keeva grabbed her purse and called for a taxi, praying the elevator was working, because once the night was done, Keeva didn't fancy dragging her drunk ass up the eleven flights of stairs.

Sensing the unease in Scarlett, Keeva pulled out her phone and made her friend pose for photos, and by the end, they were both laughing as Keeva's phone pinged to let them know the taxi was there. Scarlett's face flushed as a group of guys wolf-whistled at her as she ducked into the taxi.

The female taxi driver turned up the music at Keeva's request as they drove the short distance into the city centre down along St. Patrick's Street. Scarlett groaned at the sight of the long line.

"We'll never get in!"

"Girl, in that dress, we'll be in the VIP section."

Scarlett chuckled as they got out of the taxi, and both women headed for the line when someone called Scarlett's name. Her friend blinked at the man who waved at her as if she were trying to remember his name, and then Scarlett gave him a warm smile.

"Hey, Roman, congrats on the job!" The man grinned as Keeva took in the Sicarius Security logo on the badge. He wore a Dante's tee.

"I heard you got the job as well. So we'll be working together."

The Inferna, who Keeva thought to be a shifter, glanced over his shoulder and with a wink said, "I think the club could do with adding a little hotness to the dance floor. In you go, ladies."

Scarlett blushed as she thanked him, and Keeva and Scarlett dodged the line and slipped in the door, climbing the short few steps, the music thumping under their feet. Keeva glanced at Scarlett with a glint in her eyes. "Vita est brevior cum deformibus viris saltare."

Scarlett laughed. "Life is too short to dance with ugly men."

"Exactly, babe. Let's go get blind-ass drunk!"

CHAPTER FIVE

Keeva

WHEN KEEVA HAD GROWN UP IN CORK, DANTE'S HAD BEEN A record store, the best place to get music that Ireland generally did not have. Keeva had even worked there for a summer, indulging in her love of music while getting the inside scoop on bands. Two stories high, this building was the main staple on St. Patrick's Street, and now, Dante's was a beacon to all who wanted to dance and drink the night away, the logo of flames notorious among club goers even if the lines rounded the block most nights.

The ground floor by day was a bar, but tonight, the busiest of the week, the ground floor had been cleared to accommodate the extra crowd. Keeva could smell the scent of sweat and alcohol as the music pumped from the speakers. Scarlett swayed a little to the music as Keeva linked her arm, and they headed through the throng of bodies to the bar.

The music, which had been very drum and bass, switched to a more recent track by Tinie Tempah that had her friend grinning. Then her smile faltered as she glanced up at the DJ booth.

"Hey, what's up?"

Scarlett inclined her head to the blond women on the decks. "That's Jasmine Cavanagh. She interviewed me for the job on Thursday."

"What is one of the directors of Sicarius Security doing working in the club?"

Scarlett shrugged, her teeth worrying at her bottom lip. "Hell if I know. Let's go get a drink."

They shimmied through the crowd to the bar, managing to snag a nice corner with a full view of the dance floor. Keeva tapped her fingers on the solid oak bar while they waited for a bartender to come and take their order. A young human girl filling a pint called out and asked what they wanted.

"Bottle of Coors, gin and tonic and four shots of tequila."

The girl grinned as Scarlett shook her head at Keeva. "Are you trying to get me drunk?"

"Hell yeah. It's my mission tonight to get you drunk enough that sexy Scarlett comes out to play and old maid Scarlett is long forgotten."

The bartender laughed and slid two shots to Scarlett, who looked at the tequila, then at Keeva and took the first one in her hand. "Screw it," she muttered, then drank not one but two shots in quick succession, leaving Keeva to play catch-up.

An hour later, Keeva was starting to feel a little buzzed as she took to the dance floor with Scarlett. They danced and ignored all the eyes on them, and Keeva scared away a drunk idiot that got a little handsy with Scarlett, his hand cupping her ass when she ignored his advances.

Out of the corner of her eye, she glanced up and caught someone watching them, and the figure, hidden by the shadows, inclined his head toward the VIP section. Keeva caught Scarlett by the elbow and steered her toward the little steps that would bring them up to the VIP area.

"Told you that dress would get us into the VIP section."

Scarlett laughed, her eyes dancing as she inhaled. Her body trembled as she swallowed hard, and Keeva glanced to her right, where in the dark corridor that led to the bathrooms, a human couple were enjoying a drunken tryst. Scarlett licked her lips, her eyes getting that glazed-over look she got when she needed to feed.

Keeva sat her friend down on the seat closest to the bar, where she could feed off their sexual energy but still be safe until Keeva got back.

"Stay here, Scarlett. I'll be right back."

Keeva made her way upstairs, wondering why there was nobody guarding the VIP section. Keeva's gaze fell on the figure lounging in a booth, his arms stretched across the back of the velvet sofa, near enough to where the blond vampire was bopping her head in time with music.

Turning her attention back to the vampire she had come to meet, Keeva took in his rugged appearance, from the long blond hair that curled just under his ears to the cheeky frat-boy smile and the lean, muscular frame. But her eyes fell on the black T-shirt that was stretched over his chest that read Dante's.

Fucking hell, Mac worked for Sicarius Security.

"Have a seat, sweetheart. I promise not to bite unless you ask me to."

Keeva rolled her eyes, sinking down on the edge of the booth as Mac continued to grin at her.

"So, you work for Sicarius? What now? You going to take me out before I have a second shot at your boss? Why lure me here in front of all these humans?" Keeva didn't bother to hide the ire in her tone, because even though they were assassins it didn't mean they didn't live by some sort of code.

"I'm not going to kill you, Death. I'm here to strongly advise you that going after Malakai isn't your only option here. We are willing to sit down and discuss an amicable outcome."

Glancing over her shoulder, Keeva could still see Scarlett sitting at the bar with a smile on her face. She was chatting to the female bartender. She was safe and relatively content for now.

Turning her attention back to Mac, Keeva smirked. "And if I say no?"

"Then you and I will have to have some alone time."

Keeva jerked to her feet with a hiss at the sound of a husky tone behind her and came face to face with Malakai

Cavanagh, dressed in an impeccable suit of midnight black that only darkened his chocolate-coloured eyes. Dark stubble framed his jawline and full lips, which were breathtaking with his smile as he watched her much like a lion stalked its prey.

Keeva stared at Mac. "So you sold me out to the boss? And here I thought we were friends, Mac."

"The only reason I'm being so civil with you is because my brother does consider you a friend." Malakai interjected.

Hang on a damn second. Brother? Her eyes widened as Keeva's mouth opened. Mac … as in Dylan McGrath, brother of Jasmine Cavanagh, sister of Malakai Cavanagh … how could she not have figured it out? Her eyes roamed to the DJ booth, where the blond vampire waved and winked at her.

Keeva folded her arms across her chest as Malakai's dark eyes dipped to the shift in her breasts. "Eyes up, vampire. And stop invading my dreams. Now either tell me what you want or let me go so I can salvage what was a good night until you party poopers showed up."

"You been dreaming about me, little assassin?"

Before Keeva had a chance to argue, Keeva heard Scarlett call her name, and she took off down the stairs, her eyes darting from side to side until she spotted her friend with her back pressed against the wall and a very scary vampire next to her with his hand wrapped around a human's throat.

Thankfully, they were hidden from view in the darkened corridor as Keeva jumped in front of Scarlett and checked to see if she was okay. When Scarlett nodded, her big blue eyes widened as Malakai strode into the corridor. The hulk of a vampire lifted the human, his toes barely touching the ground, his eyes bulging so much Keeva was afraid they'd pop.

"Zeke," Malakai said in an even tone. When the vampire, Zeke, growled, Malakai stepped forward and put a hand on his elbow. "Ezekiel Collins, let the human go."

Power saturated the air, goosebumps pimpling her skin, and Keeva wondered if Malakai gave orders like that in the bedroom. Zeke let the human go as Dylan stepped forward, his eyes flashing red as he told the human, "Go home. Sleep it off. You had some bad drugs and can't remember any of this night. Go."

The human scurried off, leaving only the members of the Inferna gathered in the hallway. Malakai kept his hand on Zeke's arm as he peered over at Scarlett as if he were afraid of what the hulk of a vampire might do. "Are you all right, Ms. Russell?"

Scarlett nodded her head sharply as Zeke growled a little low in his throat. Keeva put herself in front of Scarlett in case the monster that she could feel lurking under Zeke's skin happened to make an appearance.

"I'm fine now," Scarlett began in a low tone, her eyes fixed on Zeke's shoulders. "I left the bar to go to the bathroom, and the human wouldn't take no for an answer. I'm not … I don't … and Keeva normally is there to scare them away."

Mac—no, Dylan—clapped Zeke on the shoulder. "And you decided to try and ride in like a white knight and rescue the damsel? I didn't know you had it in you, old man."

Keeva felt the brush of magic on her skin and shivered as Zeke seemed to relax slightly enough to turn around and hold Scarlett's eyes. Keeva looked into eyes that were so dark they were almost black and decided he was a threat. He was built like a linebacker. His shoulders nearly took up the entire space. The tattoos of black ink grasping at his neck only added to the scary MF thing this vampire had going on.

Malakai said something to Zeke softly in Latin, too low for her to pick up, but she knew the sounds of it. Then Zeke grunted out a breath before he managed to grind out in a very gentle tone that surprised Keeva, "I'm sorry if I scared you."

"I wasn't scared of you." Scarlett answered.

Keeva glanced back at her friend to see Scarlett watching

Zeke with a little bit more interest than she would expect from the quiet succubus. Then again, the rest of the vampires seemed just as surprised as she was, with Dylan chuckling softly and Malakai holding back a grin. The poor little hulk seemed shocked as he snatched his hand from Malakai's grasp and stalked off into a room that said *Staff Only.*

Malakai smoothed down his suit jacket and motioned with his arm. "Shall we continue our conversation upstairs where there may be less drama? Ms. Russell, you can join us if … Keeva doesn't mind."

Well shit, now the vampires had her name—he almost purred when he uttered it—and it would be easy now to pinpoint her identity. Keeva walked with Scarlett back up the steps and sat with Scarlett in the booth next to her, as Keeva sat on the edge to give her the quickest escape route.

"Were you aware of Keeva's need to assassinate me when you applied for the job, Ms. Russell?"

Malakai's tone and gaze were accusatory, with a little bit of menace, so Keeva answered for her. "Hey, don't talk to her like that. I knew Scarlett had been going for an interview. She was gone before I was given the contract. I didn't even know who I was killing, just given a description and location. Our little encounter was done in all before I went home and found out Scarlett got the job. She has nothing to do with this."

Malakai nodded, seemingly taking her at her word, then the bartender brought them a round of drinks and Keeva was surprised to see Malakai drinking a beer like her, just like in her dream. He tipped the bottle at her as he took a long drink, Keeva watching as his throat moved and as her mouth went dry. She took an ice-cold drink of her own to try and cool her down because she was seriously flushed right now.

Dylan's phone pinged, the blond vampire frowning at whatever had popped up to annoy him, then he held it out to Malakai, who also frowned. Her own phone pinged. She pulled it out of her bag and glanced at it, her eyes widening in surprise.

There, on the app that all assassins used to accept and reject contracts, was a contract out on her life. But it wasn't just as her alter ego: This had every single detail of her life in a dossier, from her skill set to a warning to not let her touch them, for her touch meant certain death.

Someone wanted her dead badly enough to offer a quarter of a million euros.

She should be flattered, really. Instead she was pissed off.

"Is that why you were looking at your hands? Something went wrong?"

"Nothing went wrong, bloodsucker. Normally when I touch you, you're dead. Ha ha … well, you're already dead, so deader. There is something wrong with you that my powers don't like. Most people don't get to walk away when I let loose with my powers."

Dylan grinned, his unique-coloured eyes twinkling with mischief. "I think we should test the theory. I mean, there has to be a reason why you can touch Kai and nothing happens. I've seen the aftereffects of what you do, Death, and it ain't pretty."

Keeva held up her beer bottle, not even bothering to hide her smugness. "Thank you."

Malakai chuckled, unbuttoning his suit jacket and folding it neatly on the back of the booth before he began unbuttoning his black shirt. Keeva jerked in her chair and glared at him.

"Um, what the hell are you doing?"

"Helping to test a theory."

"You don't need to be naked for that."

Malakai gave her a sly smile. "I wasn't planning on getting naked, Keeva, but I'm sure that can be arranged if you want to straddle me in my bed again."

Damn, there he went again saying her name like she was already naked and beneath him.

Keeva rolled her eyes, leaning back in her seat. "Nope, all good here. I don't do fang."

But as Keeva watched him unbutton his shirt to reveal that lickable eight pack, Keeva was seriously rethinking her aversion to vampires. Malakai dragged a chair over to where Keeva sat, invading her space so that their knees almost touched.

"This power of yours, it works on any part of the body?"

Keeva set her palms down on her thighs with a sly grin of her own. "If you are worried about little Kai, then please don't worry your pretty self about it. My hands are going nowhere near your cock."

"We'll see."

Scarlett leaned forward as the tension crackled in the air, and Keeva tried to rein in the raging hormones as her palms grew sweaty. Inhaling through her nose, she closed her eyes until Malakai said her name.

"Eyes open, little red."

With a growl of her own, Keeva tilted her head slightly, then slapped her palms down on his chest and urged her power forward. Keeva could feel it simmer under her skin, and then when it got to the palms of her hands, to her fingertips, it stopped. Scrunching her face, Keeva concentrated and pushed again with the same results.

She became hyper aware of Malakai's hands on the bare skin on her own thighs, his fingers digging in her skin and making her want to crawl into his lap, unbutton his pants to indulge in all her deepest fantasies that she had shoved down for decades, afraid to hurt a lover, stroking herself because she couldn't allow herself to lose control.

But Malakai was immune, and that made him even more attractive ... if only he wasn't so damn arrogant. If only she didn't have to kill him.

Sliding the chair back suddenly, Malakai beckoned his sister over from the DJ booth and whispered in her ear. The girl, who looked like cheerleader Buffy circa season one, grinned and rolled up her sleeves as she said with a wink, "I can strip off if you wanna fondle me like you did my brother."

Keeva glanced down at the blonde's ample cleavage and pursed her lips like she was considering it. When the vampire laughed, throwing her head back, Keeva instantly liked her.

"Oh, I like you, Keeva. My brother needs someone to ruffle his feathers."

There was no way in hell Keeva was going to answer that, so she reached out to press her finger to the blonde's arm when Malakai grabbed her wrist.

"Just because I can't kill you with my touch doesn't mean you have the right to manhandle me. Let go of me."

Malakai ignored her remark, his brow narrowing as he asked, "You can control the death touch?"

"The minimal amount of power I'll use will make her a little ill, like food poisoning. I'll use the smallest dose I can so I don't kill her. I'm not a complete idiot, Cavanagh."

Satisfied with her words, Malakai let go of her hand. Keeva pressed her index finger to Jasmine's pulse and got nothing. She added a second finger, still felt her power stop at her own fingertips. Jasmine grinned, winking as she flipped her blond hair over her shoulder, calling Dylan forward.

Her former assassin buddy raised his brows as he began to pull off his T-shirt. Keeva snarled with annoyance. What the hell was it with this lot and taking off their clothes? "I swear, Mac, if you go all Magic Mike on me too, if it works, I'm gonna make you so sick you'll be camped out next to the toilet seat."

"Spoilsport," Dylan teased but kept his tee on, pushed off the chair and then knelt down in front of her.

Keeva reached out and pressed her finger to his pulse,

wondering if her power was gone and what she would do if it didn't work anymore. Her power flared as Keeva felt it flow through her arms and into her fingertips in a rush. When Dylan groaned, Keeva removed her fingers. Sweat beaded on his brow before Jasmine passed him a bin and he vomited into the bin. He groaned again as his stomach heaved, and then he was dry-heaving into the bin and scooting away from Keeva.

Jasmine was grinning as she handed her sick brother a bottle of water, and that made him vomit again. Keeva didn't really feel sorry for him, considering Dylan had lured her here on false pretences.

"Why the hell did my powers work on him and not you two? Aren't you all related?"

"Different mothers," Malakai and Jasmine said at the same time, exchanging a little smile that had Keeva thinking they got asked that question a lot.

"To clarify," Malakai said as he slipped into his shirt, "Jasmine and I have the same mother. Dylan and Jasmine share the same father."

Jasmine tapped her finger on her chin. "So maybe our mother had a little banshee in her that makes us immune to Keeva's powers."

"Perhaps." That was all the arrogant vampire said as his eyes watched Keeva with interest; she just wasn't sure if it was because he saw an assassin that would be good to have on staff or if it was because he was *interested* in her.

"Well I don't really care about your freaky family history, but I've killed a banshee before, so there is definitely something wrong with you guys."

Rising to her feet, Keeva pulled Scarlett out of the booth. "As fun as this has been, I think we are gonna bounce."

"There is a bounty on your head, Keeva. We can keep you and Scarlett safe." Malakai's tone was cool, calm even, as if he expected her to obey his word. Then again, this was Malakai

Cavanagh she was talking about; the guy never probably heard the word no in his life.

"I can protect Scarlett just fine. I've done it for a long time, and before that, I kept myself safe. We'll be fine. Make sure he drinks plenty of fluids when he can stomach it. I'm told boiled white lemonade and toast for twenty-four hours will see him right. Might not be as long, considering you guys heal pretty fast."

Keeva steered Scarlett down the steps and into the crowd, pushing through the heaving masses and into the night air, all the while acutely aware that eyes watched her and they were probably not looking at the back of her head.

Once outside, Scarlett waved at the shifter who had let them inside, and Keeva wondered if shifter boy was in on the little ambush as well. This night had gone to hell quicker than expected, and now, not only did she have Sicarius Security on her tail, she had to contend with the assassins of the Inferna world.

"Nights out with you, Keeva, are never boring!" Scarlett chortled as they slipped into a taxi and headed for home.

"I'm not the one who was making come-to-bed eyes at a raging hulk monster of a vampire who looked like he could break your face as quick as he could break your headboard."

"I don't think I'd mind if he broke my headboard, Keeva," Scarlett admitted as her face burned bright red, and Keeva laughed when Scarlett placed her hand over her mouth.

"Who knew all it would take was a serial killer wannabe to rev your motor, Scarlett Russell. We should have been hanging out in biker bars all along!"

They both laughed, and despite the fact that Keeva was a wanted woman, she let herself enjoy the little moment of happiness ... because who the hell knew what calamities tomorrow would bring?

CHAPTER SIX

Malakai

Malakai was having a hard time concentrating, a certain flame-haired banshee wreaking havoc on his control. As soon as the sun had set on Sunday evening, Malakai had dressed with the intention of tracking Keeva down and trying to persuade her to come to Sicarius for protection. He also wanted to know how the hell she had gotten inside, because he and Dylan had spent a night with their best people trying to figure it out and they couldn't manage it.

Pouring himself a cup of coffee, he set the mug down as he rolled the sleeves of his knit jumper up to the elbow. The elevator pinged and Dylan strode in, looking none the worse for wear after Keeva had made him ill, wearing the same clothes as last night, his eyes heavy. His step faltered as he spotted Malakai, a guilty expression on his face.

"I'm not up for a lecture this morning, *Dad*." His grim tone told Malakai everything he needed to know, that even though Dylan looked like he'd had a very wild night, his brother's unique talents sometimes meant that his body was not his own.

"Can you pass me the coffee so I can at least have some caffeine with your pity?"

Malakai chuckled, poured him a cup and slid it across the breakfast bar to him. Malakai let Dylan sip his coffee as he looked around the communal living space. Most of them were content to hide out in their own rooms the majority of the time, but Malakai wanted to ensure that they remained tight-knit, a family unit.

Jasmine had worked hard to create this open planned space, none of them feeling comfortable in small spaces, and Dylan joked they were piss-poor vampires considering none of them could ever cope with sleeping in a coffin.

The kitchen area was large enough for their needs, the black marble granite tabletops and grey wood chosen by Jazz. There was a table right in front of the custom-built glass with a tint that meant no sun could penetrate. It was also large enough that it seated around eight people, and they used it for formal occasions like Christmas and other holidays. Then a large U-shaped couch in front of a massive TV was positioned in the centre of the room where they had movie nights all the time.

Malakai spent a lot of time and effort trying to make sure his family had very human moments, to remind them that they were not just vampires and that the life they were living was the one they were meant to live. It eased the guilt in Malakai that he had created a good life for those he loved and they would want for nothing. He had no need to experience any of the things his family enjoyed once they were the ones who were happy. His happiness came from seeing them be happy.

"I need to shower off the night, and then we need to talk."

Malakai set down his mug and looked at Dylan. "You get some information?"

"Is that even a question?"

Dylan pushed away from the counter with a grin that didn't quite fit right on his face today. He disappeared down the elevator, leaving Malakai on his own again, his guilt sinking in as he worried not only about Zeke but about Jazz and now Dylan. His guilt stemmed from the fact that Malakai didn't hate being a vampire; he loved feeling powerful and almost invincible. When he had awoken with the hunger, it had not bothered him to drink his fill. He revelled in death and, for the first time in his life, felt like he was finally who he was meant to be.

Jasmine had hoped that being reborn would take away her gift to see the future. When she was human, the visions had been calm, peaceful, like telling the farmers that a rainstorm was coming or that poachers from another village had come to pillage. She was revered, treated like a princess, and he and Dylan had been overtly overprotective of her. But over time, the visions brought severe headaches, nausea, and nightmares.

But becoming a vampire only accelerated her gift. The visions became more vivid, her feelings so eerily accurate that they had all decided that they needed to keep Jazz's power to themselves. He and Dylan had tried to keep her safe over the decades, shielding her from those who might want to use her. Anyone who discovered her gift was dealt with swiftly and quietly.

Jasmine had been the one to tell them they needed to find Zeke. It was nearly four decades after Malakai had been reborn when Jazz had woken them screaming, clutching at her throat, her eyes blanketed in white as she thrashed. Dylan used his powers to try and calm her, but for a split second she let Dylan inside her head, and even Dylan had looked a little green.

When Jazz had come back to herself, mumbling about their blood brother waiting for them, they'd been powerless to stop her. She dragged them to a remote monastery by the west coast of Ireland. They all smelled the blood before they stepped inside the monastery. Bodies littered the corridors; blood was splattered on the stone walls. There had been a massacre. Not a sinner was left alive.

Stepping inside the main church of the monastery, Malakai had been ready to take out the monster in the room as he counted a dozen slain monks on the ground. The scent of burnt flesh wrinkled his nose as Malakai got his first glimpse of the vampire responsible for all this death.

Taller than Malakai by a good few inches, the vampire was broad-shouldered, muscular, as if he had acquired the bulk and mass through hard labour on a farm and not from his transition. He wore the robes of a monk even though they were torn and bloodstained, as were his face and arms.

Lifting his gaze to clash with Malakai's, red bleeding through his irises, the vampire snarled, clenching his fists and taking a step toward Malakai. Then Jasmine had stepped in front of Malakai, and the vampire's nostrils flared.

"Hello, Ezekiel. I've come to take you home, brother," Jasmine said in a singsong voice, and the red receded from his eyes and the hulking frame fell to the floor, begging them to kill him, for God had punished him for his evil thoughts and now he had to walk with the devil inside him.

It was such a shame, almost five hundred years later, that Zeke still believed he had the devil inside him.

Dylan was another story. He and Malakai had been best friends growing up, considered one another brothers. When Jasmine came along, she only solidified the bond. While Malakai was the one with big plans that always led them into trouble, Dylan would just smile and divert any punishment from them. He had a way of putting everyone at ease.

When Dylan arose as a vampire, that gift seemed to have intensified to where Dylan now sensed emotions and could manipulate them. If someone was sad, he could use his influence to take the sadness away. If someone was angry, he could calm them down. However, some of their emotions became internalized. Dylan smiled like he hadn't a care in the world, but he worked too damn hard to keep Zeke level, and sometimes, like last night, after taking in some of Zeke's rage, Dylan loosened his own control. Recovering quicker than expected from Keeva's touch, he'd gone to a supernatural club that had succubi and incubi and could handle Dylan's aggressive nature.

Dylan brushed it off like this was just what he needed, what he liked; however, Malakai wasn't sure if his brother enjoyed it anymore or not.

The elevator pinged again with Jasmine and Dylan emerging, Dylan laughing at something Jazz had said. Malakai walked over to the dining table and pulled out his seat as Dylan sat at his right. Jasmine frowned, crossed the room and banged loudly on the door of the library. When she got no answer, Jazz simply grinned and continued to knock until Zeke opened the door, soft classical music drifting out. He spotted Jazz, frowned and sighed, then stepped out and closed the door behind him.

Jasmine came to take the seat at his left, with Zeke sitting next to her. His eyes were firmly fixed on the table.

Dylan leaned back in the chair. "I got offered the contract on Keeva last night after we left the club."

"As did I," Zeke muttered, not taking his eyes off the table.

Malakai knew it was a possibility, considering that Sicarius and Dylan were behind the app that allowed clients to update contracts and assassins to take them. It was the Sicarius Security technical analysts that monitored and tracked for any contracts that might be for petty reasons or go against the Inferna peace rules.

"I also got some more info on both your banshee and your new PA," Dylan said with a sneaky glance at Zeke before he continued. "It seems that Keeva Cross is currently serving a hundred-year sentence for the murder of Angus McFergus's only daughter."

Angus McFergus was the head of the Irish Scream of Banshees, and he'd also just attained a spot on the Inferna council. His request had been denied for the last couple of decades due to a number of factors, including a full table and

Malakai's dislike of the man himself, but he had recently managed to get enough votes to bring him to the table, so his motivation to want Malakai dead was minimal.

"Turns out Keeva and the girl were friends. Angus's daughter fell, and Keeva tried to save her. She panicked, losing control, and killed the other banshee. Angus sentenced her to a hundred years as his pet assassin, only gaining her freedom when she had killed a certain number of people for him or a hundred years, whichever came first. Looks like Angus, or whoever went to Angus, was willing to set her free if she managed to kill you."

"Bastard," muttered Jasmine, and Malakai echoed her words. So that was why Keeva wanted him dead so badly. And Angus had used her for his own means for far too long.

"And moving on to our reluctant succubus."

Malakai bit back a smile as Zeke's hands clenched into fists. Dylan cleared his throat with a smirk on his face. "I know we did a full background check when she applied, but some things you can't find out on a background check. Scarlett Russell, succubus, was pushed out of her Seduction, because while most succubus can't wait to have a nice hard cock in their hands, Scarlett used to get embarrassed in school."

"So the blush and shyness was not an act?" Jasmine asked quietly.

"No. You know what those schools are like. It's like training their teens to be good at sex. From all accounts, Scarlett is known to go to human clubs with Keeva to feed. Her socials are all pictures of her and Keeva. She had no other family or friends. She's definitely being legit about who she is. From the tech guys who checked her browsing history, she spends a lot of time reading romance novels."

Malakai scrubbed a hand down his face. "Good. I really liked her for the PA job. So we have a succubus with an aversion to sex and a banshee who isn't a banshee. I thought I had my hands full with you little freaks; now I'm adding more to the company."

They all laughed, Malakai dismissing them for the night. Dylan and Jasmine got up and went to the window, discussing some new music Jazz wanted to introduce to her set and maybe do a grunge night at the club. Zeke had yet to move or make a comment.

"Anything you want to add, Zeke?"

The other vampire frowned, then lifted his gaze to Malakai's. "You need to keep the damn succubus away from me."

The tone was low, held the hint of a tremor, as if Zeke was trying to hold himself in check.

"Why would I do that?"

"Because last night, when that idiot put hands on her, I wanted to fucking kill him. I wanted to tear out his throat just because he dared touch her."

Sitting back in his chair, Malakai regarded Zeke with caution. "But there's nothing wrong with that, Zeke. You wanted to protect her. I would have done the exact same thing. Why would that mean we needed to keep Scarlett away from you?"

Dylan chuckled softly as he called over, still able to hear what Zeke was saying. Zeke grunted out a breath, refraining from answering. Instead, Dylan thought it was an excellent idea to poke the angry bear. Sometimes Malakai wondered if Dylan got his jollies from living dangerously, like driving rally cars in the dark was not enough.

"I like a challenge, Zeke. I'll keep the succubus away from you. I'm pretty sure I can get that pretty little mouth of hers on my skin. That dress last night, all those curves, it could give a vampire lots of sexy ideas."

Zeke stood up so fast, the chair crashed to the ground. He pointed his finger at Dylan, his expression growing dark. "You … you … stay away from her."

Malakai got to his feet as he saw Dylan take in some more of Zeke's rage, and Dylan snarled. "I'd let you watch if you wanted, man. You could sit on that chair in your little library while I bend her over your desk and take her from behind. Those big innocent blue eyes would be watching you as those full breasts rub back and forth on the wood."

"Dylan," Malakai growled, pushing some of his power into the reprimand, but Zeke bared his fangs, spun, stalking back into the library. He slammed the door so loudly it sounded like a grenade went off.

Dylan bent over and exhaled a shaky breath, his hands on his knees. Jasmine placed a hand on his shoulder, and he brushed it off, causing Jazz to frown.

"What the hell were you thinking, Dylan? Did you want him to deck you?"

Dylan straightened, and Malakai saw something in Dylan's eyes that was startling, as Dylan rarely had use for the emotion himself, only when it was to ease another. But the anger in his brother's eyes was all Dylan.

"I'm losing my goddamn mind over him. He stopped trying to shield his emotions, and now the guilt and anger are driving me crazy. Jazz told me that Scarlett could be his way to redemption, so I pushed. You know how bloody stubborn he is, and we all can see he wants her. Now, instead of picturing himself tearing out her throat and killing her, he's gonna be picturing all kinds of ways he wants to have Scarlett. I can't deal with angry anymore, but horny I can work with."

The last sentence was meant to ease the tension in the room, but it did little to ease the knot in Malakai's stomach. He needed to feed and get clear in his head. With everything going on, he hadn't drunk from the vein in over a week. Grabbing the keys to his car, he left Dylan and Jasmine to their own devices and headed down to the car park.

Slipping inside the Aston Martin, he pulled up details

about Keeva and synced them with an audio app that read out the details over the car's speaker. He drove out into the night, meaning to head for the club, where he could sate his hunger and gain back some of the levelheadedness he was known to have.

Driving down St. Patrick's Street, Malakai couldn't bring himself to pull into his spot outside the club, the crowds of women eyeing his car making Malakai rethink his decision. He suddenly wasn't sure if he would be sated drinking the blood of just any warm body. He bypassed the club and kept driving out into the suburbs. He lied to himself that he had no destination in mind even as he pulled up to an apartment complex that looked less than secure. He could see at least seven ways to access the building if he wanted to sneak in.

Parking the car outside, Malakai headed inside, surprised that there was no one manning the security desk. A giant out-of-order sign was duct-taped to the lift, so Malakai took the stairs two at a time. Then he hesitated outside the apartment door, listening to the sound of the television, for ten minutes as if he was deciding whether or not he was going to knock.

Malakai hadn't even realized he had done so until Keeva opened the door. Her eyes narrowed in suspicion as she ran her eyes over him, her eyes widening slightly as the casualness of his clothing.

"If you are trying to slum it, Cavanagh, you might try wearing clothes that the plebeians don't know cost over a hundred euros, for that cashmere jumper."

Malakai suppressed a smile as he quirked his brow, trying to appear nonchalant. "I'll take that under advisement. Now aren't you going to be polite and invite me in?"

Keeva snorted as she held open the door wide, rolling her stunning cat eyes. "We both know you don't need an invitation inside, vampire."

"It's still polite to offer."

She swept her hand off to the side. "Then, please, oh glorious Primus, won't you enter my humble abode?"

With a chortle of laughter, Malakai stepped inside, shocked that Keeva's entire living room could fit in Malakai's closet. Keeva, with her skills, should be earning massive amounts of money, and it prickled at Malakai's temper to think that Angus has prevented her from living it up. The walls were covered with framed photos of Keeva and Scarlett.

There was a small couch and an armchair. The apartment was poky at best, but Malakai got a sense of warmth. Turning to face Keeva, Malakai ran his eyes over her. Dressed in simple camo leggings, Keeva wore an off the shoulder top with a ACDC logo. Her neck was bare, her pulse thrumming as Malakai tried to stop the innate need to stride across the room, tilt her neck as he fisted his hand in her hair and sink his fangs into her flesh.

"Why are you here, Malakai?"

That wasn't a question he could answer because he sure as hell wasn't sure. But he had been drawn to her like a siren song, and he could have smirked as he licked his lips, Keeva's haunting green eyes following the trail of where his tongue went.

"We have gathered some information and have decided that you and I, the team, we need to work together to decipher if the same person wants us dead."

"So you want a temporary truce?" Keeva asked as she tilted her head just like Malakai wanted, and his throat burned. Would she taste like she smelled, of strawberries?

And didn't that just send the blood rushing right to his cock.

"Yes." That was all he managed to grunt out before he got control of himself and continued. "Six o'clock at Sicarius headquarters. I believe you know the way."

Keeva smiled, her whole face lighting up. "Ya, but it's no fun if I'm allowed to walk in the front door."

Malakai felt the hunger build again, and if he didn't walk out the damn door right now, he would be sucking on her neck. What kind of spell had she woven on him that he was acting like a schoolboy who had a crush?

He confirmed the time again, to which she rolled her eyes, showed him to the door and closed it before he had even taken a step away.

For a second, he contemplated knocking on her door again, then shook his head and was in his car and driving away to find a warm vein before the sun rose. Something told him he wouldn't feel satisfied until Keeva was his.

If she didn't kill him first, that is.

CHAPTER SEVEN

Keeva

Scarlett was long gone by the time Keeva rose the following evening, and Keeva was grateful for the peace and quiet of the night. She had spent the day tossing and turning, her skin too hot, the sheets too heavy on her limbs. Every time she closed her eyes, she saw the hungry look in Malakai Cavanagh's dark brown eyes with a dash of red that flashed for a second. When he had run the tip of his tongue over those full lips, Keeva knew if he walked across the room, hoisted her up on the breakfast bar, she would have thrown caution to the wind and let herself indulge in the want to touch him.

But did Keeva just want him because Malakai was unaffected by her touch?

That thought both thrilled and frightened her.

Having showered away the day, now dressed in black combat pants and boots, Keeva yanked on a dark grey camo long-sleeved tee that was snug but allowed her to move if needed, and then grabbed a dagger and slipped it inside her boot. She wouldn't get away with walking in the front door with a Glock, so the dagger would have to do, though it would surprise her if she got away with that. Forgoing a jacket, Keeva grabbed her keys and then drove the short distance to Sicarius Security.

It felt strange walking in the front door with its fancy logo like a normal person, the camera in the entrance following her every move as she gave it a one-finger salute in greeting. She selected the floor she wanted, which read: Malakai Cavanagh

CEO. The lights remained red for a couple of seconds, the camera whirring until a light flashed green. Keeva tapped her fingers along to the soft rock playing, admiring the company's excellent taste in music as the elevator halted and the doors opened.

A grin broke out on her face as she caught sight of Scarlett with her back to Keeva, reaching into a cabinet. Keeva wolf-whistled as Scarlett's head snapped round, a flush on her cheeks until she laid eyes on Keeva. Then her friend scowled.

"Keeva Cross here to see his royal smugness and arrogant Primus, as requested." Keeva tapped her legs closed and gave Scarlett a salute.

Scarlett rolled her eyes as she closed the cabinet and walked back to her desk. She pressed the com on the phone and said, "Mr. Cavanagh, Ms. Cross here to see you."

"Send her on up to level six, Scarlett. You are welcome to join us if you wish."

The conversation ended as Keeva rested her hip on Scarlett's desk. "So, you laid eyes on your hot serial killer vamp yet?"

Scarlett's entire face went tomato-red. "Keeva!"

"Listen, I'm all for Scarlett finally getting some, so anything I can do to help make that happen, I will. Even if it means breakfast with the enemy."

"You are terrible. Go. I'll come up in a bit once I get some of this mess sorted." Her friend motioned to the neat-as-a-pin pile of files that had Keeva smiling.

"Aye, captain."

Scarlett was still laughing as Keeva strutted back into the elevator, pressed level six and waited as the lift climbed up. When the doors opened, Keeva's eyes went directly to the clear window. Cork city looked incredibly beautiful from all the way up here, the lights like fireflies in an open sky. Sometimes, even at night, it was hard to see the stars through all the clouds. However, tonight the sky was clear, iridescent, as stars twinkled in unison with the lights below her.

Keeva was acutely aware that someone was watching her, and she lifted her gaze to see Dylan grinning at her. His smile was genuine; however, his eyes gave Keeva the impression he had a restless day's sleep like her.

"Rough night?" she asked as she turned to face him, hoping he wasn't still suffering from the effects of her touch.

"Nightmares." Was all Mac ... shit ... Dylan said as he began setting the table with pastries and coffee.

"What kinda nightmares does a billionaire have?" Keeva teased as Dylan paused and smirked at her.

"Not my own, that's what. Not my fucking own."

Keeva made to question him more when across the room, Malakai strode out of what must be a gym, a towel around his neck, wearing joggers and a muscle shirt with bare feet. Beads of sweat coated his pale skin, and Keeva was horrified as she thought of how much she wanted to trail her tongue over his sweaty torso.

"Good evening, Keeva."

"Cavanagh," she replied to his greeting, trying to keep her face impartial.

Malakai chuckled as he motioned for her to sit. Once she had taken a seat, Dylan slid her a mug of coffee and pushed the pastries toward Keeva as if she looked like she needed a feed. He looked like he had fed last night, a quick means to sate his hunger, but now his hunger was ignited once again. Malakai reclined in the chair beside her as she bit into some chocolate-flavoured heaven, holding back a moan at the burst of flavours. Keeva opened her eyes to stare into decadent eyes that looked as good as the chocolate tasted.

"Good, huh?" Dylan said as he grabbed a pastry of his own. "Kai may be a genius businessman, but vampire knows how to bake."

Keeva lifted her brows. "You baked these?" When Malakai

smiled shyly, as if he were sharing a rarely seen part of him, Keeva took another bite and said, "You'll make a good house-husband one day, Cavanagh."

Dylan nearly busted a gut laughing as Malakai chuckled. His eyes turned dark as he reached out and brushed a crumb from Keeva's lips with his thumb, and when he put his thumb in between his lips, Keeva's face and lower body burned. Much lower.

The elevator pinged as the Cavanagh sister bounced inside like an excited cheerleader, her eyes scanning until they landed on the empty seats. "Where are Scarlett and Zeke?"

"Scarlett had some work to do but said she would come up later. Not sure where the hulk is," Keeva said as she swallowed a gulp of coffee to see Dylan watching her in amusement.

"I dare you to call him the hulk to his face."

"Mac," Keeva said, calling him the nickname out of pure habit, "do I look that stupid? I only start battles I can win. Or run very fast away from."

Jasmine slumped down in her chair, a pout on her face, as if things had not turned out the way she had planned. Keeva listened as Malakai told her that both Dylan and Ezekiel had been offered the contract on him as well as her. It was posted on the app late yesterday, so Keeva should expect to see a lot of her former assassin buddies up close and personal. She also learned all about the fact that the assassins were covertly run by Sicarius Security, and that was something she needed to keep to herself.

"As an Elder, it is my job to make sure that Inferna are not killing in such a way that could expose us. We are in direct competition with other organizations for contracts, but we only take jobs that don't compromise us morally. It's not about the money for us."

Easily said by someone who had an abundance of it.

"I understand why Dylan would get offered our contracts, considering we have been trading info for decades, but I had no clue the notorious playboy of Sicarius Security was the man behind the flirting." Keeva noted a sharp look from Malakai to Dylan, who shrugged.

"And," Keeva continued as she picked at another pastry, "I don't understand why Zeke would be offered the contracts. Is he an assassin too?"

The vampire in question walked out shirtless, glared at them, then went through the door Malakai had exited when she had arrived. Tattoos covered a large portion of his back, and Keeva could make out Jesus on a cross.

The pieces of the puzzle clicked into place, and Keeva's jaw hit the ground. Holy hell, Zeke was the infamous Monk. The stone-cold killer that all assassins strived to be. Little was known about the Monk, except that he was a vampire and apparently, he was celibate, but that was just locker-room gossip. He had entire websites dedicated to his little groupies.

Everyone was watching her, as if they expected her to bolt or be revulsed by the revelation. She knew they would all defend the other vampire as much as she did with Scarlett, so Keeva bit into her pastry and then fanned herself.

"Dude, like I can't believe you've been hiding the frickin' Monk from me! I could swoon and fangirl for reals right now."

Dylan barked out a laugh as Jasmine grinned, both seemingly delighted at her fast acceptance of Zeke. But her eyes studied Malakai's reaction as he ground his teeth together. Then his eyes danced with mischief before he pushed back his chair and got to his feet.

"When was the last time you sparred with someone you couldn't harm?"

Anticipation welled in her chest as Keeva slowly lifted her gaze to his. "Never. When I trained, I wore special gloves so as not to touch anyone. Why? You looking to get your ass handed to you?"

"You talk a lot of game for such a petite little assassin."

Keeva let a slow, seductive smile creep over her lips. "Oh, it's on, Cavanagh. I can't wait to show you up in front of your squad."

Keeva rolled up her sleeves as she crossed the room and pushed open the door, ready to show Malakai Cavanagh just how much trouble she really was. Kicking off her boots as she entered the gym, she marvelled at how nice it would be to have somewhere to work off her aggression. Keeva ran as much as possible, careful to only go to gyms that were open all night, where she could work out without interruption or anyone noticing the extra oomph in her strength and speed.

This was a standardized weight room that had a little squared circle in the middle for sparring. Keeva tested the floor, felt the slight bounce in it and grinned even more. She turned, prepared to beckon Malakai forward, when she suddenly sensed a towering presence at her back.

Spinning around, Keeva swallowed hard as she saw up close and personal just what Death looked like, and it wasn't her. Zeke had come out of nowhere, and he somehow managed to cut off her only exit route with his massive frame. Keeva took an involuntary step backward, her back hitting solid wall.

Instead of letting her fear show through, Keeva grinned. "Hello, Monk. Big fan."

"Hello, Death."

Oh, this was not going to end well. Zeke ignored the barked commands of Malakai as he leaned in, and Keeva tried to keep her own fear in check. Last thing she wanted to do was let the big scary monster smell her fear.

"They say your touch can kill a man between one blink and the next."

"Is that what they say?" Keeva croaked out, wondering

why no one was moving to help her. Out of the corner of her eye, she spotted Dylan make an attempt to reach for Zeke, but the vampire swatted him away like he was a fly.

There was this intense anger in Zeke's eyes, this pain that Keeva felt in her soul. And then, as Zeke lifted his meaty hand toward Keeva's throat, his eyes shifted, and in them she saw peace, a resignation to his fate.

Zeke was going to use her to kill himself.

Keeva ducked at the last minute as Zeke growled and swept his legs out to catch her feet. Keeva jumped to avoid the move, ending up cornered with Zeke advancing on her. Malakai would kill her the moment she touched Zeke. So Keeva yanked on the reins of her own power, internalized it, knowing what it would feel like, and oh gods, she was dying.

Zeke gripped her bare arm, lifted her hand and placed it on his flesh, smiling for a second as Keeva felt the room spin. Her organs screamed as her blood roared in her eyes and nausea rolled in her stomach. Zeke's grip on her arm was hard enough to bruise as he snarled at Keeva.

"Show me what you got, Death."

"Bite me, vampire." Then Keeva vomited to the side as the pressure in her head grew tighter and tighter. She had maybe sixty seconds before she ruptured a major organ. It would take a miracle to put a stop to this madness.

"Ezekiel Collins, what in all that is holy are you doing!"

The miracle came in the curvy frame of an angry succubus. Zeke dropped his hand as if he had been caught with his hand in the cookie jar. Keeva dropped to the ground in a heap, letting go of her power so that it no longer attacked her, and sucked in a massive gulp of air as the pain in her head eased, but she'd have a killer headache for the rest of the night.

"I asked you a goddamn question," Scarlett yelled, and Scarlett Russell never yelled. She might get cross with Keeva at times, but this was a new side to her, and Keeva liked what she was seeing!

Malakai was by her side, helping her to her feet as Scarlett marched over to where Zeke was standing and shoved him hard, yet he remained rooted to the spot.

"You planned on using my friend to kill yourself? Do you realize how selfish you are to think you could use her like that? She has been used all her life to kill, and I thought you better than that. She is all the family I have, and you do not get to use her like that. I'm so angry at you!"

The entire gymnasium went deathly silent as Scarlett blinked in surprise at her outburst, and when she realized that she stood, hands on hips, within touching distance of Zeke, her cheeks flamed, and then she managed a perfect pivot and left them all standing there dumbfounded.

Malakai smoothed Keeva's hair from her face. "Are you okay?"

"I'll survive. I hadn't reached the point of no return yet."

"And what is that point?" he asked with genuine concern in his tone.

"Dead."

Keeva stepped around Malakai as he said, "You should have killed him."

Keeva shook her head. "And always be known as the one who killed the legend that is the Monk? No thanks. Hard pass."

Zeke lifted his head, those eyes of his now back to the mixture of pain and anger. "I'm sorry."

"Next time you try and lay hands on me, I'll flay your skin while you are awake. Or maybe I'll tell Scarlett and leave her to deal with you."

Zeke grunted, storming from the room, and then Keeva closed her eyes as a wave of nausea rolled through her stomach.

Malakai took her arm, leading her from the gym and to

the kitchen, where he handed her a bottle of water, studying her as she rinsed out her mouth and spat into sink.

"I need to go lie down."

"You should stay here and let me look after you."

Keeva sighed, shaking her head, even though she was considering it. Leaning against the counter, Keeva took another drink before she set the bottle down. "I don't think that's a good idea, do you?"

Malakai gave her a grin that was wolfish and boyish at the same time, and Keeva got another glimpse of the man underneath the mask. "I think it's a very good idea to get you in my bed."

Rolling her eyes, Keeva remarked casually, "You're used to looking after other people."

"I make sure my family is happy and safe. I do the same for any vampire in my Kiss. I also take good care of my employees."

"So if something happens to me, you'll look after Scarlett?"

Malakai frowned at her. "Nothing is going to happen to you, Keeva."

The way he said her name was enough to flush her skin, but Keeva clamped down on her fickle heart and the fact that the more she got to know the enigma that was Malakai Cavanagh, the more she wanted to spend time with him.

"I've been wondering if you would taste as good as you smell. It's something that I cannot stop thinking about."

Heart racing, Keeva decided to dance with the devil as she asked, "And what do I smell like?"

"Strawberries. Ripe, plump, juicy strawberries."

The air tingled as Malakai took a step toward her. Then another. He crowded her body so that if Keeva had wanted to, she could reach out and run her palms up the planes of his abdomen and pet that muscular chest of his. Malakai leaned in and inhaled at the curve of her neck.

"Definitely like strawberries. Good enough to eat."

Keeva shook her head with a smile and moved around Malakai to head for the elevator. The vampire followed her into the elevator as if he were surprised that Keeva was holding out on him and not ripping his clothes off.

"How long has it been since you could touch someone without fear of killing them?"

"Too long," Keeva admitted in a whisper, wishing she hadn't when he grinned smugly.

"I promise to be very good and let you touch me wherever you desire."

Keeva snorted out her nose as she rolled down her sleeves. "If all I wanted was a night of sex with someone I can touch, I'd give your sister a call."

Malakai chuckled, scratching the stubble on his jawline. "Jazz might just take you up on that. But I think you want me as much as I want you."

Keeva decided it was detrimental to her health and sanity not to issue a response to that statement as the elevator doors opened. Malakai walked beside her as they went out the doors of Sicarius Security. Standing out in the cool night air, Keeva shivered, tiredness seeping into her bones.

"I could pay Angus off for you. You could come work with me, with us. I'm dying to know how you managed to get in undetected."

Knowing that his offer was sincere was the only reason why Keeva was able to quell her temper, but Malakai saw the flash of it in her eyes, and Keeva could tell he wasn't sure what he had said that had irked her. Like buying her freedom was the easiest thing in the world and maybe, to him, it was.

"Whether it's Angus that holds my leash or Sicarius," Keeva stated, careful not to suggest that Malakai would be the one controlling her, "it means I'm still stuck in that position. I want the freedom to choose, Kai. Not have my life chosen for me."

Malakai regarded her with surprise, perhaps because she had used the nickname used by his family but maybe because of the truth in her words. Malakai made to answer when Keeva heard a whistle though the air, and she moved without thinking, even as the vampire made as if to grab her.

She took Malakai to the ground as the bullet whizzed over their heads. The bullet bounced off the bulletproof glass and plonked to the ground. Keeva shifted her position and placed her hands on Malakai's chest as she glanced around, checking for any assailants.

"I think we're clear," Keeva said as she made the fatal mistake of looking Malakai dead in the eyes. Time stood still for a heartbeat, and then Malakai fisted his hand in her hair and claimed her mouth in a hot kiss that set her soul on fire.

CHAPTER EIGHT

Malakai

MALAKAI DIDN'T CARE THAT SOMEONE WAS TRYING TO KILL either of them as he slanted his mouth over Keeva's, his grasp of her hair tight as his free left hand stroked over the curve of her ass, bringing her core dangerously close to his rock-hard erection. Keeva gasped into his mouth as he lavished her tongue with his own.

She met each thrust of his tongue with one of her own, her hands firmly planted on the planes of his chest, with her eyes fixed on his, until she pulled back her mouth from his, leaving him chasing after the taste of her. Nothing had ever felt as good as that before. He had guessed correctly. She tasted like strawberries.

"I'm not done with you yet," Malakai growled as Keeva scrambled off him, her eyes darting around.

"Someone just tried to put a bullet in your head. They might still be out there. Get your ass off the floor, Malakai, and into your armoured building."

Zeke and Roman ducked out the door, Zeke picking Malakai up off the ground like he weighed nothing and dragging him inside before setting him on his feet again. When the doors to Sicarius closed behind them, Keeva slipped back outside despite Malakai's growl in a feeble attempt to stop her. Roman slipped out after her, and then the two came back in, Keeva with a bullet in the palm of her hand.

Lifting the bullet to her nose, Keeva frowned. "Coated in holy water. I can smell the blessing oil. This is also a specialized custom bullet that once it pierces the flesh, splinters.

There are probably traces of wood in the bullet that would have lodged in your heart to kill you."

Dylan strode over to Keeva, glanced down at the bullet and then back at Keeva. "Who do you think it was?"

Malakai watched the exchange, jealousy punching him in the gut that Dylan had such an easy friendship with his fiery banshee. Dylan spared him a glance with his brow raised in question, obviously sensing his totally uncalled for reaction, but Malakai shook his head and simply watched his banshee work.

Because after the kiss that they'd just shared, Keeva was definitely going to be his.

"Could have been a few of them. I could have shot that in my sleep. So could you. Ghost used to carry rounds like this, as did Harper."

"Harper's eyesight isn't that good. She's better with knives. Ghost could do it, but you know he gets his kicks from appearing out of thin air and using a garrotte."

Keeva pressed her lips together and turned to look out the window. "Shot came from that rooftop. Send some guys over to see if the idiot made any more mistakes and left something behind. It's obvious the bullet was meant for Malakai, not me. They just hadn't factored me in."

Dylan barked out an order, a team heading out to check the rooftop as Keeva turned back to Dylan. "You've obviously got security cameras all around this place. Is your server room still in the basement?"

Dylan blinked in surprise. "How the hell do you know that?"

Keeva grinned, her green eyes brightening, and Malakai saw beneath the hard exterior to a woman who liked to tease and have fun. "The same way that I know that when you fitted the building, especially the roof, with motion sensors, the idiot installing them forgot all about the air-conditioning unit and the maintenance vent. Figured someone couldn't squeeze their way in, because no one considered a short little female might at some point try."

"Son of a bitch, I'm that idiot," Dylan growled as he ran his fingers through his hair.

Keeva threw back her head and laughed as Dylan led her away, his hand on the small of her back. Malakai felt unnecessarily possessive, like an idiot, because he trusted Dylan with his life and with Keeva's. Dylan opened the door and held it open for Keeva, who snuck a glance at him, giving him a small smile before they disappeared inside to head to the basement.

Malakai turned his focus to making sure the rest of his people were safe. "Roman, lock down the building. No one goes home; no one enters. We are in total lockdown until further notice. Send someone to check on the families."

The shifter nodded and headed off without another word to do as asked, Malakai watching as Jazz's gaze followed the retreating back of the wolf with a little less contempt than their initial meeting.

"Jazz, go let Scarlett know what happened. Set up the guest room for her and make sure she has everything she needs."

"I'll do it."

Both Malakai and Jazz turned to look at Zeke as the other vampire rubbed his scalp as if uncomfortable. When neither he nor Jazz said anything, Zeke turned round and headed for the elevator.

"Zeke," Malakai called after him. The other vampire turned back to face them. "Ask Scarlett to bring her laptop to the communal dining area. Once Keeva comes back, she will feel more comfortable. And Zeke?"

"What?"

"She's bound to be a little scared. Reassure her that Keeva is fine."

Zeke read the unsaid words telling him to not scare Scarlett any more than she already was. He pondered that for a moment, as if he did not know how not to be intimidating, then nodded before disappearing into the elevator. Malakai and Jazz made a few more arrangements over the next ten minutes before they headed up to the main area to regroup.

They stepped out of the elevator to see Zeke set a bottle of water down on the table for Scarlett, who gave him a warm smile. Scarlett turned her attention to her laptop then, her face full of concentration. Malakai watched in amusement as Zeke lingered for a full minute before he turned, heading for his safe haven and sometimes his self-inflicted prison cell.

"Ezekiel."

Hand on the library door, Zeke froze at the warmth in Scarlett's voice, keeping his back to her so that he missed out on the radiant smile she sent in his direction. Malakai wondered if seeing it might have made a difference.

"Thank you for making sure I was settled. That was very kind of you."

Zeke grunted in response before he disappeared inside of the library, and Malakai headed over toward the table. Jazz tossed him a tee that was on the sofa as he sank down next to Scarlett, Jazz taking the other seat as Scarlett lifted her gaze to his.

"Interesting first day?"

"Keeva's really okay?"

Malakai reached out and gave her hand a squeeze. "I promise. I won't let anything happen to her."

Scarlett's big blue eyes held his for a moment before she dropped her gaze, her cheeks flushed. "Thank you. Keeva has looked after me for a long time. I try, but she's just a force of nature, you know. It's nice for her to have someone to look after her. She's never really had that."

Flashing Scarlett a brilliant smile, Malakai said, "You don't give yourself enough credit, darling. When you thought Keeva was in danger, you stormed in like a warrior princess in heels and got through to Zeke. I think it's that sort of empathy that means you look after Keeva as well as she looks after you. There are different kinds of care, Scarlett."

The blush on Scarlett's face deepened as if she wasn't used to such compliments. "I'm sorry I lost my temper before. I never lose my temper. I don't know what came over me. I don't even know him that well."

"And that just proves my point. We've had Zeke in the family for a long time. I love him as much as I love my other brother and sister. I think he could do with a little bit more of Scarlett in his life."

Just when Malakai thought the succubus couldn't redden even more, she did, dropping her eyes to the laptop. "I cancelled your conference call with the New York office due to the current situation, advising them you had an immediate meeting that was more pressing. You have received three calls about a council meeting this Friday, and I rearranged other meetings until end of the week, citing urgent family business."

Lifting her hand after the abrupt change of topic, Malakai pressed a kiss to her knuckles. "A godsend. How did I ever cope without you?"

Scarlett chuckled softly as she shut her laptop, excused herself and went off to the little spare room they had on this floor, citing the need to freshen up. Jasmine went with her to give her some extra clothing to wear should she want to change, leaving Malakai alone in the room.

He wandered to the window, looking out over the city until the elevator chimed and Keeva strode in. She immediately went to where he stood, her arms folded over her chest as she looked out on the city with him.

"Cameras caught an image of the shooter, but their face was covered, with no distinguishing marks or movement. Dylan said to say he came to the same conclusion, like you needed his confirmation that I was right in my assessment. Doofus."

"Dylan," Malakai said with a chuckle, "is a little pissed off that you found a loophole in his security system. No doubt, right now, he is contacting every single Sicarius Security premises to install motion sensors in the ventilation systems. Should keep him busy for the rest of the night and out of my hair."

"Well, it's a good system. I'm just better."

"And would make the perfect newest addition to the company."

Keeva tilted her head to look at him. "You know I filled out an application once. Had all the documents and everything ready to press send, and I chickened out. I didn't think I was good enough to work for you guys. I had no college degree or specialty skills like Roman. I mean, this is where one of us wants to end up when being a lonely assassin got too much. I used to tell Mac—Dylan—all the time that we could make more money and probably have a longer lifespan. To think I used to worry that Mac was all alone, especially when I could go home to Scarlett."

"Do you still get lonely?" Malakai asked, the blood he'd ingested last night allowing his heart to beat, his pulse racing as he swept her hair off her face, cataloguing each and every freckle.

"Do you?"

He refrained from answering her, checking his smart watch to confirm that his building was airtight, and then he said, "I don't want to be lonely today."

He was male enough to know when a woman wanted him, knew his lethal banshee wanted him from the way she curved her body toward him. Not waiting for an answer, Malakai dipped his head and gently pressed his lips to hers in a soft kiss. Her eyes widened as Keeva dropped her arms to her side.

"I can't decide if I want to go slow with you first, taking my time to taste every inch of that gorgeous freckled skin. To lick those pert nipples and mark your pretty breasts with my teeth. I can't wait to find out if you taste of strawberries when I put my mouth on your wet heat and lick you like a lollipop."

"Malakai." That hitch in her breath was all he needed to continue.

"Or if I fucked you with my fingers, would you already be wet and tight? Would you milk my cock so good that I'd come with one single stroke? I find myself wanting to take you from behind, your breasts pressed against the glass over-looking the city so I can see your face reflected in the glass when you scream my name, and scream you will, my little fiery banshee."

Her mouth opened as if to argue, and he kissed her again, this time taking as much control as possible to suck and bite and tease enough to leave her breathless as he broke the kiss, spun her round and pressed her front to the glass, sweeping her hair off her neck to press an open-mouth kiss to the nape of her neck before he licked up the taste of her.

Rotating his hips, he smiled smugly as she sucked in a breath at the feel of his erection against her. She pressed back into him, turning suddenly to drag his head down for another kiss that went straight to his cock. He was rock-hard and ready to strip her bare and have his way with her right now.

Her lips sucked on his bottom lip, then she used her teeth to tug gently at them. Malakai cupped her ass and hoisted her up into his arms, Keeva wrapping her own arms around his neck. Malakai walked them to the elevator, pressing the button to call it up, all while he sucked hard on the soft skin between her shoulder and neck. He bit down gently, not hard enough to break the skin, when they stepped into the elevator.

Once inside his room, she wiggled in his grasp, and he let

her stand on her own two feet, giving her a second to catch her breath.

"We need ground rules," she stated, breathless and flushed.

"Ground rules?" he asked with amusement.

Hands on her hips, Keeva backed away as he advanced, prowling toward her as he pulled his T-shirt and vest off. "Yes, ground rules. One time. We get whatever this is out of our systems, and then we part amicably."

"I was hoping for more than once, Keeva, and that's just tonight."

Keeva licked her kiss-swollen lips and swallowed hard, like she was planning to run. He was very good at stalking his prey when he needed to.

"I told you, Keeva." Malakai prowled around her, pulling her own tee over her head to reveal a green lace bra. "I want to take you slow, thrusting long and deep, so that when you come, you can't even think straight. Then I'm going to fuck you hard and fast while I taste your blood. For round three, I think I'm going to fuck you with my tongue as you fist your hands in the sheets. I want you to walk around tomorrow and with every step you take, you'll still feel me inside you."

She spun to face him, her eyes wide as he said, "What do you think about that?"

"I think you talk too much. More action, less words."

Malakai chuckled as Keeva came forward and put her hands on him, causing him to shudder under the heat of her touch. Starting at the navel, she traced the planes of his stomach before running her hands over his pecs, then up to his shoulders and down his arms, a look of pure amazement on her face like she couldn't believe she was running her hands over his body. Leaning in, Malakai felt the smile on her lips as she pressed her lips to his right nipple and then, Malakai almost lost his mind when she ran her tongue over his nipple.

Her hands tugged at his pants, but he gripped her wrists. "Not yet."

His fingers popped the button on her combat pants as she kicked off her boots, and then hooking his thumbs in the loops, Malakai slowly shimmied them down over her hips and firm thighs before she stepped out of them, and then Malakai dropped to his knees and pressed his open mouth to her damp panties, the same colour as her bra.

Keeva swore, scraping her fingers against his scalp, and he wanted to feel those nails on his flesh as thrust into her. Pushing her panties aside, he kissed the inside of her thigh as he inserted a finger into her wet, hot heat. He pumped his finger once, twice as Keeva's body clenched, and then he inserted a second finger.

"Forget slow, Kai. I need you inside me now."

He liked the sound of his name on her lips. Much like he did her combats, Malakai slid her panties down so she could step out of them, and then he stood, claiming her mouth again as he walked them back to the bed. He lifted her and had her lying on the bed as he slid off his own pants.

Keeva's green eyes fell to the bulge in his boxers as she unhooked her bra and tossed it to the side. "You are absolutely gorgeous," he marvelled as he drank in the sight of her naked and ready for him.

Keeva huffed out a laugh. "I'm already naked, Cavanagh. Cut the foreplay already."

"Oh, Red, I've just started."

His hands cupped her thighs, yanking her toward him, and Keeva let out a yelp that quickly turned into a moan as Malakai sucked on her clit like a starving man. Her moans of pleasure were like music to his ears as Keeva arched her hips to let him penetrate her deeper with his tongue. Shifting his grasp, he fingered her again, and it wasn't long until she was undone, her orgasm sending little shudders coursing through her body.

As Keeva started to come out the other side of her orgasm, Malakai let his fangs elongate, and then, as he continued to spear his fingers inside her, Malakai sank his fangs into the creamy flesh at her thigh, Keeva screaming his name.

Removing his fingers, he flicked his tongue over the fang marks on her skin to close the wound, letting her momentarily catch her breath as she panted. "Dear God, I'm dead. I'm done."

Malakai stripped off his boxers and crawled his way up her body. "I'm not done with you yet, Keeva." To emphasis the point, Malakai rolled his hips, the blunt head of his cock barely touching her molten core as she sucked in a breath.

"I wanted to take my time with you. I wanted time to play with those pretty breasts of yours." Malakai cupped her breasts to emphasize his point. "They fit so perfectly in my hands. But that can be for later. I don't think I can take my time, Keeva. I want you far too much and need to sate this hunger I have for you."

He let his hand fall to his rock-hard cock, her eyes watching him as he pumped once, twice, then Malakai positioned himself at her entrance and slowly thrust in a little, pulling out again before he went in a little deeper. Malakai felt her walls contract to accommodate his size, her nails digging into his arms as she held on to his, those eyes on him as he thrust in again a little deeper.

"Oh God, Kai. Don't stop. Please, God, don't stop."

His control broke as he sheathed himself fully inside her, waiting a full minute before she ordered him to move. So he did. Malakai pounded into her, gritting his teeth as his fangs burst out of his gums again as Keeva met him thrust for thrust, and when she managed to open her eyes, his hunger evident in his eyes, Keeva turned her head in silent invitation as if she knew what he wanted.

Malakai latched onto her flesh, piercing her skin, and Keeva cried out, another wave of pleasure sending little tremors from her body right down to his cock. He sheathed himself fully inside her as he swallowed her blood, and then with one final surge, Malakai came harder than he had in his whole life.

He reluctantly pulled out of her to roll them so Keeva was half sprawled over him, her eyes heavy with exhaustion as she patted his chest, her husky whisper like a kiss against his skin. "Not bad, Cavanagh, not bad."

Malakai chuckled as she lay down on his chest and fell asleep, so he wrapped his arms around her and simply held her, wondering how the fuck he would be able to convince her that he wanted to keep her.

CHAPTER NINE

Keeva

EYES FLUTTERING OPEN, KEEVA WAS SURPRISED TO SEE THAT THE sun had just set and darkness descended upon the city. Her body ached in the most delicious of ways, after what had to have been the best sex of her life. Keeva took in the position of her body, her leg curled around Malakai's, her head lying on his chest with one hand entwined with his. Malakai's eyes were closed, his body still in that way vampires did when they slept; however, he had his free hand curved possessively on her ass as if he thought she would bolt.

Keeva had never been a stay-the-night kind of girl. She couldn't risk it. Usually, after a quickie where she felt even emptier than she had before the tryst, Keeva was already dressed, if she had even bothered to get undressed in the first place, and out the door before the guy could ask for her number. Growing attached to someone meant yearning to touch them, and that would not be possible.

Having felt her power surge forward last night when Malakai was doing devilish things with his tongue and teeth, Keeva had felt a flare of panic, even though she knew she could not use her power against Malakai. But Keeva was an overthinker and knew she was worried that she had slept with Malakai because she didn't have to worry about killing him.

When she should have been worrying that she might still have to kill him.

Her phone buzzed indecently, and Keeva slipped out of

Malakai's grasp and bed, dropping to the floor as the vampire sat up in the bed. Averting her gaze, Keeva dove into her pants and pulled out the years-old phone. Frowning at the name on the screen, Keeva yanked on her tee as the phone stopped for a brief minute before starting again.

Blowing out a breath, Keeva pressed answer. "What?"

"You are meant to be killing the goddamn vampire, not saving his life!"

Gritting her teeth, Keeva got to her feet and strode away from where Malakai was taking a keen interest in her call. Leaning against the wall, Keeva snarled into the phone. "And if the other assassin had taken out the Primus, then I would not be free of you, Angus. If he dies by another hand, then I don't get the bounty. Call off the attack dogs on me so I can get on with the job."

"You do not tell me what to do, you fucking parasite. For every day that Malakai is alive, I will shave a year off the time you would have gotten if you had killed him. You will spend another forty years working toward your debt to me. I will ensure that you complete your full sentence for killing my Clodagh."

A hot wave of fury flooded her veins. "Clodagh was dead either way, Angus. Falling off the cliff would have killed her. I was a scared teen who tried to save her friend."

"You will do as you are told, abomination, or I will kill you myself!"

Even though Angus could not see her face, Keeva smiled a sadistic smile, knowing full well that Angus was blowing hot air into the atmosphere. "You're welcome to try, Angus. You are very welcome to try."

Keeva hung up and flung the phone at the opposite wall, the phone shattering on impact. Malakai had gotten out of bed and was striding toward her, his eyes dark and unreadable. He was gloriously naked, making Keeva itch to reach out and touch him, taste every inch of him with her tongue again.

"Keep looking at me like that, little banshee, and I'll let you take your anger out on me."

Malakai smiled, the gesture so human that Keeva could almost forget that he was the leader of the vampires in Ireland. Glancing around the room, Keeva was suddenly struck by how out of place she was here. Everything was pristine, expensive. And she was not.

Malakai Cavanagh was caviar and exquisite champagne, and she was fast-food takeout and watered-down cola. Wrapping her arms around her waist, Keeva brushed past Malakai and gathered up her clothes, ignoring the perplexed look on his face as she locked herself into the bathroom. If she had hoped some peace in the bathroom would clear her mind, she was wrong. Keeva was only reminded how far apart their worlds were.

The bathroom was all black tiles and countertops, with a hint of shimmer that Keeva suspected might be real diamonds. A shower ran all along the back wall, and it was one of those fancy showers that you saw in movies where the floor was level with the rest of the bathroom and that could fit maybe half a soccer team. Keeva wondered how many women Malakai had fucked in this shower and cursed herself for wishing she was one of them.

As Keeva began to dress, a soft rap of knuckles sounded on the door. "Keeva?"

Her heart pounded in her chest at the tone, a slightly cautious question that was tinged with sadness. She hadn't wanted to make him sad, but Keeva couldn't find the words to say that could rewind the clock and go back to when they were just flirting. Things were complicated now. Keeva heard Malakai release a frustrated growl before she heard him walk away from the door.

Keeva waited until the elevator had been called before she slipped out of the bathroom and scurried across the floor to call the elevator herself, trying to stop her gaze from wandering to the messy bed and her mind replaying last night over in her mind. Had she not been a convicted criminal and assassin and Malakai not the Primus, who knows what could have been.

The elevator doors opened to reveal Dylan standing there grinning at her. He opened his mouth to speak, but Keeva held up her hand. "Whatever smartass remark is about to tumble out of those lips, keep it to yourself. I'm not in the mood for you today."

"That is almost verbatim what Kai just snarled at me. Jesus, you'd think having sex would have loosened you both up, but you two are even bigger balls of tension."

Keeva arched her brows. "How the hell do you know that we had sex?"

"Darling, I can smell Kai on your skin and you on his." At Keeva's horrified expression, Dylan grinned and pointed to himself. "Vampire, remember?"

Keeva felt her cheeks flame as she pressed the button for the ground floor, but Dylan slipped a key into the elevator and pressed for the floor Keeva knew was the family area. Keeva stepped around Dylan to press for the ground floor again when Dylan blocked her way.

"The building is still on lockdown, Keeva. No matter what's going on now, we need to figure out who is coming for you and Malakai. The two of us know the assassin world better than our security teams, so you don't get to leave."

"You don't get to stop me, Mac. Get out of my way."

Dylan shook his head, blond hair falling into his face. "No can do, Death. I know what you're feeling and why you are running, yet I think you are getting in your own way. Give Kai a chance."

Keeva's green eyes moved from Dylan to the buttons as they neared the floor Dylan was directing them toward. Keeva didn't want to be sitting in that room eating breakfast with them, smelling like Malakai, digging into a meal with cutlery that probably came from some fancy department store. Keeva took a step back, and Dylan flashed her a grin as if he had won the fight.

The fight was only beginning.

Keeva clenched her fist, recoiling her arm before she decked Dylan square in the jaw, careful to move her hand before her power could surge forward. The vampire stumbled back as his eyes widened and flashed red. Keeva circled him, kicking out with her right foot as Dylan caught her foot and shoved her back. Keeva regained her balance, taking a breath as Dylan stalked toward her with anger in his face. He reached for Keeva's shoulders, but she ducked under his grasp and kicked the back of his knees.

Dylan went down, and Keeva pressed his back downward so that her assassin friend was lying on his stomach in the elevator. Dylan jerked under her boot and was suddenly rising up, fangs elongated and death in his eyes. Keeva beckoned him with her hands and stepped back.

On his feet in a blur of movement, Dylan came at her, his fists flying so Keeva had to block his blows. In her anger, Keeva had forgotten that Dylan was stronger and faster than she would ever be. She elbowed him in the stomach, and he grunted as he stepped back.

The elevator doors opened suddenly, causing Dylan to look over his shoulder, and Keeva attacked. Jumping up, she caught the lip of the door and kicked Dylan in the stomach with both feet, the vampire stumbling back into the living area, and Keeva dropped to her feet, pushing her power into her hands as Dylan lunged for her, stopping short at the pulse of magic around Keeva.

"Stop!"

Keeva pulled her magic back at the authority in Malakai's tone, cursing herself that she wasn't immune to him. Dylan gritted his teeth, snarling softly until Malakai came to place a hand on his shoulder. Dylan's demeanour immediately changed to his more usually aloof expression, his eyes lifting to Keeva's.

"Damn, little banshee, not one for hiding your emotions, are ya?"

Keeva shrugged her shoulders, rolling her eyes. "Well, when you try and stop someone from leaving when they want to leave, of course they're gonna be angry. I'm not a pushover."

"Bloody hell, Death. I only wanted you to hang around because we have information. If you wanted to get away from Kai so bad, you should have just said."

"I did. You didn't listen. So I enunciated with my fists."

Dylan glanced at Malakai, who nodded, and Dylan moved away from them to go sit at the table, where Jasmine was dishing out food and Scarlett was looking at her with those sad blue eyes of hers.

Slumping her shoulders, Keeva lifted her gaze to clash with Malakai's blank expression. He stepped back and indicated for her to take a seat, holding the chair out as she sat, and Keeva tried to ignore the brush of his fingers on the nape of her neck as he moved by her.

"Are you okay?" Scarlett asked, her features concerned.

"All good. This place … I just forgot who I was for a minute."

Scarlett frowned yet held her tongue as she reached for a pot of yogurt to add to her fruit. Keeva sat with her hands in her lap for a few minutes, her eyes fixed on the spot right above the cooker until Scarlett slid a plate of scrambled eggs and bacon under her nose. The scent of it made her stomach rumble. Keeva smiled at Scarlett, then picked up her fork and ate without tasting much.

Keeva was aware of Malakai studying her, no doubt wondering what he had done wrong since last night, when he had reduced her to nothing but moans and groans. She had not known that sex could be that good. Sneaking a peak in his direction, Keeva watched as Jasmine said something softly, and Malakai laughed, the sound crawling over her skin, the hint of fang causing Keeva to shiver.

Pushing the half-eaten plate away, Keeva let her hands fall to her lap as Scarlett sighed, got to her feet and began to clear the table. Dylan tried to stop her, however Scarlett simply said that as Malakai had cooked, she would clean up.

Scarlett looked like she was at home, comfortable here with these vampires. She had smiled more in the last few days than Keeva had ever seen. Keeva could leave her here and Scarlett would be looked after. She was okay at not having to leave, but Keeva felt the panic welling in her chest whenever she was stuck in a small room or when something triggered her, like there were shackles around her wrists and ankles. It was like she was back at the banshee prison and there was no sun, no air, nothing but her thoughts and her feelings, and Keeva felt herself want out. Her mind raced as her palms sweated and she felt held in place.

"Am I a prisoner?"

The words slipped from Keeva's lips before she had a chance to filter her tone, and it came out sounding rather aggressive. The conversation instantly stilled, all eyes looking to Keeva. She could not stand the pity in their eyes as if they knew her story, but they didn't, not all of it, she hoped, so when no one answered her, Keeva asked again a little louder.

"Am I a prisoner?"

"What have any of us done in the last couple of days to make you feel like a prisoner?" Malakai asked her in a deadly tone, as if he were fighting not to snarl at her. Keeva waved her hand at Dylan and clamped her lips together, closing her eyes, but the darkness haunted her when she did, and she lost herself to memories she had long failed to banish.

Drip, drip, drip.

Keeva shivered in the darkness, licking the salt of her tears to try and quench the thirst raging in her throat to no avail. The seconds bled into minutes, minutes to days, until Keeva didn't know how long Angus had kept her down in the dungeon without food or water or human contact. Keeva spent her time begging Clodagh for her forgiveness yet knowing her actions had been unforgiveable.

The chains on her arms and legs chafed as Keeva tried to move. A small sliver of light shone through a crack in the wall, but she could not get close enough to feel its heat, feel something other than cold and darkness on her skin.

Keeva prayed to whatever god would listen and begged them for a swift execution, but all the gods had abandoned her years ago.

"How long were you a prisoner?"

"Two years." It was Scarlett who answered when Keeva could not find the words to convey what was haunting her. It had been a while since Keeva had lost herself in her memories like so.

"She was fifteen at the time, and he locked her in the darkness for two years by herself. He barely sent food or water, and she saw no other person for those two years. Then that bastard dragged her out of the darkness and made her his assassin."

Keeva knew her friend was crying, but Keeva couldn't comfort her. She felt as if she were bound to the chair, unable to move, when the chair was moved slowly and Keeva was looking into chocolate-brown eyes. His hand cupped her cheek, yet Keeva was frozen in place.

"You are free to leave if you wish to do so. However, we only want to keep you safe. There is no one here who will shackle you in the dark, Keeva. I would kill anyone who dared try, if you did not kill them first."

Keeva swallowed hard at the sincerity in his voice. All she

could do was nod as Malakai brushed his lips over her forehead as he rose. Keeva righted her seat, ducked her eyes as she blew out a breath and changed the subject.

"If you had asked me last week who out of the assassin world could take me out, I would have just given four names. In the hierarchy, Mac would have been my first choice. Although being taken out by the Monk would have been legendary. I could have accepted that. The Widow only takes out men, so unless she suddenly had a change of heart, I think I'd be okay."

Dylan laughed. "I wouldn't kill you, sweetheart. I'd never have taken the job. And the Widow would have declined it as well."

"How can you be sure?" Keeva asked as she reached for a cup of coffee that Scarlett had set down in front of her.

"I'm super picky about who I kill. I wouldn't even get out of bed for that lame-ass amount."

Keeva's head snapped in Jasmine direction, her eyes wide. How had she not seen it? But Keeva had never expected Mac to be one of the founders of Sicarius Security. Jasmine had sun-kissed blond hair and was just as gorgeous as Dylan was. People who looked at her would think of her as this dumb blonde who only cared for money and expensive clothes. But was all of this just an act?

Shaking her head with a grin at Jasmine, Keeva ran through the list of suspects it could be. "Ghost wouldn't take out a fellow assassin no matter how much money he was offered. Harper doesn't have the stomach for what it would mean to come for me, and Sniper would consider it an insult to take me out with a bullet. Reaper and Romeo could be a problem, but I can handle them."

"Aren't you forgetting someone?" Dylan remarked with a grin that should have told Keeva that he was setting her up for something big, but Keeva shrugged and waved her hand in the air.

When people spoke of the hierarchy of the assassins, Keeva was third-tier. Mac, Monk and Widow were second-tier, but there was one elusive assassin who was the cream of the crop. He was so deadly that he had his pick of jobs. If he assigned something to you, then you did it without question for fear the Devil would come searching for you, and if El Diablo took an interest in you, then it was lights out, good night and sayonara.

Keeva chuckled, rolling her eyes. "El Diablo? Are you kidding me? The guy doesn't get his hands dirty for less than a million, and I ain't worth that."

"The bounty has risen to five million euros."

Keeva's mouth hung open. Bloody hell, someone wanted her in the ground bad enough to fork out five million euros? Apart from Angus, Keeva couldn't think of anyone who would want her dead that bad, and Angus sure as hell didn't have five million lying around. Her pulse raced as Keeva tried to come to terms with one of the biggest bounties in assassin history.

"If it makes you feel a little better, Malakai's bounty is double yours," Jasmine said with a grin so eerily similar to Dylan's that Keeva shook her head.

"Then it will be a mercenary that takes up the contract on me, because why would El Diablo come for me for a measly five million when he can take Malakai out and get ten million and bragging rights?"

Laughter filled the room, and Keeva felt like she was missing something important, and it grated on her temper. Getting to her feet with a growl, Keeva slammed her fist down on the table. "What is so bloody funny?"

She heard a soft, sensuous chuckle to her left, but Keeva wasn't going to look at him at all. Her eyes fixed on Dylan, her glare fierce enough that the vampire said with the biggest grin, "Oh, Diablo wants to get his hands on you badly. I can tell just how badly The Devil wants his hands on you with or without five million. But I think he has other ideas besides killing you."

Keeva still didn't get it. She was confused as hell as her eyes drifted to Malakai, who looked at her with this intense hunger that sent a thrill down Keeva's spine.

"I can think of more interesting things to do with my hands than kill you, Keeva."

CHAPTER TEN

Keeva

KEEVA HAD NO WORDS. WELL, SHE HAD WORDS, HOWEVER FOUND herself unable to speak them. Malakai was El Diablo, the assassin all assassins emulated. When Dylan had warned her that she needed to look past the thousand-euro suit and good looks, he hadn't been joking. She had slept with the most dangerous man in the world, and he just sat there grinning at her like he wanted to take another bite out of her in the most delicious sort of way. Malakai Cavanagh had been dangerous all on his own, but knowing that he was the assassin everyone called El Diablo, that was utterly terrifying.

She tried to find an eloquent way of asking her questions, but the words seemed to tumble from her lips before her brain could catch up. "How? You're Primus of the vampires and a member of the elders council ... you wear Armani suits and drive around in ridiculously expensive cars ... you run a multimillion-euro corporation ... you can't be a lowly assassin as well?"

"I was an assassin long before I became Primus or sat on the council of Elders," Malakai drawled, his eyes taking in every expression as she shook her head. Keeva couldn't wrap her head around the new information, struggled to process it. Had last night all been about lowering her defences so that Malakai could kill her?

"I won't let you kill me without a fight."

Malakai growled as he got to his feet with a predator's grace. "I have no intentions of killing you, Keeva. We make sure that we investigate into contracts before we take them. Had I not known you, I still would have declined the contract and perhaps sent one of us to have a word with the person who took out the contract."

His words seemed cold, calculated, detached—the vampire who had teased her and told her all the delicious dirty things he wanted to do to her gone. If he could change just like that, how much of what the man Keeva had witnessed was him wanting her and what part of it was keeping the mark close?

"Am I just a mark? Is that what all this is about?" Keeva demanded, waving her hands to the table, although she wasn't sure if she wanted the answer to that question.

"No."

That was all Malakai said, but Keeva didn't even hide her embarrassment as she spun on her heels to leave. It was only when she was at the elevator that she realised that Scarlett was beside her, ready to leave with her. Turning to her friend, Keeva reached out and squeezed her shoulder. "You need to stay here."

"You and me, we stick together. Ride or die, isn't that what you always say?"

It was, damn it, but this wasn't the type of life Scarlett should be forced to live. "I'm sorry, Scar, but it's the die part of the equation that matters right now, and I can't afford to lose you. Despite the fact that I'm so mad right now about all the secrets, you are safer here than with me, and I'm sorry for that. I need to find out who wanted me and Malakai dead so bad. But I need to know that you're safe."

Scarlett hugged Keeva to her, and Keeva wrapped her arms around Scarlett's waist, just in case this was the last time she laid eyes on her friend. Stepping back from the embrace, Scarlett said, "I love you."

Keeva smiled. "Me too," was all she said before Scarlett

swept away a tear and marched away, slipping into a room, closing the door behind her. Not wanting to look at Malakai, Keeva inclined her head to Dylan and said, "Look after her."

"Absolutely."

She called for the elevator as Malakai stalked toward Keeva and crowded her with his body, her back against the wall. Malakai braced his arms at either side of the wall and leaned down so Keeva had to look up at him. Taut tension snapped between them as his eyes seemed to bore into her soul.

"We have unfinished business."

"I don't think so, Cavanagh. We had sex. Good sex. We are both consenting adults who enjoyed a night together, but we would never work."

His mouth turned into a frown as he lowered his head so his forehead rested against Keeva's. "Enlighten me as to what makes you think we wouldn't be good together, Keeva, because last night would never be enough for me. And it was more than just good sex."

Unable to resist, Keeva ran her hands up his chest. "You drive an Aston Martin, and I drive a Golf that's seen better days. You live in a building that is bulletproof, and I live in a tiny apartment where the only security is me. Some days, I cannot afford to eat and pay the electricity. You have a family of assassins who anyone can see worship you, and I have Scarlett. It would always feel like you were slumming it with me, and you would be."

"Keeva ..."

Keeva went up on her toes and pressed her lips to his to stop whatever he was going to say. His lips were like fire on hers as she pulled away, ducked under his arm and went inside the elevator that had just opened. Malakai's eyes blazed with lust as the doors began to close, but Jasmine managed to slip inside the elevator before the doors shut.

"Before you start," Jasmine began as she leaned against the elevator wall, her arms folded across her chest, "Malakai is my brother, and he has spent his entire life, before and after becoming a vampire, looking after us. He never allows himself any semblance of happiness because he is constantly trying to make sure me, Dylan and Zeke are good. He works long hours to ensure that we stay financially wealthy. One day, ask him about how poor we were, and he will tell you."

"Look, Jasmine, you don't have to fight in his corner for him."

"Someone has to, because he sure as hell won't fight his own. I can tell he likes you."

The elevator opened, and they walked out into the foyer of the building. Jasmine glanced toward Roman, the werewolf security guard, who stood at the door with an impressive Colt CAR-15 strapped to his chest, and rolled her eyes. Roman grinned at Jasmine and winked at Keeva.

"Fido, let Ms. Cross leave."

Roman's grin only deepened, showing dimples that Keeva hadn't expected as she walked outside, Jasmine still walking beside her. Keeva was also surprised when Roman stepped outside, his eyes firmly fixed on Jasmine.

"I think Fido wants a little vampire in his life," Keeva said with an appreciative glance.

"Never gonna happen." Jasmine snorted as she dismissed Roman's presence with the wave of her hand. "Listen, we are trying out a new grunge night at Dante's tomorrow night. Come along. I'll make sure Scarlett is there, and it's Malakai's night to work the bar, so he will have his hands full and shouldn't be too distracted by you."

"Malakai works the bar?" Keeva couldn't imagine Malakai serving shots to humans.

Jasmine smiled her girl-next-door smile. "There are a lot of things about my brother that might surprise you. Come by the club. I can promise free drinks?"

Keeva laughed, surprised as her car was driven to the front of the building and keys were tossed in her direction. "If I'm not dead by then, maybe I will."

Jasmine held her hands up in triumph. "My work here is done. Hey, Keeva, trust your gut … it might just save your life."

Keeva had been around banshees her entire life, and when Jasmine spoke, she had the glassy-eyed look that banshees got when they predicted death. Then her eyes were blue again, and with a wink, Jasmine flipped her hair off her shoulders and whistled at Roman to come.

From the look on the poor guy's face, the werewolf was smitten.

Keeva strode over to her car, unlocked the door, feeling eyes on her. Glancing over her shoulder, she could make out the faint outline of Malakai watching her from the window. Shaking her head, Keeva slid into the car and drove away as fast as she could, considering the Golf spluttered before it came back to life. Keeva was going to have to try and figure out who wanted her dead, but as Angus had offered her the contract, he would be the person she had to pay a visit to.

However, getting to Angus would not be easy, and her best bet would be right after a council meeting when he was alone. Right now, Keeva needed to get home and shower and change, especially if she was going to be around other Inferna who would take one sniff and know she had gotten up close and intimately personal with Malakai.

After driving the Golf across the city, Keeva parked up and was bounding up the stairs minutes later, the damn lift still out of order. Her senses prickled even before she reached her floor, her gut clenching, as she knew that something was waiting to pounce. When she neared the door, Keeva saw that it was open, and when she inhaled, sulphur crinkled her nose.

Jasmine had been warning her about this.

She cautiously pushed the door open. Keeva needed to get

to her bedroom and her array of weapons. The growling and sniffling, accompanied by the scent, meant that Keeva had a fifty-fifty chance of slipping unnoticed through the room. Her apartment wasn't big enough that it would fit a whole pack of hellhounds, so Keeva assessed that there were two, maybe three.

While the whole debate of Heaven and Hell was still open and up for debate in both the Inferna world and the human world, there were half-breeds out there that happened to be demonic. Hellhounds were like demonic sniffer dogs, and once they were given a scent, they did not stop until they found their quarry. The only thing with hellhounds was that they had terrible eyesight and relied on their enhanced sense of smell.

A five-foot-tall monster with black coarse hair stalked out of Keeva's bedroom, his eyes blood-red, drool dripping from its maw as it moved its monstrous paws, almost as big as Keeva's head, the sounds like gunshots in her ears. Keeva wondered why they hadn't sniffed her out yet, remembering what Dylan said about her smelling like Malakai. The hounds could not make out her scent because it was mixed with his.

As the hounds began chewing on her couch, one even pissing on the leg of where Keeva usually sat, she wiggled her nose in disgust before she darted forward toward her room and flattened herself against the wall before throwing caution to the wind. Rushing to her wardrobe, Keeva pulled open the doors and dragged out a rapier, the blade curved and perfect for hacking through hellhound hide.

A snarl sent the hairs on the back of her neck standing to attention as Keeva spun and braced herself, the hellhound watching her, its nostrils flared as if concentrating. Keeva didn't wait for him to realize that she was the one he was looking for. Keeva struck with the rapier and sliced through the thick skin of the hairy beast, taking it down as she pulled the blade out and then drove it up through its throat.

The hound collapsed in a heap, dead, as its partner surged forward. This one was a whole foot bigger than the slain beast. He leapt forward, taking Keeva down to the ground, his massive paws holding her down. She drove the blade over and over into its stomach, hoping to perforate a vital organ, but the bastard wouldn't die.

His massive teeth snapped, sinking into her arm and shaking it as Keeva screamed, letting go of the rapier. Fire burned through her arm as the hellhound put its full weight on Keeva, and she struggled to breathe. Reaching deep inside her, Keeva yanked her magic free and used her uninjured arm to grab the hound's leg.

The hound shrieked and convulsed as Keeva emptied her magic into him, and the hound collapsed on top of her, crushing her. Keeva tried to move the dead monster, but she was tapped out. Keeva reached into her pocket for her phone before she realized that she had smashed the thing back at Sicarius.

Keeva steeled herself against the pain and dragged herself backward, the weight of the hound causing her lungs to heave. She pushed back another few inches and then reached for the burner phone she kept in her assassin bag. Flipping the phone open, she pressed in a number.

"Keeva?"

Dylan's voice sounded concerned, and Keeva managed to groan as her arm seeped blood and dizziness swam.

"Hellhounds."

"Fucking hell! Where are you?"

Keeva could hear him running as she gritted out that she was at home, asking him to come alone. Dylan swore as Keeva repeated what she had just said, and when Dylan tried to argue, Keeva managed to bark out, "Half the pack will be hunting Malakai as well. Keep him away."

Then Keeva lay back and waited. Her arm continued to burn. The feeling of blood seeping from the gash sent a wave of nausea rolling her stomach. Keeva closed her eyes, losing herself to the darkness. She wasn't sure how long she was knocked out, but suddenly the bulky weight was lifted off her, and Keeva let loose a moan of pain.

Dylan dropped to his knees beside her and tore her tee off to get a look at the wound. "Jesus, that's deep, Keeva. You need stiches. Hound tried to rip your arm off."

"It hurts so much that I wish he did."

Dylan chuckled as he pulled her into his arms, jesting for her not to tell Kai. "I can heal the wound, but I need to bite you first. Once I've drunk from you, I can seal the wound. It will still hurt like a mutha, but it will stop the bleeding."

Dylan waited, as if he would not do what he had said without her permission. With a brief nod of her head, Dylan lifted her arm and sank his fangs into the flesh just over where the hound had latched on to her arm. Keeva couldn't tell what was Dylan drinking her blood and the seeping from the original wound, but then she felt Dylan lick up her skin, and the ache in her arm eased.

"Once you can stand, I need you to shower and clean the wound. I also need you to wash my scent off your skin, because Kai will have my balls if he scents me on you. Not sure I'll still be able to speak if he catches my scent before I explain what happened to you. Male vampires can be a little possessive."

Keeva rolled her eyes as Dylan helped her to her feet. Blowing out a breath, Keeva waited until the nausea settled and then stepped away from Dylan.

"Thank you for coming."

"Anytime, Death."

Keeva flashed him a smile before she took in the carnage and her shoulders sagged. "We can't stay here anymore, can we?"

"It's not safe." That was all Dylan said, but his voice was sympathetic as Keeva tried not to let her emotions swarm her.

"This was the first place I called home. Besides my car, it's the only thing I owned. I used the last of my money, after decades of saving up to buy this place. Scarlett moved in with me, and this was our home. I made sure my assassin jobs never impacted this, our safe haven, and now, now I'm back to scrimping and saving to try and find something new. It will take years to sell this place. It's not exactly a palace."

"If I have learned anything in my long life, it's that home doesn't have to be a roof over your head. It's the people that you surround yourself with so that when you are somewhere, anywhere they are, it makes you feel at home. Jazz, Kai and even Zeke are my home. You still have Scarlett and, if you let us, you'll have us too."

Keeva looked at Dylan to see if the blond vampire was being real with her, but one glance at his face and Keeva knew he meant every word. She looked around the room, grabbing a duffel and shoved some clothes in before she gathered up her assassin bag. Dylan took the bags from her as she gingerly walked outside.

"I'll need to get rid of the mutts," she muttered as Dylan steered her out the door.

"We have a clean-up crew on the way."

Of course they did. There wasn't a doubt in her mind that by tomorrow evening, any evidence of this would be wiped away, for fear the humans might stumble upon it. The hounds would reek quicker than any dead body would, and it was punishable by death for anyone to expose the Inferna.

She wasn't taking any chances that she might get blamed for their presence in the human complex.

Keeva hesitated, not wanting to shut the door on the happiest part of her life, but maybe Dylan was right. Maybe home was the people who made you feel like you were safe. Shutting the door behind her, she walked down the stairs, and when Dylan made to head toward a black BMW, Keeva called his name.

"I'm not going to Sicarius, Dylan."

"Don't be stubborn, Keeva. Let us help you."

"If the tables were turned, would you take handouts?"

Dylan shook his head and frowned. "No one is offering you a handout, Keeva. What we can offer is a steady income, a place to belong, no shackles, just support. When you are one of us, we come when you call, no questions asked. We will never leave you alone in the dark."

Her heart clenched. Her breathing hitched. Thinking back to the time when she had filled in the application, having read exactly what being a member of the Sicarius Security family meant, Keeva had been afraid of herself being hopeful.

Shaking her head, Keeva took the bags from Dylan and opened the boot of the car. Setting the bags inside, she shut the boot with a bang. She headed for the driver's door when Dylan asked her where she would go.

"I'll be fine, Mac. I'll see you tomorrow night at the club. If I don't show up, then I won't be your problem anymore."

Keeva was inside the car and driving away before Dylan could stop her. Night was waning. Even as Dylan tried to follow her, she knew he would need to go soon, as the sun would rise and he would be forced indoors. Uncertain of where she could go, Keeva drove around until morning, parked in town, and when the shops opened, she got a replacement sim card with a cheap prepaid phone.

Then Keeva snuck inside a shopping centre where they had shower facilities for the homeless, washing the blood and gore from her skin, dressing in leggings and a hoodie before dragging her tired ass back to the car. She stopped to spend her last available money on a day-old sandwich and a coffee, which she inhaled like it was her last meal on death row.

Returning to her car, Keeva drove to a parking lot, her little car hidden in a darkened corner. Climbing into the back seat, Keeva locked the doors and pulled a blanket over her head, closing her eyes and dozing, her arm in savage pain, her heart empty as she shivered, pulling the blanket closer, wishing she was not alone and that a certain vampire was holding her in his arms.

CHAPTER ELEVEN

Malakai

WHEN DYLAN ARRIVED BACK AT THE COMPOUND, MALAKAI WAS seething that Keeva wasn't with him. He launched into a rant demanding to know why the hell he had let her go off when there's a contract out on her life. Dylan stood in front of him, face impassive, as he knew Malakai rarely lost his temper, especially around Dylan, who would feel his anger deep inside him.

When Malakai finished, Dylan went to the fridge, removed two bottles of beer and handed one to Malakai. "This one's gotten right under your skin, Kai. What's so special about this Keeva that makes you act so irrational?"

Malakai didn't have an answer for Dylan that couldn't have sounded crazy; Malakai could *feel* that she was meant to be his. He barely knew his little banshee; however, what he did know was that he wanted to take care of her like no one had ever really taken care of her. It was in his nature to protect, yet Keeva was so stubborn from years of going it alone that Malakai feared she would not let him all the way in. When Scarlett had revealed a little of Keeva's past, Malakai's blood had been boiling, ready to go and slice Angus's throat for what he had done to her teenage self.

He was surprised Keeva had not done the deed herself.

Dylan cleared his throat and dragged Malakai from his thoughts. Striding around to the couch, Malakai sank down, stretching his arm over the back of the couch. Dylan joined him, kicking off his shoes and stretching out on the other side of the couch with his feet dangling off the edge.

"So this is what I think," Dylan mused, his eyes sparkling with a mischief that Malakai remembered from when they had been human. Dylan had always been the one to initiate all the trouble they had gotten into in their youth, even if Malakai had been more than willing to participate. His part in their elaborate schemes was to execute the plan ... Dylan's was to talk them out of trouble.

"Women throw themselves at your feet," Dylan continued after taking a drink from his bottle. "Human or Inferna. There's no challenge in it. Keeva doesn't do that. She doesn't care about the money or the cars or the clothes. That doesn't impress her, and that's why you've taken an interest. You've always been the father figure who looks after us, Kai. Keeva has looked after Scarlett, and you think you could have a life with her. You guys seem to fit."

"Perhaps." That was all Malakai replied to Dylan because his fellow vampire was right; he saw Keeva, and suddenly his life was complete. He revelled in his vampire nature, was not ashamed to admit it; however, forever was a long time as an immortal, and even when he was human, he dreamed of having a wife and children. He had set all that aside for his family, was content to do so.

"Then don't lose your head over her, Kai. I think the little redhead is used to running. Used to going it alone. If you try and be overprotective, Keeva will not thank you for it. I've known her a lot longer, and she is smart, capable, vicious when she has to be, with a good heart."

Malakai lifted his brows. "Sounds like you have a little crush there, brother."

Dylan barked out a laugh, shaking his head. "Keeva and I will always only be friends. Now your personal assistant is all kinds of fine. I would love to see what other parts of her blush when she's naked."

Malakai leaned forward in his seat, the bottle hanging from his fingers. "Dylan, no. You might be able to feel and drain his emotions, but he is acting like she is already his. If you and Zeke end up falling out over a woman you don't intend to keep, you will break this family apart. Promise me you will keep your head and not do anything stupid."

Before Dylan had the chance to offer a rebuke, the doors to the elevator pinged, opening to reveal Roman carrying Jasmine in his arms, their sister's eyes bone-white as she mumbled to herself. The scent of copper permeated the air, a trickle of blood coming from Jazz's nose as she leaned into the crook of Roman's shoulder, the werewolf's face marred by concern.

They were both on their feet a heartbeat later, Dylan holding out his hands to take Jasmine, and Malakai supressed a smile when Roman hesitated a moment before handing Jazz over to Dylan. Roman stood rooted to the spot as Malakai thanked him, not wanting to leave as Dylan cradled Jasmine to him and whispered to her. Jasmine jerked in his arms, the blood from her nose flowing more now, the scent strong enough to drag Zeke from his library.

"What happened?" Malakai asked Roman.

"Jasmine called me to her floor and asked me to take some stuff over to Dante's for her DJ gig tonight. We traded barbs, and then her eyes rolled in her head and she started saying a whole lot of nonsense, sir. Then the blood started before her knees gave out and I brought her straight up here."

Malakai clasped him on the shoulder. "You did good, Roman. We've got it from here."

"I'd like to stay, sir, to make sure she's okay."

Malakai smiled, holding the other Inferna's eyes as he said, "There are Inferna who would exploit Jasmine for her gift if they knew what she could do. If I find out that after centuries of keeping it a secret, suddenly everyone knows what Jasmine is, I will end you."

"Understood, sir. Both man and wolf simply need to know she's okay before we can rest."

Malakai left the man standing there, sat down beside Dylan and ran his hand over Jasmine's hair. She was muttering low, twitching, as Zeke came over and knelt down in front of Jasmine. The moment Zeke reached for her, Jasmine sat up and placed both hands on the side of his face.

"Rivers of blood tempting faith. Salvation comes when innocence cries. Death is the catalyst; Fear is the end. He comes, he comes, Darkness to swallow us whole. The city will burn, and hope is lost."

Her hands dropped from Zeke's face, and he sat down on the floor, his face ashen as Jasmine blinked, shaking her head as she ran a finger under her nose. "My head hurts like I've been on a three-day binge of nothing but tequila. What happened?"

Malakai gently turned Jazz to face him so he could get a better look at her face. "You don't remember what you said? When did your nose start bleeding during visions, Jazz?"

His sister ground her teeth tight as she glanced over to where Roman stood watching her. "You sure it's okay to have this conversation with Fido in the room?"

"Roman carried you to us, Jasmine. He merely wanted to make sure that you were okay before he continued on the task you had sent him on."

Roman ran his eyes over Jasmine, nodding his head, and then spun on his heels to head back out when Jazz called his name.

"Thanks."

"Anytime."

It was the most pleasant conversation the two had ever had, and Malakai considered that progress. Jasmine rubbed her head as Zeke pulled his knees to his chest and rested his chin on his knees, as if he were trying to make his bulk smaller. Dylan shifted so that Jazz was now seated on the couch beside Malakai as Dylan went to fix her a drink.

"What do you remember, Jazz?"

"I remember giving shit to Roman, and then I woke up here. Gods, my head is really pounding."

Dylan returned with a sweet-smelling tea and handed the mug to Jasmine. She sipped it gingerly, her eyes heavy, and Malakai knew she would be asleep in the next half hour. They needed to figure out what the hell was going on and what the words she had said meant, but sometimes the words were jumbled, like when Jazz had warned him to "Beware the kiss of Death." Not in a million years would he have considered that it was the assassin known as Death Jazz had been referencing.

"What did I say?" Jazz asked quietly, her hands firmly grasping the mug of tea. Malakai made to answer, but it was Zeke who answered her.

"Rivers of blood tempting faith." Zeke repeated the words with an even tone. "Salvation comes when innocence cries. Death is the catalyst; Fear is the end. He comes, he comes, Darkness to swallow us whole. The city will burn, and hope is lost."

"Well, that's not ominous at all, is it? Why can't I have visions that say hey, sale on that Dolce dress you've been drooling over."

Malakai chuckled as he brushed his knuckles under Jazz's chin. "They are your visions, Jazz. You own them. Try and decipher them for us."

They all waited patiently as Jazz sipped her tea again before she closed her eyes and spoke. "The streets were covered in blood—both human and Inferna. I see flame-coloured hair, and I can sense you, Kai, but I can't see you. Oh God, the pain, the terror. I know Death is Keeva and Fear is an Inferna; I just can't *see* them."

Jasmine's hands trembled, letting the cup go, and it smashed loudly on the ground, but none of the vampires took any notice, continuing to watch Jasmine as she muttered, "Where is the innocent? What is it? Why can't I focus?"

Jazz growled in frustration, and they were all so focused on Jazz that none of them heard another person enter the room until a soft voice said, "Is everything all right? I heard something breaking."

Zeke's head snapped around as Scarlett stepped farther into the room, her feet bare and her face flushed with sleep. She wore red flannel pyjamas that covered most of her skin, her jet-black hair swept off her face in two pigtails that should have looked ridiculous on her but simply added to the succubus's charm.

Malakai got to his feet, ignoring the slight growl in Zeke's throat as he moved around him and went to Scarlett. Turning her so that her back was to the vampires, Malakai suppressed a smile when she glanced over her shoulder at Zeke, who snapped his head back around so fast, it had to have hurt. From the sadness in Scarlett's eyes, the reaction hurt her as well.

"Everything is okay, Scarlett. We are sorry to have disturbed you. Jasmine was just feeling a little unwell. We will all be going to sleep soon and promise not to wake you."

"I'm the one that's encroaching on your home, Malakai. I should be apologizing to you. My presence obviously upsets Ezekiel."

The succubus sounded tremendously sad at the thought that Zeke was upset or uncomfortable around her. Once Scarlett was safely deposited back in her room, Malakai gave her a big smile and said, "The old man could do with being made a little uncomfortable. Sometimes, we pander to his whims because we love him. It is a very good thing that you make him uncomfortable. Get some rest. We have a long night ahead of us at the club tonight."

Malakai left Scarlett as she closed the door after him and made his way back toward the vampires. The broken cup had been swept up and Jazz was sleeping on the couch, her legs draped over Dylan, her hands under her face with her body still. Dylan inclined his head, then hoisted Jazz into his arms and went for the elevator, leaving Zeke and Malakai alone.

They sat in relative silence for about ten minutes when Zeke began to speak. "Jasmine was touching me when she got a clearer vison. What if I am the reason there are rivers of blood on the city's streets? What if I am the end of it all? Keeva may be Death, but what if I am Fear? Even the succubus is afraid of me."

"You think yourself a monster because centuries ago, you believed that God was all-seeing, that the Devil was inside you. Your parents didn't help that when they burned you with crosses and holy water. Do you know what Scarlett said to me mere minutes ago?"

Zeke lifted his dark eyes to watch the words coming from Malakai's mouth. "She was not afraid of you; she was worried that her presence here upsets you. She was more concerned for your welfare than her own. You are a smart man, Ezekiel Collins. Think about that."

"She does not know all the horrendous things I've done."

Malakai knew what horrendous things he was referring to. Slaughtering the priests, gorging on blood until his hunger was sated, and it was never truly sated. Killing with his bare hands when those hands used to be free of callouses, clasped together in prayer. Bodies blazed a trail on Zeke's path, and he despised himself for it.

"It is hard for you all to understand how I feel about being a vampire because you all are in control of yourselves. I am not. I ache with hunger every moment of every day. I am consumed with my need for blood. I am alive because none of you can bring yourself to end me, and despite my actions with Keeva, I'm not sure if I can continue my sins by ending my life."

Zeke got to his feet, shoving his hands in his pockets. "I do not feel that I can be redeemed, Malakai. For when I die, it is not heaven that I will go to but a fiery pit in hell, where I will relive my greatest atrocities. I cannot be saved."

Zeke left him alone then, and Malakai made his way up to his own room. Pulling off his clothes, Malakai lay down on his bed but could not stop thinking about what Zeke had said about the fact that he could not be saved. Malakai doubted that very much, and he would be damned if he would let his brother in all but blood suffer because of his own stubborn beliefs.

After tossing and turning for hours, Malakai sat up in the bed and took out his laptop, getting some work done before his shift tonight. He went through the financials, the numbers as soothing to him as they always had been as he checked the stock markets, purchasing a few shares here and there, selling his shares in a company he knew would flatline in the next couple of days.

Malakai responded to some emails from the Elders, some from clients, and sent a quotation to a company in Monaco who wanted to hire Sicarius Security to remodel their security features on their premises. Dylan loved Monaco, so he would send him to give the building a once-over.

Logging into the secure black-market website designed for the assassin community, he logged in as El Diablo, checking out where the assassins were talking about the contracts on them both. He weighed up the seriousness of the conversations and decided that he could end them all if he wished. But good assassins were hard to find.

Setting the computer aside, Malakai checked the time, and since it was around four in the afternoon, he considered it an appropriate time to try and contact his little banshee, hoping she had replaced her phone, having smashed the old one. If not, he would ask Dylan for her assassin number and call her.

He pressed the number he had for her, letting it ring once, twice, a third time before he heard the call connect and a sleep-laden voice say, "Hello."

"You sound as if you slept as well as I did."

"Malakai?" Keeva obviously wasn't fully awake yet, as he heard her shifting, then a bang and a curse.

"Are you okay?"

"Sure," Keeva answered, not sounding sure herself. "I just forgot what it was like sleeping in a car with a low roof. Hit my head."

Malakai bit back a snarl, unable to mask the annoyed tone in his words. "Keeva, why are you sleeping in your car?"

"Well, Mr. Cavanagh, as hellhounds broke into my home and pissed on my furniture, played with my arm like I was a chew toy, and I spent my last few euros on a sandwich that tasted like feet, I didn't have enough money to afford a hotel."

Malakai ran his free hand through his hair as he huffed out, "You could have come here."

"That would not have been a good idea."

"And sleeping in your car was?" he snapped, instantly regretting losing his temper. He was about to apologize when Keeva snarled down the phone.

"You don't know me well enough to comment on my life choices. I am not some child to scold, Malakai. Now if all you called to do was mess with my head, then you can fuck right off."

"Keeva ..." he began, but she cut across him.

"Don't Keeva me. I can't deal with you this early in the afternoon, Cavanagh. I need to get my ass up and out of this car park and try and scrounge up some breakfast with maybe two euros to my name because I can't use any of my cards because like a dumbass, I left them all back in the apartment that Mac said I couldn't go back to."

"Let me take you to breakfast? Please?" Malakai just wanted to take care of her. It was in his DNA, from very early on, just like Dylan had said, and now—now he wanted to look after Keeva.

"I'm not gonna let you buy me with food."

Swinging his legs out of the bed, he planted his feet on the wooden floor. "Then come by Dante's at five. The changeover from the days bar to nightclub should just be happening, and we always have food left over. You can eat while I work. You don't even have to be in my company. I'll bring Scarlett with me."

There was silence on the other end of the phone, and if his hearing hadn't been supernatural, he would have missed the rhythmic sound of her breathing as she mulled over his offer. Then she let loose a sigh of resignation. "Fine. But I need another shower and change as well because I still smell like hellhound. If I go by at five, will someone let me in to change?"

Malakai smiled to himself. "Roman is due to be on-site early, so I will let him know you are stopping by and to get you anything you want. My office has a bathroom, and no one will disturb you."

"Thanks," Keeva ground out as if she was not used to accepting help from anyone. It made him even more attracted to the resilient banshee and more determined to convince her that he wanted her for keeps.

"Keeva."

"Yes?"

"I'm looking forward to seeing you," Malakai admitted honestly, as he had a feeling that Keeva appreciated honesty and integrity in a person.

"Whatever, Cavanagh. I'm only interested in the free food."

Keeva disconnected the call to Malakai's husky laughter as he sauntered into the shower to get ready. Keeva thought that they were entirely different, that his money and prestige made them completely incompatible, when that was the furthest from the truth.

Malakai knew what it was like to sink his fingers into dirt

in order to ensure crops grew. He knew what it was like to work long hours for a pittance. None of them had known how to read or write before their transition, and Malakai had taught himself so he could teach Jasmine and Dylan.

It was Malakai who started work as an assassin so his family could go to college and have the money to do whatever took their fancy as Malakai took online classes. It had taken decades of hard work for them to feel comfortable and build the life they had together.

Keeva saw the money and the clothes and thought he had been dealt a silver spoon. It was time that Keeva learned that Malakai was self-made and that his wealth was simply a means of protection against the world.

It was time Keeva realized exactly who he really was.

CHAPTER TWELVE

Keeva

KEEVA PARKED HER CAR DOWN THE SIDE LANE OF DANTE'S AND climbed out of the driver's side. After a quick rummage around in the boot, she slipped some of her weapons under the lining where the spare tyre should be because she was almost certain that she was safe inside Dante's, and if someone managed to break into her rust bucket, the last thing she needed was some idiot running down St. Patrick's Street with an illegal weapon. Hauling her duffel out, Keeva closed the boot and headed to the top of the lane, not surprised when Roman stood waiting for her.

The werewolf wore a Sicarius Security tee that had that styled S against what looked like bulletproof glass, that was tight over his chest and well-defined arms. Combat pants and boots completed the look, and Keeva knew he must have been military at some stage, for the way he held himself, dressed, screamed military. The longer hair and scruff meant he probably wasn't your typical soldier but special forces.

"Why do I get the feeling you're sizing me up and not in a fun way?" His voice was a low rumble of amusement that made Keeva grin.

"Because I am," Keeva replied with a shrug of her shoulders, ignoring the burning pain in her forearm.

"And what have you decided?"

Keeva gave Roman her assessment, the werewolf's smile deepening as she explained why she thought him to be military. When Keeva asked him if she was right, the Inferna inclined his head and then motioned for her to move with him.

They went into Dante's, the place in the middle of transformation. Tables were being moved, chairs stacked and wheeled into a back room. Alcohol was being restocked as lighting was tested, the dark room flashing with multicoloured strobe lights. Humans and Inferna worked side by side, the humans having no idea that their colleagues were creatures who could kill them between one breath and the next.

Roman pointed to the stairs, and they went up to a door that was at the top of the stairs. "Malakai called ahead. Shower is in the room at the side, and I brought coffee and some of those pastries he likes to bake. Take your time. The vampires are due in about an hour."

Roman closed the door, leaving Keeva to take in her surroundings. The room was small, compact, with a glass window that looked out over the entire bar, the glass tinted. A metal desk in black was in front of the window, long enough for a laptop so Malakai could keep an eye on the club. Pictures on the wall were of Malakai and the rest of the vampires, smiling, laughing—exactly how Keeva imagined family photos would be.

As a wave of sadness washed over her, Keeva snatched up the pastry that was sitting on the table and devoured it, draining the coffee seconds later. Needing to wash away the day, Keeva opened the door to the bathroom. She emptied her bladder before stripping off her clothes and turning on the small shower.

Stepping under the spray, she scrubbed her skin under the warm water, using Malakai's shampoo to wash her hair, her mass of curled Irish red hair the bane of her life. Running her fingers through her curls in the hope to detangle some of the knots, Keeva waited until her skin had been so thoroughly scrubbed that her skin was reddening.

Turning off the water, Keeva used one of the fresh, flowery-smelling towels to dry herself and dressed in black skinny jeans and one of her many Nirvana T-shirts. Slipping her feet into socks and her boots, Keeva swept the steam from the mirror to look at herself.

Red hair framed her face in a torment of curls, freckles covering her face, which had a pale complexion, and her eyes, green eyes, seemed sad as Keeva stared at herself. Full lips held a scowl as she towel-dried her hair, shoving it back off her face. She gathered up her stuff and headed outside.

Malakai Cavanagh leaned against the table, looking up when she exited the bathroom with a devilish smile that flushed her skin. Setting her bag down, she ran her eyes over him, surprised at how casual he looked. He wore a black Dante's T-shirt that clung to his very muscular body, well-worn blue jeans and Nike trainers that were scuffed. His brown eyes studied her as she watched him, and the air crackled with tension.

"Keeva."

That was the only notice she got before he surged forward, capturing her mouth with his. Keeva groaned, her entire body coming alive as Malakai devoured her with his mouth, a tangle of tongues and teeth. Keeva gasped as he turned them so that her butt hit the edge of the desk, then she was sitting on the edge of the desk, her legs wrapped around him, her booted feet digging into his ass as he rocked against her and she sucked in a breath.

Her skin burned as Malakai trailed his lips along her jaw, down her neck, nipping slightly as Keeva arched into his touch, his hands on her breasts, his finger flicking her nipples through her T-shirt so that Keeva could only moan her pleasure as her body ached for him to touch her more, everywhere.

Knocking sounded on the door. Malakai snarled, ignoring the sound as he rocked his hips again. The brush of his erection against her denim-clad core sent a shudder through her. Keeva roamed her hands under his tee, stroking his chest and running nails over his nipples, earning a growl from Malakai as she repeated the action.

His teeth scraped the pulse at her throat as the knocking became insistent, causing Malakai to swear, step back from Keeva, march to the door and swing the door open. Dylan stood with his fist raised, ready to knock again with a knowing grin on his face, and said in a very Malakai tone, "You are here to work, not have fun. Have fun on your own time."

Malakai pushed him hard, causing Dylan to let lose a chortle of laughter as Malakai slammed the door shut and turned back to Keeva, heat blazing his eyes. "Dylan always had piss-poor timing."

His voice was husky as Keeva slid off the desk, snatched up her bag and went to go around him, but Malakai blocked her way. He leaned down, pressing his lips to hers quickly, then stepped aside to let her by as he grinned. "Scarlett is in the VIP section, and she ordered food for you both. I'll bring it over in a bit once I do some strategic rearranging."

Keeva immediately dropped her gaze to the erection straining against his jeans. Feeling brave, as Keeva went to step around him, she cupped the bulge, and Malakai jerked against her palm. Then with a silly smile on her face she removed her hand and left him alone, swearing.

It made her a little smug to know that she could affect him as much as he affected her.

Jogging down the stairs, Keeva rounded the corner and then climbed up the steps to see Scarlett sitting in the booth, her fingers typing on her laptop as she sipped her coffee. Dressed in black pants, blouse of the same colour and a red blazer, her friend glanced up as Keeva approached and smiled. Scarlett scooted over so Keeva could sit in beside her, and Keeva bumped her shoulder as she did.

"Are you okay?" Scarlett asked as she closed the laptop and set it aside.

"Arm still sore, but I'll be okay. It's been a fun twenty-four hours. Nearly got eaten by hellhounds. Almost had sex with Malakai in his office, but we don't need to talk about that right now."

Scarlett blushed as she rolled her eyes at Keeva. "I ordered you a proper breakfast because I assumed you would forget to eat, and from the looks at the bags under your eyes, you haven't slept either."

"I'll sleep when I'm dead. If the assassins get me, then that could be sooner."

"I really don't know how you can be so glib about this, Keeva. As if dying is nothing," Scarlett chastised her, even though there was no anger in it.

Keeva shifted in her seat so that she could look at her friend's sad face. "I have to pretend it's nothing or I'll curl into a ball and wait for it to come, terrified." Taking her friend's hand, she gave it a squeeze. "I'm not afraid to die, Scar. I'm afraid of leaving you behind. But you would be fine without me. The guys in Sicarius would take care of you."

"No, I would not," Scarlett retorted, now letting a little bit of anger seep into her tone. "I know that I'm a nuisance. I'm useless and have to be protected. I want you to train me to fight. If you are going to be blasé with your life, then I need to know how to protect myself."

Tears glistened in those bottomless blue eyes of hers, and Keeva embraced her. "You are not a nuisance. You are far from useless, Scarlett Russell. I'll teach you some self-defence moves if you want, but I will always do my best to protect you."

Keeva sat back with one more squeeze as Malakai climbed the steps with two plates in his hand, Dylan behind him carrying a pot of coffee and a few mugs. Setting the plates down on the table, Malakai pushed a full Irish in front of her and then set an omelette in front of Scarlett.

Keeva focused on the food and began to dig in as Malakai said, "We were all just about to have breakfast as well; would you mind if we joined you?"

"Not at all." Scarlett smiled as Malakai nudged Keeva to slide over. Keeva rolled her eyes as Dylan moved to sit beside Malakai. Zeke and Jasmine came up the steps with Zeke carrying a platter of plates. Jasmine sank down to the floor, eating her breakfast from her lap, a sandwich that looked like it would be far too big to fit in her small mouth, but the vampire was munching away on the breakfast sandwich.

The only seat left was next to Scarlett, and as Zeke sat down beside her, his body was rigid. He sat on the very edge of the booth as if he didn't trust himself with her. Scarlett's cheeks were flushed as she nibbled on her own food, her eyes on the eggs. The vampires each took a plate and fell into easy conversation as Keeva watched them.

Dylan and Malakai engaged in a conversation about sports, wearing easy grins as they ate. Keeva reached for some toast only for Malakai to take it, buttering the slice before sliding it toward her without even glancing in her direction but not before taking a bite himself.

Keeva rolled her eyes as she made quick work of her food, absolutely ravenous, sliding the plate away when it was empty and sitting back in her seat. Closing her eyes, Keeva let herself be at ease as Dylan asked Malakai about a project in Monaco, to which Malakai remarked that Dylan was long overdue a holiday.

When Dylan said the same about Malakai, he chuckled. "I'm the boss. I don't get holidays."

"I'm sure you could make an exception if it meant getting Keeva in a bikini."

Keeva snorted and waved a hand down her person. "Dude. Have you seen my hair? My freckles? The sun is not my friend, and I don't fancy looking like a tomato, thank you very much."

"Keeva has always wanted to see the northern lights," Scarlett said, something in her tone dragging Keeva's attention. She opened her eyes to see a bead of sweat on her friend's forehead, her eyes wild, a slight tremble in her hands.

Damn it!

Keeva let her hand rest on Malakai's thigh, giving it a squeeze as she inclined her head toward Scarlett. Malakai immediately began talking about how he had never seen the northern lights either and would very much like to go there one day as Scarlett shivered.

"Scarlett, honey, when did you last feed?" Keeva broached the subject carefully, because as much as the vampires made them feel like part of the group, there was still a lot about Scarlett and Keeva that they did not know.

"I'm okay."

The entire table was quiet as they looked at Scarlett, her face as red as her jacket. Dylan cursed as he shifted, the effects of Scarlett slipping her reins as he licked his lips, his eyes blazing with lust.

"Scarlett, if you are hungry, there is nothing to be ashamed of. We know what it is like to be hungry." Malakai's tone was reassuring, calming as Scarlett swallowed hard.

"She can't be hungry. She just ate," Zeke said in a confused tone that made Keeva want to laugh and throttle him at the same time.

"Not that kind of hungry, you idiot," Dylan growled, his eyes darkening as he looked at Scarlett like he was minutes away from devouring her on the table. Keeva was beginning to put the pieces together as to some of the comments Dylan had made and if the look of sexual hunger on his face was down to Scarlett's own hunger.

Realization dawned on the big vampire's face as his nose flared and Scarlett shuddered. Keeva wondered what would happen if Scarlett touched him. He was coiled full of tension but had this deer-in-the-headlights kind of look. Keeva fought against the irrational feeling that she wanted to laugh.

"Scar, when was the last time you had physical contact to feed?"

"Keeva, I can't. Not with them all … it's unprofessional."

"Someone needs to make a decision here because unless she brings it under control, I don't care who watches, but she's gonna be naked," Dylan ground out as Zeke growled at Dylan and Scarlett's gaze darted to Zeke.

Her hands dug into the table as if she were trying not to reach out for someone, anyone, but when Dylan got to his feet, Zeke flashed his fangs, the aggression feeding into Scarlett's lust as she whimpered. Scarlett got to her feet and stumbled, reaching out and putting a hand on Zeke's elbow to steady herself.

Zeke jerked out of her grasp as if her touch burned him, stumbling back out of her reach as if all he wanted to do was sink his fangs into her skin. And wasn't at all happy with himself because of it.

"Don't touch me."

Keeva was shocked at the brute, bluntness and disgust in his tone. Scarlett's eyes filled with tears as she stumbled out of the booth to run and hide from her embarrassment, with Zeke backing up against the rail. Jasmine had gotten to her feet during the incident. Dylan stalked toward Scarlett. This had gone to hell in a handbasket rather quickly. Maybe she shouldn't stop this; maybe Dylan was a safer choice for her friend. Keeva scooted over to go with Scarlett when a flurry of movement stopped her.

"Oh, for fuck's sake!"

Jasmine took Scarlett's tear-stained face in her hands and kissed her. Scarlett sagged at the physical contact and energy exchange as Jasmine kissed Scarlett until her body stopped trembling and she took a step back, her cheeks flushed but the lust dampened. Jasmine winked at Scarlett before she waved her hands in the air.

"Problem solved." Then the blond vampire punched Zeke hard in the arm. "You are an absolute buffoon. You of all people should know what it's like to have a hunger you can't control. Scarlett has been nothing but nice to you, and you act like she's contagious! I'm so furious with you right now!"

To emphasis her words, Jasmine stomped down the stairs, flicking her hair over her shoulder as she stormed away from them. Zeke looked sheepish as he rubbed the back of his neck. Scarlett grabbed her laptop and asked Malakai if there was somewhere quiet where she could work in peace.

Malakai gave her directions to his office, and Scarlett scurried away without looking at any of them. Keeva stayed rooted in her spot as Malakai pushed Dylan out of the way and went to Zeke.

"Ms. Russell is who she is. You are who you are. She sought you out to ease her pain because for some reason, she feels safe with you, and you turned her away. I understand your fear, Zeke. Truly I do. But for a man who once gave his shoes to a homeless man so his feet would not get frostbite, or the man who donates to the local children's hospital for kids who are forced to reside in a hospital during Christmas, you showed no compassion for Scarlett."

"Malakai … I …" Zeke began, but Malakai held up his hand for Zeke to stop.

"No. You hurt her because you were afraid of your own reactions. I think you should stay inside the security room until it's time to leave, because right now, I cannot stand to look at you."

Malakai turned his back to Zeke, whose shoulders slumped as he stalked away and disappeared from view. Malakai slipped in beside her, his body flush against hers, and she leaned into him as Dylan mumbled about getting laid and left them alone.

They sat in silence for a while as she felt Malakai release some of the tension in his body the moment that they were alone. He slipped his fingers into hers and lifted her knuckles to his lips. Her stomach fluttered as she looked up into his eyes and knew he wanted her still.

"It hurts you that he has disappointed you. But not as much as he hates to disappoint you."

Malakai was quiet as he mulled over her words, and had she not been looking at him, Keeva would have missed the slight incline of his head. "It feels like I am failing him. And it will be my hand that kills him should I need to. I will lose a part of myself if I do, and we all will mourn. We have already lost one brother, many years ago, and it still hurts."

Dipping his head, Malakai brushed his lips against her neck, inhaling her scent as he pressed an open-mouth wet kiss to her neck, the slight graze of teeth delicious with a promise of more to come.

"I don't want to talk about Zeke. I don't want to be responsible. When I'm with you, I can let go because you want the man and not the persona. I told you that one night would not be enough for me, Keeva, and it's not. I don't indulge in my wants and needs very often, but I find that I want to with you."

Keeva's heart was breaking open as Malakai nipped on her flesh. "Come home with me tonight, Keeva. I would rather not sleep alone."

Malakai backed off, waiting for a response from Keeva, but she knew, had always known that she wanted him. Rising up slightly, Keeva gave him a quick press of lips before pulling back. Keeva nodded her head, earning a sly, smug smile from Malakai that was as sinful as the man himself.

They had hours before the club would close, and as Malakai left her with another blistering kiss to return to work, anticipation coiled inside her at the promise of the night ahead.

CHAPTER THIRTEEN

Keeva

KEEVA FOUND HERSELF WATCHING MALAKAI WORK. AS THE Primus of vampires, even as the CEO of Sicarius Security, Malakai gave off this wave of authority, this "I am alpha" vibe. He was a born leader. But right now, as he pulled a pint and smiled with a human male, tossing banter around with a boyish grin that made her stomach dance, the wall around her heart crumbled slightly. He seemed comfortable here, as if this was more of who he was rather than who he had to be.

It was the same aura that Keeva felt when he was with his siblings and Zeke. He relaxed around them, probably didn't even realize it, and had Keeva not known that he was the deadliest assassin or that there was a ridiculous amount of money out on his head, she would have never guessed that death lurked around the corner.

Leaning over the balcony, Keeva took in the crowd enjoying the throwback to grunge and rock as Pearl Jam's "Jeremy" pulsed from the speakers. The melody died out as Jasmine worked her magic on the decks, and Nirvana's "Smells like Teen Spirit" sent the crowd into a frenzy. Whoops of joy rang out as the crowd moshed to one of Nirvana's most famous tunes, none of them really old enough to have heard the music when it was released nor to have the opportunity to see the band when they played live at Sir Henry's nightclub back in '91.

Sir Henry's was a legendary nightclub that broke many a heart when it closed in June 2003. The '90s was its best decade, providing music from all genres for you to enjoy. If you wanted ear-bleeding dance music, there was a floor for that. But Keeva loved the grunge or rock music played in the club, and the closest she had gotten to enjoying music like that in a bar in Cork was Black Dog Saloon & Mezcalaria—or BDSM, as it was affectionately known.

Keeva had been in the crowd the night Nirvana had played support to Sonic Youth, the first time this track was played live to any European audience. Most people were there to see Sonic Youth, but Keeva had fallen love with the sounds of Soundgarden, Nirvana, Pearl Jam, as well as Black Sabbath, AC/DC and later on, after Kurt Cobain's death, Foo Fighters.

The Nirvana set was sheer brilliance, even though some disagreed with Keeva, but when Kurt's voice filled the room, the two hundred people who showed up were as transfixed by the band as Keeva was. By the time their set was nearly over, two hundred people had multiplied into about five hundred.

It was a little slice of grunge heaven, and Keeva was addicted to the thrill of it, that feeling of standing in a crowd of people who you didn't know, but you all were there for the same reason and it united you all. She might be a supernatural creature with the ability to deal out death with her hands, but being in the middle of a crowd of music-goers was the closest to magic Keeva could imagine.

Glancing over at Jasmine, Keeva flashed the vampire a grin as she changed it up again, and Soundgarden's "Black Hole Sun" now blared from the speakers. Keeva caught movement out of the corner of her eye as Zeke made his way up the stairs toward where Scarlett was hiding. Keeva gave them a few seconds and then she left the safety of the VIP section, bounding down the stairs before she slowly made her way up the stairs to the office. She'd hang back, of course, so Scarlett could handle the situation as she saw fit, her bestie finally finding her wings, but Keeva would step in if needed.

Keeva leaned against the wall outside the office, the door slightly ajar so that she could see what was happening. Scarlett had turned the chair around to speak to him, a small smile on her full lips as Zeke ran his hand through his black hair.

"I came to apologize for how I acted before."

Scarlett didn't respond as she blushed, her eyes watering as she bit her bottom lip. If the hulk made her cry again, Keeva would have his balls. Scarlett had her own scars to deal with; Keeva knew each of them as if they were her own. She was ashamed of her species, of who she was, and Zeke did not get to make her feel worse than Scarlett already did.

"I ..." Zeke began. He must have realized Keeva was outside before he said, "It was wrong of me to react as I did. I ... I ... understand when a hunger is yours but you do not want it. I should have been more considerate."

"I understand that being a succubus is the lowest rung on the Inferna ladder. We are considered parasites. I think, if you find me so aversive, that we should try and avoid each other or at least remain civil. We have to work in close proximity; however, I will ask Malakai to limit our interactions."

"There is no need for that," Zeke grunted out; Scarlett's cold tone shocked even Keeva.

"I think there is. Now, I accept your apology and need to get back to work."

Zeke blinked as Scarlett turned round and gave him her back. He stood there for a good five minutes before his feet started moving, bringing him face to face with Keeva. Reaching around his hulking frame, Keeva gently closed the door and set her hands on her hips.

"You hurt her and I won't kill you; I'll just make it so that you end up with a fate worse than death. Scarlett is one of the few good souls left on this planet, and I will protect her with my life."

Zeke's dark eyes betrayed nothing as he ground his teeth

together and said zilch. Keeva could see his brain overthinking, so Keeva decided to throw the guy a bone.

"Scarlett has been told all her life she is an abomination. A succubus who doesn't want to screw every guy or girl in sight. All she wants is to fall in love and like those goddamn romance novels she loves to read, have someone see *her* and sweep her off her feet. You know, after she feeds off people having sex, she cries? She says it makes her feel so empty. I swear to the gods, Zeke," Keeva warned, "I have no qualms in making you feel every ounce of pain you inflict on her. Either respect her wishes and keep your distance or try and be the man she deserves. That choice is yours."

Keeva went around Zeke, slipping inside the office as Scarlett's head snapped around. She smiled at Keeva, a flash of relief in her eyes as Keeva closed the laptop and leaned her butt against the desk, trying not to think of the last time she'd been up here, a few hours ago.

"How' bout you stop hiding away down here and come keep me company?"

"I'd rather stay here until we can leave."

Keeva rolled her eyes as she pulled Scarlett to her feet giving Scarlett just enough time to gather up her stuff and dragged her out of the room, Zeke already gone so Keeva led her back to the VIP section. Setting her belongings aside, she joined Keeva as they looked out over the crowd, laughing and dancing along with the humans that moshed below. For an hour they were able to forget assassins and vampires and just enjoy the merriment.

When the club was cleared out, Scarlett sat down on the seat and closed her eyes before lying down on the seat completely, drifting off to sleep. Jasmine left her DJ booth, draped a blanket over Scarlett before Keeva went down and began to clear glasses from various ledges around the club.

Arms wrapped around her waist, teeth on the nape of her neck. "You don't have to do that."

Keeva smiled as she slipped out of Malakai's arms. "I've worked in bars before to make some extra money. Washed my share of glasses. It's no trouble."

Malakai left her to continue his own sorting out with a smile, and once the bar was cleaned and set out for the next day's opening, Malakai went to the VIP and carried a sleeping Scarlett in his arms so she could rest, the succubus not even stirring. As Keeva studied Zeke, his eyes lingered on Scarlett, her head on Malakai's shoulder. Once they were outside, Malakai put Scarlett into a black Mercedes that Dylan strode round to drive. Jasmine opened the back door to get in beside Scarlett, and Zeke reached for the passenger door, meaning Malakai meant for Keeva to go with him.

She glanced at the sleek cars parked in the alley and then to her own little Golf, instantly feeling self-conscious. "I'll drive over myself."

"You can drive over with me. Roman will bring your car over later."

Keeva shook her head, making her way over to the Golf as Malakai came after her. She had the keys in the door, ready to open, when Malakai inhaled, growled and tackled her as she twisted the handle. The Golf exploded, flames engulfing everything Keeva had in a matter of minutes as the car lifted off the ground before it hit the ground again.

The heat of the blaze made her skin sweat. Malakai's body blocked her from the brunt of the heat as he dragged her up to her feet. Her ears rang, making her shake her head to try and stop the ringing. Malakai asked her if she was okay. It took another few shakes to clear the ringing.

"Keeva!"

Scarlett's freaked-out tone sounded, and Keeva tried to brush past Malakai to go to her. Shots rang out, a bullet pinging the wall just over Scarlett's head. She screamed and put her hands over her head as if that would stop the hail of bullets. Keeva lunged forward, jerking back when a bullet went into the wall by her.

Everyone was taking fire, and Keeva could not get to Scarlett, who was standing out in the open and target practice for anyone who wanted an easy mark. Keeva ignored Malakai's shout of warning as she dove forward, rolled, shoving Scarlett back, but whoever was firing had decided that Scarlett was the weakest link and kept aiming for her skull.

For Keeva, time seemed to move in slow motion as she tried to get in front of the bullet, arms around her waist dragging her back. Malakai ignored her own growl of frustration as shots rang out again and Keeva was certain that Scarlett was dead.

The bullet never hit her.

Zeke had Scarlett pressed up against the wall as if they were caught in a passionate embrace, his blocky frame shielding her as he took a barrage of bullets into his back. Zeke jerked with every hit, his head leaning against the wall until the firing stopped. Dylan returned fire with two handguns as a shadow moved along the roof, and Dylan and Jasmine went off after the person who tried to kill them.

Keeva darted forward as Scarlett screamed. Zeke dropped to his knees, taking Scarlett with him. Malakai grabbed Zeke and ripped off his T-shirt, and Scarlett sucked in a breath. His skin was a medley of tattoos and scars, so much so that an untrained eye would not know where the scars began and the tattoos ended. Or were the tattoos scars in their own right?

Blood seeped from the wounds as Zeke groaned, the only indication that he was still hanging in there, as Malakai assessed the damage to his back. Keeva tried to count all the bullet holes, but the vampire was bleeding so damn much that she couldn't see, especially in the dark.

Scarlett got to her feet and hugged Keeva. "Oh my God! I thought we were all going to die. He took bullets for me. I'll never forgive myself if he dies."

Roman burst out the side door with two more Sicarius employees. Malakai barked at Roman to get the van, tossing a set of keys to another employee who got into Malakai's Aston Martin, edged it carefully around the burning Golf and then sped off into the night. Keeva stood in the alley, on full alert, Scarlett still hugging her as tyres screeched behind her.

Jasmine dropped down off the roof, Dylan following her a second later, murder in their eyes. "Fucker got away."

Roman rushed forward. "Emergency services are on the way, sir. We need to get out of here."

It took Malakai, Roman, and Dylan to carry Zeke to the van, laying him down on his stomach. Roman ran around to drive the van, and surprisingly, Jasmine got in beside him. Malakai gave out a few orders as the doors to the van were closed, but not before the rest of them all clambered in.

Dylan sat on the ground with his hand on Zeke's bare shoulder, wincing every so often as if he had been the one that was shot. Scarlett, who had been huddled next to Keeva, crawled over to the other side of Zeke, opposite Dylan, and began brushing her fingers through Zeke's hair.

Dylan shuddered, causing Scarlett to stop and glance at Dylan. "Keep doing that, sweetheart. It's calming him."

So Scarlett did, her eyes full of concern for the vampire who had definitely saved her life. Keeva leaned her head against the cool panelling of the van as Malakai called ahead asking for supplies and to clear all non-essential employees to the bunker. He snapped the old-school phone shut and then said, "I'm sorry about your car."

"I'm just surprised the old thing didn't blow up long ago. Seems fitting it went out in a blaze of glory. But all my stuff was in that car. Well, I'll have to go back to the apartment and try and salvage some things. Damn, some of my favourite weapons were in the boot."

Malakai made to speak as the van rounded a corner and ground to a halt. The doors were flung open, a stretcher and two vampires in medical coats waiting. They gently lifted Zeke onto the stretcher and wheeled him inside. Zeke started to get agitated, and Dylan called Scarlett forward, the vampire stilling when Scarlett held his hand.

The vampires wheeled him up into the family room, the table they had all sat around eating dinner now covered in a white sheet as Zeke was lifted and laid down on the table. Malakai went to the head of the table, asking Keeva to take Scarlett out, but the succubus refused to budge.

Malakai put his hands on Zeke's shoulders, a hum of power from Primus to a member of his Kiss, as Dylan started to pluck the bullets from the wounds on Zeke's back. The wounded vampire groaned, then growled as Dylan extracted near to twenty-five bullets from Zeke's back. It seemed the only thing that kept Zeke from rearing up was Malakai.

"He's lucky they weren't wood, or it would have hurt a hell of a lot more. Now comes the fun part."

Keeva was confused as to what could be worse than having been shot and then having twenty-five bullets removed when Malakai and Dylan pulled Zeke into a seated position. Zeke's head lolled to the side, and Keeva wondered why his body wasn't healing like a vampire's usually would do.

Malakai must have read her thoughts because he said softly, "We need to have human blood in our systems to accelerate the healing process. Zeke has about a pint glass of blood left in him now that he's bled so heavily. Considering he doesn't feed that often, he had not much to give. He needs to feed."

"He can drink from me," Scarlett offered, stepping forward.

"No!" Keeva wasn't surprised that both Malakai and Dylan were against the idea, but a throaty growl from the big man had Keeva thinking Zeke wasn't opposed to it.

Malakai smiled over at Scarlett. "We appreciate the offer,

but we would not trust him with you like that. In the same way you do not like having to feed your hunger, neither does Zeke. I implore you both to leave so you do not have to witness this."

"I'm staying."

Well, if Scarlett was staying, then so was she. The elevator pinged as Jasmine strode out with a very human man, his eyes wide as he regarded the room. His hands were cuffed, and he was dressed in a grey woven tracksuit that had "prisoner" across the chest. The man sneered in Scarlett's direction, and Jasmine smacked him hard at the back of the head. The prisoner stumbled forward as Zeke made to get up off the table, stumbled and almost smacked his head off the floor.

Malakai and Dylan righted him, holding his arms by his side as Jasmine shoved the prisoner forward, glancing over her shoulder at them. "This is about to get ugly. Last chance to leave."

When neither Scarlett nor Keeva moved, Jasmine nodded at Dylan, who said, "Sicarius, initiate ripper protocol."

"Initiating." A computerized voice responded to Dylan's command, making Keeva wonder what other commands the system had in place.

The lights flickered as Keeva heard locks bolting. The elevator powered off, and Keeva felt like she was stuck in a horror movie. Scarlett clung to her side, trembling. Keeva could only watch as Jasmine pulled the jumper off the prisoner, flashed her fangs and sank them into the throat of the human.

The human jerked, reaching up to try and stop the gush of blood as Zeke's eyes sprang open, his scarred lips curving into a snarl as his nose flared. He backed away, shaking his head, until Dylan grabbed the back of his neck and shoved his head toward the blood that was spilling from the wound.

The moment Zeke's lips latched onto the blood, an animalistic growl ripped from his chest. He surged forward, yanking the human from Jasmine's grasp and tearing at his throat like a wild animal. Blood dribbled down his front, and Keeva fought the urge not to vomit. Zeke bit down so hard on the human's neck, Keeva heard the sickening sound of a neck snapping. Zeke drank and drank, long after the man had stopped twitching, as if he were trying to drain every last drop of blood.

Suddenly the body dropped to the ground. Zeke whirled on Malakai, grabbing him by the neck of his tee and yanking him closer. "More."

There was a demand in his voice that set the hairs on Keeva's arms standing to attention. This was what Zeke was afraid of. This was the monster that lurked under his skin. Malakai shook his head, setting his hands on Zeke's arms. "You have had enough, Ezekiel Collins. Release me."

Zeke roared, the sound almost as loud as the explosion that had assassinated her car, as he hoisted Malakai up like he weighed not a thing and tossed him across the floor. Malakai hit the glass and slumped to the ground. Dylan lunged forward to grab Zeke and got a sucker punch to the jaw for his trouble.

Zeke beat his fists against the sides of his head, his face contorted as his blood-red eyes scanned the room. He took a step toward Jasmine, who held up her hands in a sign of peace as Zeke snarled, "I fucking want more. I *need* more."

CHAPTER FOURTEEN

Malakai

THIS WAS THE NIGHT MALAKAI WOULD HAVE TO MURDER HIS friend.

This was the very night Malakai would give up a sliver of his soul.

Malakai had been the only thing for decades that had been able to subdue Zeke when his bloodlust became so ferocious, so vicious, that he would hurt them in order to quench his hunger. Zeke had broken bones before; however, this time, when Malakai had no choice but to end his life, their family would be heartbroken, and he was not sure any of them would recover. They had known loss before, had taken an age to claw themselves back from the loss of their brother, Dante; however, Malakai felt as if this death might unravel them all, including him.

Slumped against the window, Malakai was struck by a memory, when after a particular bout of bloodlust, he and Zeke had spent time together. It had been quite a long time ago, in a castle in the west of Ireland, the dungeons below the surface where Dylan had managed to pull some of the bloodlust from Zeke but ended up being lost to it himself. Dylan, who had not killed a human in half a century whilst feeding, had been a victim of Zeke's hunger. For that very reason, Malakai could not let his brother take Zeke's emotions from him, for Malakai could not bear to lose two brothers. One would be hard enough.

The castle was eerily quiet after a night that had reigned with screams and death, the sound still lingering in Malakai's mind as he sat vigil beside Zeke, waiting for him to awaken. Blood stained Zeke's face and torso. His lips were coated in dark red dried blood that was now caked to his skin. He was naked, stripped of all his clothing for fear he would harm himself, and Malakai counted the scars on his skin over and over, ticking off the seconds with each burn mark of the cross, each holy-watered blade that had tried to pull the monster from his body.

Scrubbing a hand down his face in an attempt to negate the tiredness in his bones, leaving Jasmine and Dylan to bury the dead, some of whom had served them for years, Malakai regarded Zeke as his dark eyes opened slowly, confusion on his face for a brief, peaceful moment before the events of the night before crept into his mind.

Sitting up straight and pulling his knees into his broad chest, Zeke lifted his gaze to meet Malakai's. "You should have killed me."

"It is not your fault that the hunger consumes you."

"That is not what you really think, Malakai. I can smell the lies on your tongue."

It was true, the words Zeke spoke. However, Malakai had embraced his vampire nature, had relished the fact that he was now stronger, faster, deadlier than his old human self, who probably would have died from famine, war, or disease by now. Zeke was the only member of their Kiss who fought his nature, hindering his control over the hunger.

Malakai leaned forward. "You cannot change what you are, Zeke, yet you can learn to live with it. We are slaves to the hunger; however, it grants us the chance to do great things."

"You mean like murder young women who we have known since they were babes suckling at their mothers' breast? Is being a vampire such an enlightenment that I would be given this immortality and be a monster I once thought only existed for me to exorcise? Does it not prove how demonic in being we are that once we are remade, we cannot stand under the rays of God's sun and bask in its warmth? We are forever beholden to the night and the parts of the devil that cling to us."

Ezekiel's hatred for himself was soul-deep, and considering he wondered if their kind even had souls, that was the major reason why Jasmine, Dylan and he had spent four decades keeping him alive. Once, Zeke had tried walking into the sun, and Jasmine, the only one with him at the time, had burnt the flesh right off her in an attempt to get him back inside. The only thing that lured Zeke back into safety was the fact he knew that Jazz would die alongside him.

Even to this day, Malakai questioned Jazz about her reasons for keeping Zeke around and what she had seen, yet Jasmine never divulged the full extent of her visions, simply giving Malakai a small smile, saying, "Our destiny is tied to his. Should we fail, then our fates fail."

"*Parce mihi, Pater, quia peccavi,*" Zeke muttered to himself as he made the sign of the cross. *Forgive me, Father, for I have sinned.* Malakai couldn't understand his faith, never had understood the Catholic ethos, although he understood having some sort of faith. Malakai's origins, his ancestry could be traced back to Scandinavia, and Dylan always teased that Malakai, with his dark hair and sallow skin, was a piss-poor Viking.

Of course, with blond hair and blue-green eyes, Dylan proclaimed he and Jazz were exactly like a Viking should be. He even had the axe to prove it.

"Do you not think, if you were not so resistant of your hunger, if like us, you drank from a willing partner daily, stopped this self-imposed hunger strike, that when it was absolutely necessary for you to feed, then it would not be so brutal?"

It was an old argument; one Malakai had no chance of winning. Zeke's scars ran deeper than the marks on his skin. Raised to become a holy man, Zeke had God as his saving grace, and when vampires had raided his monastery, Zeke had fought to save the weaker monks and priests who hid. Zeke was changed and left to deal with his sudden vampire state. The relics he once polished and cleaned now singed his skin. He implored the monks to stay hidden, but when they came out, ready to embrace their brother who had saved them all, he killed them one by one.

That was how they had found him, drenched in the blood of the inhabitants of the monastery. Zeke's introduction to his second life had been bloody and brutal. However, he had sought absolution, leaving them a mere few days later to travel the short distance to his village, returning home to his parents, who had tortured him.

"Do you not wish to find someone to love you? Do you not want someone to wander the earth with who can share with you a contented life?"

Zeke snorted, shaking his head. "I pledged myself to God even if I had yet to take my final vows. I remain faithful to those vows because I have broken most of my commandments. I remain devoted to God as penance he has inflicted on me for whatever wrongdoings I have done. I do not seek or deserve the right to love anyone."

Zeke held out his hand, and Malakai waited for the longest time before he sighed and handed over the cross to Zeke. The other vampire took the cross into his palm, sparking the scent of burning flesh as Zeke dropped off the stone bed and to his knees, making the sign of the cross, touching the cross to his forehead, cheeks and then his lips and holding the cross to the scar that puckered his lips.

Malakai could not stand the smell of Zeke's torment, so he left the cell and locked it behind him. The bars were iron. Zeke was strong enough to break them; however, he would hide himself away in the dungeon until he felt he had offered penance. Malakai strode up the stairs. He could hear Zeke as he cried, reciting the "Our Father" in Latin as he often did, and Malakai sighed, feeling that constant awareness that each night when he opened his eyes, tonight might be the night when he said goodbye to his friend, his brother.

Crashing back to the present, Malakai got to his feet at the same time that Dylan did, as Zeke stalked toward Jasmine, who was holding her hands up and telling Zeke that the buffet was closed and she was not dessert. It was the slightest stroke of luck that Zeke had not turned his attention to Keeva and Scarlett.

Pushing his thoughts from his mind, he let the order flow

to his sister and brother, including Keeva in his little chat. *If Zeke makes a move to you or Scarlett, Keeva, kill him.*

Malakai?

Keeva's surprised thought came back at him, and he inclined his head. Keeva frowned at him for a split second before she nodded, the movement snagging Zeke's attention, and the angry vampire turned to latch his gaze on Scarlett and Keeva. His spine straightened. He shoved Jasmine out of his way as he stalked toward them.

Keeva stepped in front of Scarlett, earning a roar from Zeke as Keeva backed them away from the raging vampire. Malakai rushed forward, grabbing hold of Zeke's elbow, but then Zeke wrapped his hands around Malakai's throat and flung him across the room, barrelling into Dylan, who was coming to Malakai's aid. They crashed into the breakfast bar, wood splintering, as spots danced in Malakai's eyes.

"Fucking hell, I feel like I have a hangover without the fun beforehand."

In other circumstances, Malakai would have laughed at Dylan's remark, but he got to his feet as Keeva withdrew a dagger from somewhere on her person.

"Hey, big man, don't make me kill you, okay? I mean, you'll kill any chances of me getting a job here if I murder one of the partners. Or ruin my street cred as the idiot who assassinated the infamous Monk. Plus, banshee blood prob doesn't taste very nice, especially mine. I'll taste of sarcasm, spite, and a little vinegar. You really want that to be your last meal?"

Keeva sprang forward, slicing her dagger down on to Zeke's forearm. Zeke reared back with a bellow of anger, his clenched fist aiming for Keeva's head. Malakai let loose a cry of warning as he stumbled toward them, but his little banshee ducked under the blow, driving the dagger into the back of Zeke's thigh.

As if it were nothing, Zeke reached down and yanked out the dagger with a grunt and threw it at the wall, where it embedded in the cupboard with precision. Zeke caught Keeva by the arms, careful to avoid her uncovered hands, and flung her at Malakai, who caught her before she could fall and hurt herself.

Keeva flashed him a sexy little smile as she patted his cheek. "Smooth, Cavanagh, very fucking smooth."

That made Malakai chuckle. He set Keeva down on her feet as Zeke came toward them, thankfully taking his eyes off Scarlett to deal with the bigger threats in the room. Just like any predator worth his salt, Zeke would take them out first, leaving Scarlett undefended. Keeva brushed her hair from her face, rolling up her sleeves, bracing herself to fight.

None of them could have predicted what happened next.

"Ezekiel Collins."

The words were spoken in a sultry tone that brushed against Malakai's skin and sent a shudder down his spine. The room seemed to freeze, the wave of power in the air, halting them as Zeke slowly turned to the succubus who had uttered his name.

Scarlett Russell closed her big blue eyes for a moment, and when they reopened, Malakai saw glimpses of stars in them. He himself took a step toward her, toward the sexual energy that seemed to shimmer on her skin. His body stirred as he wrapped an arm around Keeva's waist and pulled her back flush against him, and from her low moan, he wasn't the only one who was affected by Scarlett's powers.

"Ezekiel Collins," Scarlett said again, her lips curving into a seductive smile that had Zeke stopped dead in his tracks, his head tilted to the side as he growled. "You don't want to drink any more blood, right? You don't want to hurt anyone anymore, right?"

The red receded from Zeke's gaze as a hunger of a different kind filled his eyes. Scarlett's knees trembled as she walked around Zeke, trailing her fingers along his bare skin, tracing the tattoos and the scars on his arm. The only sign that

Scarlett was terrified was the way her throat swallowed hard when Scarlett sent a quick glance over at Keeva.

Then she turned her attention back to Zeke, his chest heaving as he inhaled Scarlett's scent. He reached out and wrapped a hand around the throat of the succubus, who smiled, batting her long lashes at him before another wave of sexual energy had Malakai rocking against Keeva, wanting nothing more than to strip her bare and bury himself deep inside her.

"Kai," Keeva breathed out as Scarlett reached out and ran her hands up Zeke's torso. That was enough to snap the control Zeke had.

Before any of them could react, Zeke had Scarlett up against the wall, her legs wrapped around his waist, her arms around his neck as he ripped open her shirt to reveal her creamy skin and full breasts covered in a black lace bra. It was then that Malakai was able to clear his head and see the panic in her eyes.

"Fuck ... we have to stop this."

Keeva slipped from his embrace as Dylan called his name, tossing him a tranq dart, which he caught. Zeke cupped Scarlett's breast, and the succubus moaned, throwing her head back and exposing her throat. All the air was sucked from the room as Zeke struck, sinking his fangs into Scarlett's neck, the Inferna crying out but not in pain. She dug her nails into Zeke's skin as she said softly, "Zeke, please. I don't want to die."

A single tear slid down her throat as Zeke snarled, his fangs still in Scarlett's throat as she begged him to stop. But it wasn't until Zeke began to reach for Scarlett's pants that he heard the succubus beg him to stop, saying, "I'm a virgin."

With that surprising revelation, a miracle happened. For the first time since Zeke became a vampire, he stopped. He pulled his mouth from Scarlett's throat, licking the wound closed as if on autopilot. As the fog of hunger cleared, Zeke took in his position, Scarlett's exposed breasts, and he sucked in a breath. He stepped back, Scarlett's legs unwrapping from his waist as he set her gently on her feet.

Not a single soul moved for fear that whatever Scarlett had done to cast a spell on Zeke would break. The succubus flushed crimson as she wrapped the torn shirt around her breasts. Her body trembled, sending little waves of energy throughout the room. Zeke backed away from her with a growl, licking his lips and letting out a groan as he dropped to the ground, sitting with his head in his hands as he barked for someone to get Scarlett a shirt.

Jasmine pulled her own tee off, seemingly not at all bothered that it left her in the same position as Scarlett, her sports bra more modest than Scarlett's own lace one, and handed it to Scarlett as Dylan shook his head, trying to clear his head from all the emotions swirling in the air. He glanced at Malakai, and the moment Malakai nodded, Dylan shouted to lift ripper protocol, and he was in the elevator faster than Malakai had seen him move before.

Keeva cautiously made her way toward Scarlett, who was shaking uncontrollably as her eyes hungrily watched Zeke. Scarlett stepped out of Keeva's reach, shaking her head. "I can't. I used too much, and now, oh gods, Keeva, it hurts."

Keeva muttered reassuring things to Scarlett as the succubus ran her fingers over where Zeke had bitten and moaned, as if he still had his fangs at her throat. Zeke shuffled back on the floor, away from Scarlett, as if he did not trust himself, and Malakai crouched down in front of him, blocking Scarlett from view.

"Are you yourself?" he asked the other vampire, to which Zeke gave a nonchalant shrug of his shoulders.

"I am not sure. I do not hunger for blood. What sorcery has she wielded over me?"

His words were a whisper, so Malakai was the only one who heard him, not wanting the vampire to blame Scarlett for using her powers to stop him from draining her. "One that has cost her a great deal. One that saved your life. Tell me, what do you want to do right now, Zeke?"

"I want to strip her bare and fuck her." It was a guttural response, the evidence of his arousal in his body and in his tone.

"And before she used her powers on you? Did you feel the same way?"

Zeke was silent for a moment before he grunted out a yes, getting to his feet and taking a step toward Scarlett, who sucked in a breath. "Keeva, it hurts. Please, someone, make it stop."

Scarlett's hand dipped inside the waistband of her pants, searching for a release, and she moaned again. Zeke backed away as Scarlett's eyes watched him, her lips parted, and Malakai felt uncomfortable watching as tears slipped down his assistant's cheeks. It was painful to witness.

"It's okay, Scarlett. It's okay."

Keeva stalked forward, taking the tranquilizer from Malakai's hands. She glanced up at Zeke and arched her brow. "You're level now, right? You don't need this?"

Zeke nodded mutely as Keeva walked right over and struck her friend in the shoulder with the dart, pushing only half of the tranquilizer into Scarlett. The succubus's eyes rolled back in her head, and she dropped, Keeva catching her before she cracked her skull on the wooden floor.

Keeva lifted Scarlett into her arms, declining any help as she carried Scarlett to her bedroom and locked herself in. Both Malakai and Zeke waited a couple of minutes before either of them dared speak.

"Are you all right?"

Malakai shook his head, reaching for a cloth so Zeke could clean himself up. "I did not know she had that kind of power. I can still feel it on my skin," he admitted, wondering exactly what kind of power Scarlett Russell could wield.

Zeke didn't say anything as he surveyed the damage around the kitchen while he wiped his face and torso. Malakai left him to clean up, pressed a buzzer, and after a few seconds, the elevator whirled to life and one of his elite employees stepped out.

Isolde was almost six feet, with short hair shaved at the sides and a Mohawk down the centre of her hair. She was broad-shouldered, quick on her feet and was a stand-in for Dylan when he was not at Sicarius. She was also a fire-breathing dragon and one of the last of her kind.

"Sir."

"Have a clean-up crew get rid of the body, and once Dylan and Jazz come back, we remain on lockdown for the next twenty-four."

The dragon nodded and barked orders into her mic. Malakai went to where Zeke was trying to clear up the kitchen and advised him to retire for the evening. When Zeke went to protest, Malakai smiled and said, "I've been thinking of a remodel. Perhaps this will lead me to finally take some time off and indulge in my carpentry skills. I have not done so in over a decade."

Zeke looked like he was about to argue again, his eyes darting to the door that held Scarlett and Keeva, before he paused and said, "The banshee ... you've fallen for her, haven't you?"

Zeke didn't wait for a response as he left Malakai alone in the room, contemplating the answer to that question. If he were being honest with himself, the very thought of watching Keeva leave made his heart hurt.

CHAPTER FIFTEEN

Keeva

DAWN HAD JUST ABOUT BROKEN WHEN KEEVA MADE SURE THAT Scarlett was tucked up and safe in bed. She had spent most of the evening making sure that the sedative hadn't caused her best friend any discomfort. Instead, Scarlett slept like the dead, peaceful even, so Keeva knew she could leave her. It hurt her heart that Scarlett had been forced into action to stop Zeke, telling her deepest secret in order to stop him even when Scarlett had hurt herself because she hadn't fed.

She guessed when a guy took a hail of bullets for you, you found a way to reach inside the darkest regions of yourself to come to his aid.

Keeva brushed her lips over Scarlett's forehead, the succubus remaining still as Keeva stepped outside and closed the door quietly behind her. Keeva glanced into the kitchen area, surveying the damage as she whistled between her teeth. Zeke had caused some serious damage to the breakfast bar, a Malakai- and Dylan-size hole in the wood.

Walking to the fridge, Keeva took out a bottle of water and drained the bottle, her bones weary and her mind tired. By God, she wanted to sleep, but she was full of pent-up energy that couldn't stop her mind from racing. She considered heading out in search of a fight but turned and spotted a bulky figure on the sofa. Keeva took another bottle out of the fridge and walked around to where Zeke sat on the couch and handed him the bottle.

The vampire sat wearing a tee and a pair of basketball

shorts. He stared at the ground, as if he were merely waiting for it to open up to swallow him whole.

"Is she okay?"

Keeva gave him a small smile. "Sleeping. Probably will for a while. I haven't seen her use that much power in a while. She tends to keep it under lock and key."

The vampire said nothing as Keeva sank down on the couch. Running her fingers through her hair, Keeva glanced at Zeke and took a chance, because if her gut was right and Zeke cared for Scarlett, then he had to go into this with a certain expectation.

"What do you know about succubi before they graduate?"

Zeke glanced in her direction. "Graduate? Like from school?"

Okay, so this was going to be a revelation to Zeke, probably shatter his impressions of what an Inferna child went through, and Scarlett might be pissed that Keeva was telling him some of it, but she could scold her tomorrow. "Scarlett always had power, was expected to be top of her class. Already had her pick of jobs. But she got embarrassed easily, you see that. The leader of her Seduction, her class of succubi and incubi, thought it was a ploy to pretend to be coy. They were delighted. Her bashfulness intrigued them. Some men like that."

The bottle crunched in Zeke's hand, but Keeva continued. "It wasn't an act. From an early age, she was taught to use her sexuality to feed from humans or other Inferna. It's the nature of her species. Told me she was violently sick before and after. The leader had ways to nullify her power, mute it, but Scarlett's power was so off the charts, it was only ever diluted. When it came to graduation, she couldn't go through with the final test. It wasn't pretty, what happened, and they cast her out like a leper."

Zeke's teeth ground together as Keeva got to her feet and regarded the vampire. "If you ask her, she will tell you she wishes she were not born an Inferna. She hates that people are drawn to her because she is what she is, a species who preys on sexual desire. That is not Scarlett. But no more than I can wish away my death magic, Scarlett is who she is."

"What happens at graduation?" Zeke asked with a quiet determination. But this was Scarlett's story to tell, not Keeva's. The rituals and rites of the Seduction were known by so few, and Scarlett would tell Zeke if she wanted to.

Keeva shook her head. "Not my story to tell. Ask Scarlett; she may just tell you. But one thing you need to know. Scarlett is a Hallmark kind of girl. She wants the big romance where she's swept off her feet by the one person who is not swayed by her magic. She wants to be seen as herself, not her species. She hasn't shown interest in a member of the opposite sex in all the time I have known her. However, she likes you."

"Why would you tell me this? Should you not be warning her away from me?"

Keeva strode toward the elevator with a sigh. "I'm not sure. I've known Scarlett for nearly twenty years, and I've never seen her act like she does around you. Who am I to stand in the way of happiness?"

"You would be best to tell her that I am not for her. She is kind and gentle, and I am not."

"Whatever you say. I think you don't give yourself enough credit. You try to hide in the darkness, but as someone who lived in it for two years, the darkness won't bring you peace, only pain."

Keeva stepped into the elevator, letting the doors close before staring at the options for buttons to press. Moving subconsciously, she pressed the button that would take her to Malakai's floor, her body tingling at the anticipation of getting Malakai naked again. He'd somehow wormed his way past her defences, and although Keeva still worried that they were too different, she didn't want to die not knowing if the second time round would be better.

The doors opened and Keeva stepped out, her jacket already in her hands as she smiled at the sight before her. Malakai was stretched out on top of the covers, his torso bare, his back leaning against the headboard as he read a novel that certainly wasn't in English. Keeva ran her gaze over him as she kicked off her boots. Delicious muscles had Keeva's mouth-watering at the thought of tasting him and sating her appetite.

"How is Scarlett?" Malakai said as he set the book aside, his brown eyes watching her as she came toward the bed. Stripping off her tee and pants, Keeva crawled up the bed and straddled Malakai.

"Sleeping." Keeva leaned in and pressed a kiss to Malakai's jaw, nipping gently on the curve of his strong jawline. Malakai slipped his fingers into her hair and pulled her down for a mind-numbing kiss that clouded Keeva's mind.

Dragging her lips from Malakai's, Keeva grinned. "I'm not finished yet." Malakai let Keeva roam her hands over his body, tasting and feeling every plane of his torso, getting to know his skin, what he liked by the tiny tremble in his body or the sharp intake of breath when her teeth scraped his flesh.

This was the drug that Keeva craved, touching a lover without fear, without trepidation, to lose herself in the sensations of being able to run her hands all over his body as she longed to do.

Rocking against his boxer-clad erection, Keeva kissed her way down his stomach, flashing him a wicked smile as she dipped her hand inside his boxers. Her fingers grasped the hard steel of his cock in her hands. Malakai blew out a harsh curse as Keeva slid her hands up and down his hardened flesh before she leaned down as if to take it in her mouth, until Malakai growled.

"I'm not sure I would last very long if those kiss-swollen lips wrapped around my cock. I've been hard for you for days, Keeva Cross, and I want your wet pussy to feel me as I fill you completely."

Wetness soaked her panties as she stripped Malakai of his boxers, her vampire shifting to allow her to free his erection. Then she slipped her own panties off, returning to her previous position. Never before had she indulged in any of her own wants. Those quick fumbles where her hands were placed over her head so she wouldn't kill anyone had been about sating the needs of her body. This was about the needs of Keeva herself and of her heart.

Keeva took Malakai's cock in her hands again, shifting her body so that she knelt up and positioned the blunt head at her entrance. Slowly, she lowered herself down, taking him inside her body inch by glorious inch, her body clenching, stretching to accommodate him until he was buried deep inside her. They moaned together as Malakai's hands gripped her hips, and he lifted his own hips slightly to intensify the sensations rippling through her body.

Keeva held herself in check, wanting to savour this moment as she reached down and dragged Malakai close for kiss. She began to move the moment his tongue licked against her own, capturing the sounds of her pleasure as they touched and tasted each other until Malakai dragged his lips from hers. As Keeva lifted her body and then sank back down, she groaned. "Kai, I'm so close. Now, do it now."

Gods, he had already addicted her to his bite, but it was because it was Malakai.

Malakai sucked at the sensitive spot on her neck, and Keeva hissed, her entire being on fire as Malakai leaned in to her ear and said in that husky fucking tone of his, "Ask me nicely, Keeva."

Her words were a purr, a caress on her skin as she ground out, "Bite me, Cavanagh."

Keeva threw back her head as Malakai struck, his fangs sinking into her flesh as she came, hard, lights in her eyes as Malakai wrapped his arm around her waist to stop her from collapsing. His hips surged up, sending her cresting the wave again until Malakai thrust into her one last time before his spine locked and he came, shuddering with her name on his lips.

They stayed entwined, both of them breathing hard, until Malakai withdrew from her, sending little aftershocks through her. He positioned them so that Keeva was snuggled against his chest, where his heart was beating against her palm. She traced her fingers along his arm, lifting her head to look up at Malakai.

His eyes watched her with a smile as he brushed her curly hair from her face. "I like being ridden by my sexy little banshee."

Keeva swatted him but laughed as she stretched out her limbs, moving to lie on her stomach to get a better look at him. His skin was slick with sweat, his smile dangerously smug as his eyes looked at her like she was the most beautiful woman in the world. Keeva had always been right to think that Malakai Cavanagh was dangerous and deadly, but now, now he held her heart in his hands and had the power to crush it.

"Tell me, how is it that your heart beats?"

Malakai reached his arms down and wrapped them around her waist, pulling her closer as he spoke. "The human body needs blood to be pumped around the body in order for organs to work. Vampires are essentially the same; however, as we are not technically alive, our bodies require blood in order for our organs to function."

"And what happens if you don't feed?"

Tugging on the strands of her hair, Malakai gave her a warm smile. "We are husks; our bodies stop working, and while our minds and the hunger still are there, we do not have the strength to go find a meal. It's like we are paralyzed until we are fed on blood, and then, when we have had our fill, our bodies start to work again."

Keeva placed her hand over the place where his heart beat, marvelling at the steady thump, thump that pulsed against her palm. "Is it true that a vampire can father a child?"

Malakai quirked a brow with a little smirk. "Thinking of having a kid with me?"

Keeva blushed, digging him hard in the ribs as she blew out a breath. "Well, we've just had sex, and neither of us thought of you wearing a condom. Just thinking about the future."

"And to answer your question, no, we cannot father a child. Vampires are made, not born."

Keeva fell silent, lost in her thoughts, relieved a little, because try as she might, Keeva never saw herself as a mother. It pierced her heart to think of subjecting a child to inheriting her powers.

A memory flooded her mind, and Keeva's breath hitched.

The sound of the rain was her only friend as Keeva huddled in the corner of the cell, her fingers touching the moonlight that breached the confines of the darkness. She was not sure when was the last time she had seen the sun or how many days it had been since she had tasted freedom. The days bled into one another, a wave of thirst and hunger and crippling loneliness.

Closing her eyes, Keeva pictured herself roaming the forest with Clodagh, rolling down the grassy dunes as they picked flowers and spoke of their future. Clodagh was destined to take over from her father as head of the scream. Already she had numerous offers of marriage. She promised to take Keeva with her, because as Angus told her on numerous occasions, no one wanted the dud banshee.

Keeva imagined, even at fifteen, that there would be someone, someday who could love her, kiss her like she was the air needed to breathe, who chased a red-haired little boy around the garden as Keeva watched from the kitchen window.

And then Keeva opened her eyes to the darkness. The reminder that Clodagh was dead and that she had no chance at that future sent a river of tears cascading down her face.

Sucking in a breath at the memories, Keeva shivered at the reminder of the person she used to be and the person she had to become to survive. Keeva did not regret the decision to become an assassin, for it meant she was released from the prison of darkness; however, Keeva felt as if she would always be a prisoner of Clodagh's death.

Offering up a little piece of herself to Malakai as if speaking the words aloud would free her of some of the burden she carried, Keeva said softly, "When I was locked in the darkness, I dreamed of having a family. When I felt lonely, I would imagine what it would be like to be happy. Clodagh was there, smiling and laughing as we picnicked at the beach with our kids and the sun shielded me from the darkness."

"Keeva." Malakai uttered her name like it was a prayer, leaning down to kiss her. "I cannot offer you the sun or that image in your head, but I can promise to never leave you alone in the darkness. I can promise you a place in our family, as unconventional as it is, if you want it … if you want me."

Keeva kissed him then, not knowing how to answer, for she was not used to getting what she wanted in life. She had lost Clodagh, lost the spark of life that burned inside her in the darkness, and now, a chance meeting with a vampire had ignited the embers inside her, threatening to unravel the careful shielding around her heart. She wanted Malakai, wanted to be part of his family maybe since the day she had seen the love and bond they shared.

Suddenly, Malakai shifted so that Keeva lay on her back, and he leaned down to capture one of her nipples between his teeth. Keeva arched into him, his hands gripping her right leg and bending it back as he thrust into her slowly. This was not the fast, desperate need of two people unable to put a halt to their attraction; this was a slow proclamation of intention as Malakai made love to her with a slowness, a tenderness that threatened to undo her.

Each kiss, each pant, each sharp intake of breath shattered Keeva as she felt herself be loved for the first time in her life. Each thrust was a branding, a claiming where Malakai was telling Keeva with his body just how much he wanted her. She loved that he was as affected by her as she was by him, evident in the growl deep in his throat as she bit down playfully on his shoulder.

He kissed her slowly, each press of lips telling her that he craved her, not just for this brief period but to claim as his. Keeva let Malakai seduce her, powerless against the vampire as she rode the waves of pleasure until she came. Malakai tensed, dipping his head to press his lips against hers as he gave one final slow thrust and then collapsed on top of her.

"Are you trying to kill me?"

Malakai chuckled, easing out of her and onto his side. "Maybe I'm trying to convince you to never leave this bed." To emphasise his point, Malakai dragged the duvet up over her waist as Keeva hooked a leg over his and curled into his side sleepily.

Keeva yawned. "Did you forget that you have a security empire to run and I have the little thing called a prison sentence hanging over my head? Plus, we have a reluctant succubus, a blood-lusted vampire, a smart-ass blond and Jasmine to keep on the straight and narrow."

"We?"

Keeva closed her eyes and patted his chest. "Don't think too much about it, Kai. You've sexed me into oblivion. My brain isn't working very well right now. Ask me again when I've had a little sleep."

Malakai laughed, making Keeva smile as he wrapped his arms around her and pressed his lips to the top of her head.

She was almost asleep when she heard him mutter absently to himself.

"I have wandered this earth for hundreds of years and always felt like I was missing a piece of me. The moment you barged into my life, I felt as if I had found that missing piece. I cannot picture my life without you, little banshee. I want you in my life, my bed, my home."

Keeva sighed, contented in her drowsiness as Malakai continued. "All my life I have dedicated myself to ensuring that everyone around me was safe and happy. Now, I crave something for myself. There is a myth within the vampire community that there is a mate out there that is meant for us. I never believed that until I laid eyes on you."

Keeva didn't say anything as Malakai simply held her, and the safety of his arms around her allowed her to relax and fall into a deep sleep that halted even the worst of nightmares.

CHAPTER SIXTEEN

Keeva

KEEVA WAS STIRRED FROM SLEEP BY THE RINGING OF HER PHONE. Malakai tried to keep her in the bed with a growl, and Keeva was tempted to let him, but whoever was blowing up her phone kept calling. Fishing inside her pants, Keeva flipped open the phone and pressed answer to the private number.

"What?" she barked into the phone, already annoyed.

"Still alive then?" Angus. Trust that smug bastard to sour the mood as Keeva sat down at the edge of the bed, as Malakai feathered kisses along her spine. Swatting him away with a grin, Keeva turned her attention back to the asshole on the other end of the line.

"What do you want, Angus?"

"Is the vampire dead?"

Keeva paused for a second before she answered Angus in a bored tone. "You already know the answer to that or you wouldn't be harassing me. If the Primus of vampires was dead, I'd be in your office now, showing proof of death so I would be free of your leash. You would make my job a lot easier if you called off the hit on me."

Angus snickered down the phone, and Keeva could almost see his smirking face in her mind. "Perhaps if you stopped spreading your legs for him, then you might be able to kill him. Get to my home in the next hour, or I'll add another twenty years to your sentence. Come alone, Keeva, and wash the scent of that vampire off you, or I'll make sure you never see the light of day again."

Keeva screamed in frustration as Angus hung up, tossing

the phone across the room, and the cheap thing broke apart. Balling up her fists, Keeva punched the bed before she jerked to her feet and began to dress. Screw Angus and his demands. She wasn't going to give him an inch. She was tired of all this bullshit.

"I'm starting to get a complex here. Every time we have sex, you end up breaking a phone."

The words were a sensuous purr that had Keeva spinning round to face Malakai as he lounged in the bed. The sheet barely covered his hips as he leaned against the headboard, his lips curved into a small smile, but there was a darkness in his eyes. Keeva pulled on her pants, reaching for the tee that Malakai had worn last night to the bar, and pulled it on over her head. The tee was far too big for her, so she bunched it up and tied a knot at the side.

"I'm frustrated that I have to go face that dickhead when all I want to do is spend the rest of the night with you. I've never done that before. It seems like there are forces who just don't want Keeva to get what she wants."

"Talking about yourself in the third person is a little weird. I think that might be a deal-breaker."

Keeva let loose a bark of laughter at his teasing tone, leaning in to press a quick kiss to his lips. "Well, if I have to become a fugitive and make a break for it, you fancy coming with me? I hear Norway is nice this time of year."

Malakai shifted in the bed, slinging his legs off the mattress to the floor and giving Keeva a spectacular view that made her legs quiver. He pulled out a panel from the side of his bed and handed Keeva a new phone. "Grab your sim card on the way. It should fit in this. Text me when you're free of Angus. I'd offer to go with you or send one of the guys with you, even though I don't want to let you out of my sight, but I know that you are capable. Had I known that Death would be this interesting, I would have asked for a face-to-face long ago."

Running her fingers through her hair, Keeva rolled her eyes. "And had I known that the CEO of Sicarius was actually El Diablo, I might have just come."

"I think you've already done that. A few times, if I remember right."

Keeva's mouth dropped open at the innuendo, to which Malakai chuckled. He pressed his lips to hers once, twice, and then in a slow devouring of her mouth that had Keeva arching into him. Malakai stepped back, a fierce expression in his eyes as he said, "I don't hear from you by dawn and I'm sending in a team."

"Thank you."

Malakai strode off naked in the direction of the bathroom, and Keeva could see the tension in his shoulders with every step he took away from her, spotted the clenched fists. It was only when he stepped out of view did she exhale a breath.

Spinning on her heels, Keeva finished dressing before she headed for the lift, surprised when it opened and a soldier stood in the lift waiting for her: tall, with muscles that made Keeva intensely jealous, hair that was shaved at the sides and a spiked mohawk that looked sharp, giving Keeva the strangest urge to reach out and touch the bristles ... but she wasn't sure her petite frame could reach.

With eyes a shock of amber, skin sun-kissed and a power omitting from her that had Keeva taking a step back, the other woman smirked, folding her arms across her chest as she ran her eyes over Keeva.

"You don't look much like Death." Her accent was not Irish, had a thickness of its own as Keeva let a slow, deliberate smile tug at her lips.

"That," Keeva said with amusement in her tone, "is what they all say—right up until I put hands on them and then they feel it. Wanna have a taste?"

"I have already tasted death, banshee. I need not dance

with it again. The Primus asked me to show you to our weapons cache. I do as asked to do."

There was a chilly undertone to her words that had Keeva studying the other woman. It was obvious that whoever she was didn't like Keeva … but why?

It only took Keeva a few minutes to see the spark of jealousy in the woman's eyes. Jesus, she had the hots for Malakai … probably had slept with him and now, she saw Keeva as a rival.

"Listen," Keeva broached with the other woman. "Us women have enough to contend with as Inferna than have this animosity between us because you fancy Malakai."

"I do not fancy Malakai." The words were sharp, indignant as if she were horrified that Keeva had even suggested that she might be attracted to Malakai. Her eyes flashed like flames, and it was Keeva's turn to study her.

"Malakai is my boss. I would never blur those lines. I am a soldier. His and my relationship is like one of mentor and apprentice. There was no trouble until he met you. I think you bring chaos and calamity with you."

Keeva perched her hands on her hips. "Well, if Malakai decides that he wants my chaos and calamity around, then that's on him. He's a grown vampire. Doesn't need you to try and scare me off."

The other woman pressed her lips together, running her eyes over Keeva as the door to the elevator opened and Dylan leaned in the archway.

Keeva stepped into the basement room, her eyes wide. "Oh my God, is this heaven?"

Dylan chuckled as the elevator doors closed, taking the soldier with it, who had no qualms in casting one last disapproving glance at Keeva before she left. Keeva felt a little angry and then pulled it back as she glanced at Dylan sheepishly.

"Making friends with Isolde?"

"You read that with your special Spidey senses?"

Dylan grinned, pointedly ignoring her question as he stepped farther into the bunkerlike room. Wall to wall were guns of every calibre, knives and blades of every length and size. Her eyes roamed hungrily over the assortment of weapons. Keeva reached out and took a pair of black-tipped daggers from the table and rotated her wrists. The blades were feather-light, and Keeva wanted them so badly.

"I'll make sure to tell Kai that if he really wants to make sure he keeps you, that this is the way to ensure it."

Keeva rolled her eyes, casting a withering look in the vampire's direction as Dylan sorted through some weapons belts and then slipped one around her waist. Keeva placed the daggers into the sheaths and sighed.

"You know how to use a gun?"

"When I need to."

Dylan handed her a Glock 17, modified from the standard gun Keeva was used to, complete with the Sicarius Security logo etched into the grip. When Keeva quirked her brow, Dylan chuckled and leaned against the table.

"As a global security company, Sicarius has some leniency with carrying a gun in Ireland. Since we have you on file as a current employee, even if it's just a cover, if you have to use that, then we can come up with a plausible reason for you having it."

Keeva slipped the Glock into the waistband of her pants. "And if I get arrested for shooting someone?"

"We have a badass lawyer who can scare the bejesus out of most Inferna. Humans, piece of cake!"

Keeva reached for a grenade with a grin, and it was Dylan's turn to quirk a brow. "You think you might need that?"

"The way things are going lately, you never know. Best to be prepared."

Dylan's laugh rebounded through the bunker as he

called for the lift and then handed Keeva a set of keys, to which Keeva frowned. "Before you argue with me, it's an old model hatchback. If Malakai had a choice, he would have given you one of the armoured SUVs we have. Hell, I think he'd even let you drive his pride and joy if you asked him."

Keeva stepped into the elevator. "Aw, is Mac not allowed drive the Aston Martin?"

With a look that asked if she were crazy, Dylan said with a bright smile, "I have a tendency to crash cars. I'm not even allowed to wash the damn thing."

Keeva was still laughing as she made her way into the parking garage, stopping to admire the array of spectacular vehicles that lined the private car park. The modest little Honda Civic that was nestled in the middle of a bright yellow Mini and Dylan's own car looked out of place with all the fancy cars, and Keeva wondered if this was a metaphor for how she would fit in with the Cavanaghs.

Keeva unlocked and sat in the car, took the gun out from her back and placed it on the seat beside her. She drove the car out of the garage and into the night, heading for the motorway to bring her into the light midweek traffic. The humans were heading home from their jobs, and Keeva wondered what it would be like to live not knowing that there were others among them.

Huffing out a breath, Keeva veered off the motorway and onto the road that would lead her to Angus's estate, one that Keeva had grown up on. Her heart clenched at the thought of being there again, because even though she was not your average banshee, Keeva had survived among her kin because of Clodagh.

Her childhood hadn't been that bad considering; at one point she even had Angus as a father figure to her, but when Clodagh's mother died in childbirth and then they lost Clodagh, Angus had turned bitter, twisted. It was hard to believe that the man who had once braided her hair had turned her into an assassin.

Yanking the steering wheel to the left, Keeva drove up the gravel. The sprawling bungalow looked dwarfed by the forest that surrounded it. Keeva halted the car outside the main door, killing the engine. Grabbing the gun, she repositioned it at the small of her back and got out of the car, jutting out her chin and striding toward not the main door but the side entrance that led directly to Angus's office.

Stepping out of the shadows, a figure that smiled warmly at her came into view. Angus might be the leader of their Scream, but there were quite a few who thought his second-in-command, Ivan Dunne, was a better fit. Younger than Angus by about fifty years, Ivan had looked like he was in his twenties when she and Clodagh were teens. Clodagh had a massive crush on the older man; Keeva just liked that he was always patient and kind, the complete opposite of Angus.

It was only after she had been released from her incarceration that Keeva found out that Ivan had spent those two years advocating for her release.

"It is good to see you, little one. Aye, it is good to see you."

Keeva allowed herself to be engulfed in a hug as the older man whispered in her ear. "He is in one hell of a foul humour, Keeva. He is feeling nasty tonight, aye?"

Stepping out of the embrace, Keeva smiled fondly at the other banshee. "I might just kill him then for any nasty thing he may have said to you."

Ivan laughed, shaking his head. "You were always trouble. A little hellraiser. We should have known when we saw the hair."

The gate swung up, and they both looked over to where Angus stood, fuming. "If you have finished flirting with *my* assassin, Ivan, let her by. I don't have all night."

The gate slammed, and Keeva was surprised that the gate

didn't break off the hinges as it did. Keeva looked at Ivan as the other man watched her with an interest that was not there before. Tall and lean with an easy smile, blondish-brown hair and dark blue eyes, Ivan had been a handsome teen, even more so as he grew into his own power and held on to his calm, easy personality. It was easy to see why Clodagh had fancied him, but as Keeva stood looking at him, she couldn't help comparing him with a tall, dark and handsome vampire who drove her crazy.

Damn, she was falling for Malakai and falling hard.

"Why do I get the impression that I'm being compared to a rather handsome vampire?"

Keeva shrugged. "Sorry ... I guess."

Ivan chortled and stepped aside, but not before he said, "Do not be a stranger, Keeva Cross. You are banshee, no matter what others say, and we look after our own."

Keeva reached out and gave his arm a squeeze before she pushed open the gate and tracked Angus to his office. She slid open the patio door and stepped into the room, her eyes darting to the pictures on the wall of Clodagh, of Clodagh's mother, Niamh, and one of her and Clodagh right over Clodagh's shoulder.

"I do not have all night, Keeva."

Keeva let her eyes fall to where Angus sat behind his mahogany desk, his fingers clasped together over a diary, his eyes full of contempt as he ran his eyes over her, his gaze snagging on the tee she wore, and his scowl deepened.

"How does he fuck you, Keeva? Like an animal so that you cannot kill him?"

Keeva was used to the crude remarks and nastiness from Angus; however, the fact that Angus didn't know that she could touch Malakai as much as she wanted made her smirk. Something else that Keeva knew would enrage the other banshee.

"Oh, Angus, the sex is mind-blowing, I mean earth-shattering. And the fact that I can touch him all I want. Wrap my hands around his—"

"Enough!" Angus roared as he stood and beat his fists on the desk, sending papers flying to the floor. "I do not wish to hear your lies. You have a job to do, and you will do it. I'm owed a vast amount of money once you kill the vampire, and I will not be denied. I own you."

Keeva had enough of his bullshit, pulled the grenade from her pocket and held it up as Angus stepped back. "I am not your property. You do not own me, Angus. For too long, I've let my guilt over Clodagh cloud my judgment and I let you use me. I am Death, and I am not afraid to die … are you?"

Despite the fear that leaked from his pores, Angus took a step toward her, and Keeva shook the grenade. "Clodagh loved you like a sister, and you took her from us. I will never let you forget that, nor will I ever let you go. You will always be mine to command, Keeva, and once the vampire is dead and you have nowhere to turn, I will make you my bride and you will never leave this house."

Keeva stepped up to the desk and pretended to pull the pin. "You see, I would never be that desperate, Angus. Death would be better than any fate you tried to impose on me. I'd kill you the first chance I got. Don't be so eager for the kiss of Death. It might be the last thing you see before you go to hell."

Keeva whirled round and stormed out of the office, her heart beating like a drum inside her chest as she hurried to the car, getting in and setting the gears into reverse as she backed out of the drive at speed, spinning the car in the middle of the road, driving down the road until her eyes blurred with tears and she jammed on the brakes, skidding to a halt in the middle of the country road.

The tears came freely as Keeva beat her fists angrily on the steering wheel, a scream building up in her throat, gathering inside her chest as Keeva struggled to breathe at the enormity of the weight of it, the force, until it ripped from her, the sound devastating and beautiful at the same time. Keeva let go of her guilt, her anger, her sadness, keening for the loss of her friend and for a part of herself until the scream turned into a whimper. She let her head fall to the wheel as she cried herself dry of tears, not noticing the tiny sliver of glass that had cracked on the back window of the car.

CHAPTER SEVENTEEN

Malakai

MALAKAI DONNED THE ARMOUR THAT WAS HIS ARMANI SUIT, fastening the cuffs of his shirt before slipping into the jacket. If the years had taught him anything, it was how appearances were deceptive and most people—whether they be Inferna or human—made an assumption of character based on their first impression of an individual. Had he stridden into the Inferna council dressed in jeans and a tee and advised them he had killed the previous Primus and would now rule the Irish vampires, they would have not taken him seriously.

Instead, Malakai had walked through the doors carrying the ashes of the previous Primus in a jar, dressed in a black suit that had felt ridiculous on him at the time, but they had taken one look at his suit, glossed over his blood-streaked face and hands and welcomed him to the council with open arms.

Grabbing the collar, Malakai smoothed the jacket before contemplating a tie, then dismissed the idea. His phone buzzed, and he slipped it out of his pocket with a smile as he read the text from his fiery banshee.

Just left Angus. Still a dickhead. Need to drive to clear my head. I'll be back before dawn.

Malakai typed in a response as he strode out of his walk-in wardrobe, the silliest of grins on his face. *Are you okay? I'm just about to head to a council meeting but could be persuaded to blow it off.*

Malakai watched the dot, dot, dot that indicated that Keeva was typing, then it stopped, as if Keeva had stopped herself. It surprised him how anxious that made him, waiting for the dots to appear again as he strode to the elevator. The typing started again as Malakai stepped inside and pressed for the lobby.

I'm fine… came Keeva's response. *Angus has a hard-on for you and is in a bitch of a humour. Watch your back, Kai.*

A shiver of delight coursed through his body at the nickname, as if Keeva was slowly dropping her defences and letting him in. When he was with her, he felt his calm exterior slip away to something more primal in him, as he sought to claim her mind, body, and soul. He thought about what she had said, about not taking the time to enjoy a lover's company, and he told himself that he would try and romance her, give her the time she deserved.

A smile on his lips, Malakai reread Keeva's text and then responded, hoping she could hear the amusement in his tone. *Have you anything to do with his humour.*

I threatened him with a grenade so probably.

Even in her texts, Malakai could hear the sarcasm in her tone, see the glint of mischief in her eyes as she recalled the incident. He was typing a response to the message, trying to play it cool, when he nearly walked straight into Scarlett.

"I'm sorry, Scarlett. I didn't see you there."

The succubus was dressed in a black suit of her own, a red blouse that made her features even more striking and a pair of heels that were high enough to bring her almost to Malakai's height. Scarlett offered him a coy smile, heat creeping up her face as she waited for him to mention last night, but Malakai simply asked, "You sure you feel okay to join me tonight?"

Scarlett nodded, swallowing hard. "I could do with getting out of the office."

And away from Zeke, Malakai thought as he called for the car, almost walking into the door as he tried to articulate a message to Keeva. If Scarlett had not jerked him back,

Malakai would have embarrassed himself in front of a lobby full of employees.

"Oh for the love of God, tell Keeva you will see her later and hand me over the phone. That's an order."

Malakai chuckled as he shot off a text to Keeva to tell her he'd just been chewed out by his assistant for not paying attention and she was confiscating his phone like he was a naughty schoolboy.

The response was a variety of emoji of a crying laughing face that made Malakai smile. His black town car pulled up outside, and Roman stepped out of the driver's door, glancing around and then motioning for them to come out.

Malakai paid attention to Scarlett best he could as the succubus gave him a brief rundown of the calls and messages he had missed while they slept. He nodded at her, pretending to listen, as Roman held open the door for them, his most recent employee turning out to be a solid investment. Scarlett ducked into the car first, then Malakai, and soon enough, Roman closed the door behind them.

"A request had been made by some Arabian prince for a quote on adding security to his extensive compound. From what I have in regards to his wealth, he owns a number of racehorses, a football club in the UK and a chain of hotels."

Malakai reclined in his chair at the wonderment in Scarlett's tone as he replied. "That is probably the public view of his wealth. Jazz will run a full background on him. Possible that he is a Jinn or some rare Middle Eastern Inferna. If it's a sound investment, I'll send Dylan out to charm him."

"When I was a girl," Scarlett mused with a little smile on her face as she flicked through some pages, "I always wanted to learn to ride a horse. Or even pet one. Not much calls for horses when you're a succubus. Do you ride?"

Malakai chuckled, glancing out of the window. "I have not ridden a horse in a very long time. I am quite happy with having horsepower under me in the shape of a car." Testing the water, Malakai continued to look out the window, making his comment as innocent as possible. "You should ask Zeke. When he was a boy, he kept horses. Still rides on the occasion we can drag him from his library."

He heard his assistant sigh and decided not to comment any further about it until Scarlett cleared her throat. "I understand if you wish for me to step down. I embarrassed myself last night, and I was not professional. That's twice now I've behaved in a manner that's unbecoming, and I would fully understand if you wanted to hire someone else."

Malakai turned his gaze back to Scarlett. "In the week since I've hired you, I'm finally organized so that I have time for myself. I can be a little bit of a control freak if left unchecked. I need someone who will argue with me and tell me to put my phone away so as I don't make a fool of myself. Unless you wish to leave, Scarlett, and I would offer you any amount of money not to, you will always have a job with Sicarius."

Scarlett let a smile curve her lips. "Is this the perfect time to ask for a raise?"

"I'll have to speak with my money man, but if it means locking you into employment, then I would ask him to agree."

Though Zeke was cautious when it came to money, Malakai was almost certain Zeke would pull the funds from somewhere.

Scarlett chuckled as they drove up to the front of the Inferna council offices. The building was warded, masked to look like a private bank. Malakai slid out of the car, holding his hand out to help Scarlett out, and then they strode inside, the shiver of magic itching his skin as they crossed the wards.

Once inside, Malakai hurried down the steps that led to the round table where they would all sit. Members of the council were already gathered, and Malakai cast a glance over his shoulder to where Scarlett had taken a seat, Roman beside her. She began typing on her little laptop.

"Malakai."

At the sound of his name, Malakai turned to the shifter standing in front of him and reached out his hand. "Duncan."

They shook hands as Duncan lifted his head. "You employ wolves now?"

"Why? You looking for a job, Duncan?"

The alpha of the shifters chuckled, but his eyes stayed on Roman sitting beside Scarlett. "I've tried for decades to put a leash on his rebellious nature. He's not one for authority, Malakai, despite his stint in the army. Even the quietest of wolves keep secrets."

It was Malakai's turn to offer a chuckle. "Roman has been a model employee. No bucking authority and even calls me 'sir.' Maybe he just didn't like taking orders from you."

Duncan growled softly as he pulled his hand from Malakai's grasp. The gong sounded to bring the meeting to attention. Malakai took his seat, keeping his expression blank as Angus glared at him from across the table. The lights dimmed as the high elder lifted his hands, and magic pulsed as a barrier fell into place, cloaking sound from those outside the circle.

Around the table, you had the high elder, a fae from the winter court who was chosen as a representative from the fae kings and queens, his Gandalf-like appearance not at all masking the true deadliness of the fae nature. Next to him, the seats were empty as the representatives of Heaven and Hell only appeared when it was a mandatory meeting, traversing the planes too much trouble for the superior beings.

Duncan was next to the angelic seat and Angus next to the demonic, as ironic as it was. Malakai was next to Duncan, followed by Miranda, high succubus of the Cork Seduction, her eyes amused at the sight of Scarlett, yet the Inferna chose not to remark on the company Malakai was keeping. The succubus had caramel-coloured hair, a skirt that barely covered her ass and a blouse that gave everyone on the council a view of her cleavage. Malakai mused at how so unlike her kin Scarlett was and was grateful for her.

The only portion of the Inferna society that was not represented was the witches, the covens remaining cloistered for the most part. Though Malakai had a witch he could call upon, it took a lot of money to draw them into society. Some suspected that the witches were consolidating for a coup, but Malakai thought they just wanted to live a simple life with nature. The movies were wrong about witches being dark and evil—they were mostly peace, love and nature, but like all species, there were exceptions to the rule.

Malakai listened as they discussed various things, including a zoning issue where the fae wanted to encroach on part of the banshee land due to a doorway to their home that had opened. Angus offered it to them at a price, in a few seconds earning a couple of thousand euros for his effort. Then matters went to things Malakai just had no interest in at this time as they droned on with the same arguments that always held their attention.

"Malakai, I believe you have had some threats upon your life?" Angus's smug tone carried across the room as Malakai reclined in his seat and shrugged.

"Nothing we at Sicarius cannot handle. I would rather the person who ordered the hits would just step forward, be a man, and come face me. It has been a while since I've gotten blood on my hands; I would very much like to see I haven't become rusty in my old age."

That earned a chortle of laughter from the rest of the Inferna council as they studied the interaction. Malakai made a show of cracking his knuckles and then brushing imaginary dirt from his sleeve as if the line of questions bored him. Duncan, thankfully, changed the subject, advising that the wolves had decided to have a party on their plot of land during the next full moon due to a mating that would be blessed during the change.

After a long, tedious hour, the meeting drew to a close, with the high elder offering Malakai support should he be unable to take care of his little problem, a slight against the vampire's ability to quash the rebellion in his own camp, even if it was said in polite terms. Malakai gritted his teeth, offered his polite thanks but assured the council there was no need to be worried; anyone who was found to have been involved in his assassination attempt or the harm caused to his employees would feel the full wrath of the vampires and Sicarius, as he was allowed under the purview of the council and as an Elder.

Malakai left them on that note, stopping to hold out the crook of his arm to Scarlett. She rolled her eyes but linked her arm in his as they continued up the steps and exited the chambers into the night air. Magic again rippled on his skin as they crossed the barrier into a light drizzle that had started falling in the time that they had been inside. Scarlett chatted away happily as Roman opened the car door, allowing her to slip inside.

"Malakai, a moment, if you please."

Malakai turned, deliberately slow, to face Angus as the other Inferna sauntered toward him. He stopped just outside reaching distance, yet Malakai knew Angus was not a threat to him or even Keeva. "What can I do for you, Angus?"

"Do you know where your little whore was this evening?"

"Do you mean before or after Keeva left my bed?"

Angus clucked his tongue in disgust. "Does it jar you that she came running the moment I snapped my fingers?"

Malakai laughed unreservedly. "If you think that's what she did, then I feel sorry for you, Angus. Truly I do."

"I'm the one who yanks her leash, Malakai. She belongs to my species, which means I own her. She does not so much as get on her knees without me telling her to. If she truly cared for you, then I would not have happened upon her in an embrace with my second. Keeva has wanted nothing more in her life than to be accepted by her own kind. Tying herself to Ivan would bring her back into the fold. That is if I do not tie her to me."

Malakai fought the urge to strangle Angus, hearing lies in his words as he spoke, smelling them with his nose. Instead Malakai reached out, grasping Angus by the shoulder, digging his fingers into his skin.

"I would gut you from sternum to stomach if she asked me to. I would rip out your innards while your heart still beat or flay the skin off your bones as a gift to Keeva. You took a terrified teen who killed by accident and held her prisoner in the dark until you broke her enough to wield her into a weapon to try and put a halt to your own grief. Now, the weapon has decided she does not need a master. It is a dangerous thing, Angus, to give a deadly predator a taste of freedom, for it will always try to bite the hand that holds its chain."

Malakai grinned, causing Angus to step back from the menace in his gaze as Malakai let his fangs elongate, felt the red bleed into his eyes. "I shall enjoy watching as she exacts her revenge."

Angus paled even as he looked a little green around the gills. Malakai gave him his back and headed for the car, where Roman leaned against the door as if he was carefree, but Malakai knew the wolf was ready to engage if needed. Angus was not a threat to him or his; Angus was a man who used his power to assert control but could not stand to get his hands dirty himself.

"Malakai."

Letting an annoyed growl rumble in his throat, Malakai cast his gaze over his shoulder, not bothering to turn back to face the banshee. Angus had retreated slowly, halting just shy of the magic barrier as he smirked. "I hope it's slow. I hope you feel every single ounce of torture. I hope she bears witness to it all."

The moment Angus stepped inside the barrier, Malakai felt something pierce his shoulder. For the briefest of moments, he felt nothing, wondered if he had imagined the sharpness, then an inferno caught fire in his veins as Malakai tried to yank the arrow out, the hilt burning his fingers as they came into contact with gold, the poisoned weapon glinting in the moonlight. His skin burned as his bloodstream filled with gold, for nothing could seep into the veins of vampires and wield so much pain as gold. When the pain drove him to his knees, he let loose a roar of agony as another sting just at the base of his spine sent another shockwave throughout his entire being.

Silver was the fabled nemesis of vampires and werewolves, and while a silver bullet to the head would kill a wolf, vampires kept the secret of their aversion to gold a closely guarded one that was forbidden to be spoken outside your Kiss. It was a law punishable with death, it was such a crime to disclose that information to anyone.

Either the person who had fired the arrows knew of their secrets, or they were a vampire themselves. That meant that someone had betrayed their own kind in order to remove Malakai from the world. This was the first shot in a war Malakai wasn't sure he was ready for.

Malakai felt his muscles lock as he was dragged to the car by Roman, each pull sending fresh waves of agony throughout his body as the wolf barked at Scarlett to call Dylan. White-hot flames burned his skin from the inside out as he felt the weapons of his agony being ripped from his back, and he let loose a snarl as Roman set him down on the back seat, stomach down, leaving Scarlett locked in with him while Roman drove off so fast he heard tyres squeal.

His body seized, the gold flooding his senses, blinding

him, as he trembled, feeling the burning in his veins travel to his organs, felt them rupture as his lungs struggled to take in a breath. His body felt like he had not drunk in decades as his skin flaked, his mind spluttered, and as Scarlett cried down the phone, Malakai succumbed to the demands of his body and ...

CHAPTER EIGHTEEN

Keeva

KEEVA BURST THROUGH THE DOORS OF SICARIUS SECURITY, HER eyes wild, her heart pounding in her chest as she spotted Roman waiting for her in the lobby. His face was drawn into a grim scowl, his teeth gritted together, and Keeva froze, convinced that Malakai was dead and she had not been there to say goodbye.

Keeva had known what it was like to lose someone she cared for more than herself, had been forced to live through her grief with no support or safety net. If she lost Scarlett, it would crush her, but something told her that if Malakai was dead, then that would break her utterly and completely. In the short time they had known each other, Malakai had chipped away at her resolve, and now, now Keeva wanted for the first time in her life.

When she'd lain in his arms, discussing the future, it was the first time Keeva even considered she could have a future with someone she could care for. Damn it to hell, if Malakai had died, she would dig her way to whatever afterlife there was and sucker-punch him right before she killed him herself.

As if sensing her thoughts, Roman held up his hands. "Keeva, he's not dead. Probably wishes he was, but Malakai is a tough SOB."

"Where is he?"

Roman pressed the elevator. "His floor. Come on. Scarlett sent me down to get you."

The elevator moved painfully slow as Keeva tapped her foot on the floor, earning a slight growl from Roman. She ignored him as he spoke until suddenly, through the fog of her mind, she heard him mention Angus.

"What did you just say?"

"We were clear. He was getting in the car when Angus called him. He taunted Malakai about you, and then when he couldn't get a rise out of Malakai, Angus told him he hoped it hurt. Then he was shot with the arrows. Angus knew."

Anger boiled in her veins as the doors opened and Keeva snarled. "Angus won't live to see the sun rise."

Keeva heard the arguing as she stepped out into Malakai's private space. She nodded to Scarlett, who was standing off to the side, careful not to get in anyone's way, as Keeva walked all the way around the family and climbed onto the bed next to Malakai, who lay propped up on his side. His skin was dry, flaked, his body rigid, his eyes watching her as she ran her eyes over his naked body to assess the damage. He looked like a body who had been in the ground for days, and Keeva had to swallow the bile in her throat.

"Well, Cavanagh, you look like shit."

Amusement sparkled in his eyes and then pain as his body creaked. Keeva went up to her knees and looked at the vampire. "What the fuck happened?"

"Someone shot him with arrows dipped in gold." Dylan snarled, holding up an arrow that the vampire had wrapped in a towel as he showed Keeva.

"Still not getting why Malakai is trying to audition for *The Mummy?*"

The vampires glanced at one another, none of them rushing to fill Keeva in until she pulled one of the daggers from her waist and growled. "Someone better start fucking talking, or I'm going to make one of you bleed."

Jasmine rolled her eyes. "I'm already in trouble with fate, so let me. Kai was shot up with arrows dipped in gold, a poison to vampires and a secret we cannot speak to outsiders. Silver is a myth that we spread, knowing that it would be believed because of the mutts. Getting shot up by gold is like boiling our organs."

Keeva glanced down at Malakai's body. "Okay, whatever. Make him better."

Dylan rubbed the back of his neck. "That's what we were arguing about. He needs to feed, but first we have to make sure we get the gold out or it will only hurt him tenfold."

"Then get the gold out of him, damn it. Why are you all acting like idiots, standing around like muppets!"

"We have to cut it out at the source, and we find ourselves unable to hurt him any more than he already is."

Keeva got off the bed and stalked toward them, pointing her finger. "You do this for him, or I swear that I will hurt each and every one of you. For days. Months. I'll gut you in your sleep and then slit your goddamn throats. I don't know what to look for, so sort your shit out and deal. I'll take care of Angus."

Handing Zeke her dagger, Keeva turned round, leaning down to kiss the top of Malakai's head as she said, "I'll find out who did this, and I'll kill them. I'll make them suffer as you did, and then you and I will have a chat about the future."

None of the vampires had moved as she straightened, their eyes watching her with emotions Keeva couldn't deal with right now or she might just crumble. Instead, she glared at Zeke until he edged closer to Malakai, waited until he muttered in Latin and then used the dagger to cut the flesh at Malakai's shoulder.

When Malakai jerked, releasing a pained sound in his throat, Keeva stalked to the elevator and beat the buttons with her fists. Tears streamed down Scarlett's face as she tried to get Keeva to stop, but as she stood inside the elevator, it was Roman who joined her.

"Take me as backup."

Keeva inclined her head, considering it, but then she

shook her head. "Thanks, but they need someone here watching their backs. None of them is thinking clearly, and should someone take advantage of that, I need to know they have someone standing sentry."

"And are you thinking clearly?"

As the doors pinged, releasing her into the lobby, Keeva grinned, though she felt no happiness inside her. "Angus and I have been dancing around one another for decades. It ends tonight. One of us meets their maker, and I hope it's not me. But if I don't come back, make sure Malakai remembers he promised to look after Scarlett."

Keeva darted out the door into the night before Roman could convince her to let him go with her. She ducked inside the car, checked the magazine in her Glock and then drove toward the banshee office where Angus would be at this time, so soon after an Inferna meeting. Keeva paused inside the car to pull her rebellious curls from her face.

Getting out of the car, she stalked toward the building, ignoring the call of the receptionist to stop as Keeva crossed the call centre floor, ignoring the early starters, and headed for Angus's office. Keeva kicked the door hard and it crashed open, hitting the wall hard enough to dent the plaster in the partition wall. Angus slammed down his phone and glared at her.

"How dare you simply walk into my office like a maniac. Get out, Keeva, or I will have you imprisoned."

Keeva laughed, the sound bitter and not at all humorous. Cocking her head to the side, she pulled the gun out and levelled it with the middle of Angus's forehead. "Who hired you to kill Malakai?"

"Oh, is the Primus unwell? Please send him my regards."

Keeva growled, inching closer, urging her hand to remain steady as her temper flared. The leader of her Scream never imagined that she would pull the trigger, his smirk full of slime that Keeva could feel on her skin. She fired off a warning shot, the bullet lodging in the wall, just to the right of Angus's head. The banshee shrieked as Ivan and the security guards came rushing down the hall.

Keeva spared a glance over her shoulder, watched as Ivan held up a hand for the security guards to stop, thankful that they did. "Tell me who wants Malakai dead and I might let you live."

When Angus smirked at her again, Keeva fired off another shot. "Next one goes in your head, Angus."

"You cannot kill me, Keeva. The council would lock you up for crimes you cannot even fathom. You would never be free."

Keeva shrugged as if she didn't care what was done to her. "You were heard by numerous witnesses threatening the Primus of the vampires. He is alive, you know. He sent me to kill you. The council is aware that I'm here now in retribution."

Bluffing with an ironclad poker face, Keeva felt a surge of delight as Angus paled before he stuttered. "I don't know who he is. I've never seen his face. Only ever identified himself as Vindicta."

Vengeance.

Keeva needed time to consider who Malakai could have pissed off enough to earn someone's vengeance. Keeva felt power bubble up in her chest, much as it had in the car, and Keeva gave herself over to it, sucking in a breath as she let loose a scream that was decades in the making. She screamed out her anger at Angus until she heard the glass shatter around her, Angus ducking as his office crashed down around him.

When her scream died, Keeva shook out her shoulders and lifted the gun once again. "You, Angus, leader of the Irish Scream of Banshees, are sentenced to death for the attempted murder of Malakai Cavanagh, Primus of the vampires and by far a better fucking man than you could ever be. Do you have any last words before you die?"

Coming forward, Angus made to reach for her, but Keeva dodged his hands, cold-cocking him with the gun so that Angus went to his knees. She pressed the gun to his temple as Angus begged her. "Please, Keeva. Kill me like you killed my Clodagh. I want to know what it felt like when you murdered her."

His words were the desperate last attempts of a man who wanted Keeva to live on with her grief and guilt. Keeva wasn't sure when it had happened, but she had forgiven herself for what had happened, and Angus's words slid off her without penetrating her heart.

"You don't deserve to know what my gift feels like."

Keeva fired point-blank into Angus's skull, already turning away as his body hit the ground. Holding up the gun and her hands as she stepped out of Angus's office, Keeva made her way toward Ivan, who was watching her with admiration and a little fear.

"I see you finally found your scream."

"What can I say," Keeva snorted with a smile. "I must be a late bloomer."

Ivan chuckled, motioning for the security guards to go forward, and they did so, dragging Angus from the office and off the floor as work continued around them. Seemed like not even a little assassination could put a halt to the banshee show.

Keeva lowered her arms and stashed the gun away as she regarded Ivan cautiously. "Are you going to arrest me?"

"Are you guilty of a crime?" Ivan asked her, his smile deepening to show off his dimples.

Keeva shook her head. "No, I never was. I just cleaned up a mess that should have been cleaned up decades ago."

"Then I see no need to apprehend you."

Keeva could have sagged in relief as she inclined her head

to Ivan, walking by him as he reached out and rested his hand on her shoulder. "You could stay, Keeva. You could stay and help me change things from Angus's rule. Come be the head of my security, and we can start to fix what Angus broke."

Keeva glanced down at his arm, and Ivan quickly dropped his hand. "Thanks, Ivan, but I already have a new gig lined up. You don't need me to change shit around here. Just be better. Do better. Make sure what happened to me happens to no other little girl or boy. If you don't, some night, I may have to pay you a visit just like I did Angus. None of us wants that."

Ivan quirked his brows, even though he smiled. "Malakai is a lucky man."

Keeva waved him off with her hand as she sauntered out of the banshee headquarters, the employees acting like Keeva had not just blown Angus's brains out. Keeva had barely stepped out onto the pavement when the hairs on her neck alerted her to danger.

Keeva spun. Had the gun in her hand as a figure clouded in darkness stepped into the night. Dawn would be approaching in the next half hour; the dark of night was starting to fade in the distance as Keeva took in the figure.

Dressed all in black, he wore a hood that blocked his face from view. The blades that hung loosely from his waist glinted in the moonlight as Keeva set her feet apart, ready for a fight. He had a set of arrows slung over his shoulder, a bow nestled within easy reach, the glint of gold on the arrows making anger coil in Keeva's chest.

"I've already killed one Inferna this night … or morning, whatever. Do you want me to make it number two?"

A chortle of husky laughter broke through the night air, the sound of it crawling over Keeva's skin like oil as he circled her. "I can see why Malakai is so taken with you. A war is coming, little fire, and you are on the wrong side of it."

"Dude, seriously," Keeva questioned with a snort. "The winning side is whatever side I'm on. Stop hiding behind this bullshit Legolas outfit and let's be done. Dawn is beckoning, and I guess I'm the only one of us who can stand under it without frying to death."

The vampire pulled out his daggers as Keeva fired a shot at his feet when he tried to come a little closer. His entire body was covered from head to toe, as if he were cast in shadows, and Keeva could not see an opening to use her powers on him. The vampire moved, knocking the gun from Keeva's grasp with an ease that surprised her.

Yanking her dagger free, she slashed back and forth as the vampire moved out of her reach with every strike. She kicked out, hoping to catch him off guard, but the vampire caught her foot and twisted, yanking her legs up so that she crashed to the concrete.

Pain bloomed in her spine as Keeva rolled, groaning as she got to her feet and blew her hair from her face. The vampire sheathed his daggers and engaged in a fist fight with Keeva, who hated to admit that the vampire was faster and stronger than she was. He punched her hard, pain surging in her eye as spots danced in her vision.

Her attacker wrapped a hand around her throat, Keeva struggled for air as the vampire leaned in, and Keeva could feel his breath on her face. "I could kill you and break his heart right this very moment, but no, I'll wait. I have waited such a long time to have my vengeance, and now that he has something he truly cares for, it will be all the sweeter. I will see you soon, little banshee."

The vampire flung her with ease. Her back hit the side of the Honda, the metal creaking at the impact, and Keeva groaned. Her new friend had vanished. Keeva glanced around. The sun broke through the clouds, its rays spreading out along the pavement as Keeva wiped her nose, her hand coming away bloody. She managed to get to her knees, her entire body in shards of agony as she managed to get the door open and drive back to Sicarius.

She stumbled into the lobby before she dropped to her knees and vomited from the pain. She leaned against the wall as Dylan crouched down in front of her, and she wondered where the hell he'd come from. Keeva's eyes were blurry as she tried to get to her feet, stumbled and had to lean on Dylan for support.

"What the hell happened, Keeva?"

"It's okay … you should see the other guy. No, wait, he handed me my ass and then some. I need to close my eyes for a bit."

Dylan lifted her into his arms, telling her she needed to stay awake, as she might be concussed. When he brushed the hair from her face, she winced and said, "I'm sorry, Mac, but I think I'm in love with your brother. Not sure why I'm saying sorry though."

A soft chuckle brushed against her senses. "It's 'cause I'm so irresistible. And you liked me first. Don't want to hurt my feelings, do ya, Death?"

"Is Kai okay?" Keeva muttered sleepily, trying to block out the pain thrumming her body.

"The poison is out of his system, and he's resting with a full stomach. Should be out for the next day or two while his body recovers. Think you can stay out of trouble until he wakes?"

Keeva reached up and patted his cheek. "Not making any promises."

Dylan was laughing as he made his way into the living room and plopped Keeva down on the couch, letting her rest her head on his shoulder as he tried to keep her awake. She was aware of Jasmine holding an ice pack to her face as Scarlett fussed over her and asked her what had happened with Angus.

"I blew his brains out with the Glock. Might have said I'd

gone on official council business, so Kai's gonna need to write me a permission slip. Then I had a fist fight with a ninja called Vindicta. He sounded like he knew you. Who'd you guys piss off enough to have a ninja come after you?"

"That could be a very long list, sweetheart."

Keeva huffed out a breath. "He wants to hurt Kai badly. He said that Malakai would have more to lose if he left me live. He could have killed me. I couldn't take him. He took me by surprise. Next time, I'll be ready."

"Sure you will, Keeva. Now just relax and let us look after you."

Keeva lifted her head to see Scarlett crouching down in front of her. Keeva grinned, her vision swimming as she said, "I killed him, Scar. Angus is dead, and now, Clodagh can rest in peace."

"You're finally free, Keeva. You're finally free."

But was she though? Her hundred-year service was the property of the leader of her Scream, and until Ivan granted her freedom, she would be bound to fulfil the binding that was hers. She should have asked him while she had the upper hand. She should have pointed the gun at Ivan's head and demanded her freedom.

It's too late now, Keeva thought as she succumbed to the seductive pull of darkness, like an old friend that rocked her to sleep.

CHAPTER NINETEEN

Keeva

"ARE YOU SURE YOU'RE UP TO THIS?" SCARLETT ASKED HER FOR like the hundredth time, worry marring her beautiful features.

Keeva rolled her eyes as she watched Scarlett stretch out her long legs, dressed in a pair of skin-tight leggings and a bright pink string top with the word "Juicy" embossed in sparkles. Scarlett had let Jasmine loan her some clothes to work out in, and Keeva was certain Malakai's sister was trying to be funny, considering Scarlett's ample cleavage, but apparently it was a brand name and not meant to be funny.

Craning her neck, Keeva rolled her shoulders. "I'm sure. My pride was hurt more than I was, but it's been five days, and Malakai still hasn't woken. If I have to sit around waiting for sleeping beauty to wake, then I'll go stir-crazy."

Keeva couldn't mask the worry in her tone as she bent down to touch her toes. Her body still ached, and her eye was a rainbow of colours. They were all worried, the vampires, that Malakai had yet to wake, and they decided, despite the fact that Malakai was back to normal, if he didn't wake tonight, they'd go back in and see if any gold was still embedded in his skin, leaking into his bloodstream.

Keeva had slept by his side every day, filling him in on everything that had happened during the day, unsure if he could hear what she was saying or if Keeva was just talking to herself. Most days, she curled herself against his body, leaning her head against his chest to listen to the beat of his heart to remind herself that he would be fine. She read to him, even tried singing to him as if her shrill voice might rouse him from slumber. Nothing worked.

One night, Keeva had gotten so angry that she yelled at him for being selfish and stubborn and having a long old nap while the rest of them were out here falling apart. She had broken another phone in temper when his prone body remained so.

It had been an adjustment, having the vampires include her in decisions, as if her opinion meant that she spoke for Malakai. She had seen them together, knew the bond they shared, but they were intent on making Keeva and Scarlett part of the family. Dylan consulted with her about security stuff, and the company would have fallen to pieces if Scarlett and Zeke hadn't stepped in.

Keeva had been shocked to find out that not only was Zeke the company's accountant, but also their lawyer. When she heard that, she chuckled, knowing Dylan was right about having lawyers that would scare anyone shitless. He and Scarlett worked long hours keeping the company going, getting on everyone's nerves, being all cordial and civil. Everyone but the two Inferna seemed to notice the crackling tension between them that even had Dylan in a foul humour.

Keeva had sat down with him the second night, thanking him for looking after her, to which he replied that someone had to while Malakai was out cold. Keeva had laughed, curling her legs beneath her as she simply stayed with him as he worked through his own emotions. As someone who tried to put hers in a little box the majority of her life, Keeva knew a little about it.

"It's strange, seeing Kai look so vulnerable."

Keeva said nothing as Dylan leaned forward, scrubbing his hand down a face full of blond scruff that made him seem harder, less surfer boy. His eyes usually held that glint of mischief, but now, they were serious.

"When we were younger, Kai was the one able to talk us out of

trouble that I got us in. He sees it different, but I don't. He shielded me and Jazz, even when I was made a vampire and developed my powers; Kai kept me safe when I was trying to figure out what the hell was going on."

Keeva had figured out Dylan was empathic long ago, had been a witness to Jazz having a vision a day ago, but she would never divulge their secrets. But Keeva had taken Dylan's hand in hers as she said, "Malakai is too stubborn to give up. He loves you guys."

Dylan had squeezed her hand back with a small smile. "I'm just struggling to keep my gift in check. Everyone in this goddamn building is so emotive! I can't sieve through their feelings to find my own."

"That's 'cause your emotions are their emotions, Mac. We are all walking this taut rope waiting for a change. We are all scared. We are all sad. There's nothing wrong with that."

Dylan leaned in after a second of contemplation and kissed her cheek before he rose.

"What was that for?"

"For loving my brother in the way that he deserves."

Keeva shook the memory from her mind as Scarlett propped her hand on her hips and pressed her lips into a perfect pout. "When do I get a gun?"

Keeva chuckled, shaking her head. "When hell freezes over. Remember, the point of all this is to defend if absolutely necessary. If something happens when you are with us, then you run, Scarlett. You run your fine ass away from danger and leave Sicarius to get bloody."

"Does that mean that you're staying?"

Was she? She still had twenty years left on her sentence, and she hadn't plucked up the courage to call Ivan and ask for her freedom. And then there was Malakai. She had fallen for him so fast and hard, it had been unexpected. What if he didn't feel the same way? And if she was free, then there was a big world out there for her to explore, one that she had longed to see outside of an assassin gig. But why did the thought of leaving make her blood run cold?

Choosing to avoid answering Scarlett's question, Keeva told Scarlett that the best way to improve on her fitness was to run, build up the stamina, get fast on her feet. Scarlett took in every piece of Keeva's advice, leaving Keeva to her own devices as she went to the treadmill.

Keeva's ears were ringing in the silence of the gym, the sound of Scarlett's trainers on the treadmill echoing in her ears. Walking over to the stereo, Keeva turned on the CD player that was in the corner. A healthy dose of Black Sabbath came from the speakers. Keeva smiled, grabbing a belt of throwing stars, and setting her feet apart, practised her aim over and over until she felt like herself again.

Yesterday, when she had tried to bench-press, the vampires had lost their minds and told her she wasn't rested enough. Keeva had shrugged, going back to her workout until Dylan had lifted the weight with one hand, and all Keeva could do was look at him open-mouthed. But then again, it seemed that just like their ninja friend, the true extent of these vampires' strengths was a mystery.

Keeva finished throwing when her arm started to ache, just in time for Scarlett to finish up her run. The damn succubus got off the treadmill with that healthy glow of sweat that Keeva had always been envious of. When she worked out, she sweated like a pig and looked a hot mess.

"What next?" Scarlett said eagerly, bouncing on her feet with excitement.

"Next you get to run some more."

Scarlett rolled her eyes, punching Keeva in the shoulder lightly with a grin. Keeva took Scarlett's clenched fist and tucked her thumb inside the fist. "Second rule of fight club, tuck in your thumb so you don't break it."

Scarlett scowled as she practised clenching her fists with her thumb tucked inside. She had obviously missed the joke or reference to the movie, because the succubus tilted her head to the side with a serious expression on her face. "What's the first rule?"

Keeva laughed, making to answer when a deep voice rumbled behind them. "The first rule of fight club is you don't talk about fight club."

Scarlett's face flushed crimson as Zeke strode into the gym dressed in basketball shorts, trainers and nothing else. Swallowing hard, Scarlett tried not to look at Zeke's physique, but damn, even Keeva was looking at him.

His hips were surprisingly slender. The muscles on his stomach told Keeva that his body had not an ounce of fat on it. Zeke had the V that sculpted his lower half and made most women go crazy. When someone roamed their eyes up to his ripple of muscles that were lickable, he looked like an MMA fighter … like Tom Hardy in *Warrior*. Keeva could make out the puckered scars on his skin, surrounded by tattoos of Oni and dragons, and Keeva knew he had Christ on a cross on his back.

Zeke snorted out his nose, rolling his eyes at their obvious appreciation of his body, but Keeva was certain she could see a faint tinge of red creep up his neck. He turned, as if to head back out, but Keeva called him back, devilment in her eyes.

"Hey Zeke, come here a second."

The hulking vampire strode over to them, inclining his head to the radio as AC/DC's "Thunderstruck" began. "I had wondered where I had left that CD."

"You listen to Black Sabbath and AC/DC?" Keeva asked with a chuckle as Zeke shrugged his massive shoulders.

"Just because I happen to be religious does not mean I cannot appreciate good music. I listen to classical in the library, but Jazz has dragged me to a concert or two."

Well, the big guy was surprising them all now, wasn't he.

"And on that bombshell"—Keeva waved her hand in front of Scarlett, who was indeed turning as red as her namesake—

"Scarlett wants to learn how to defend herself in case any more assassins come for us."

"Scarlett does not need to learn to defend herself because we will protect her." Zeke's tone dropped an octave, to which Keeva grinned.

"Scarlett can make up her own mind, and she hates when people talk like she's not in the room."

Keeva had to admire the sass in Scarlett's tone as she glared at Zeke, who was trying to look anywhere but at Scarlett. This was going to be fun.

"That's what I tried telling her, but once she sets her mind on something, there's absolutely no talking her out of it." Keeva let loose a sigh of frustration as Scarlett punched her again, and Keeva grinned.

"How can I help?" Zeke asked, his face neutral even if his body seemed coiled with tension.

"Will you just try and attack me, and we can show her how to run away?"

Zeke's answer was to lunge for her, sending Scarlett shrieking as Keeva ducked and rolled on the mat before getting to her feet with a grin. Keeva bounced from one foot to the next, waiting to see how Zeke would move, and then when he telegraphed his movement, because he knew what Keeva was trying to achieve, Keeva went right when he went left.

Holding up a T to indicate a timeout, Keva looked at Scarlett. "It's important to watch your opponent and see where they expect you to go. Then you get the hell out of dodge. As soon as you see an opening, you run. Someone of Zeke's size will always be stronger than the likes of me and you. They expect us to be weaker, but that's why we learn how to run like hell.

"Zeke, grab me from behind so I can show her some moves." The vampire hesitated, then locked his muscular arm around Keva's neck as Scarlett watched with wide eyes.

"If you are grabbed from behind, then stomp down on the foot like so." Keeva demonstrated to Scarlett but didn't put much force into the action. "If your elbow is free, then dig that right into the ribs, knock the wind out of them, and then you can run away."

Turning to Zeke as he released her, Keeva chewed on her lip. "I want to show Scarlett where to hit, should she need to. Do you mind if I put on gloves and …?"

"I trust you, Keeva. And I am not feeling suicidal today, so we have no worry between us."

Well, okay, then. She wasn't sure if Zeke was trying to be funny or if he was just stating a fact, but Keeva had enough going on in her own head to try and psychoanalyse Ezekiel Collins.

Facing Zeke, she beckoned Scarlett closer. "If you find yourself face to face with an attacker, go for the nose first." Keeva clenched her fist as if to punch Zeke, stopping shy of actually really hitting him. "A punch to the throat will always make someone back up. If your attacker is female, don't be afraid to go for the hair. If it's a man, go for the balls. That never fails to take a fucker down."

Keeva grinned as she played out the moves a few times so Scarlett could absorb it all. Scarlett nodded, her eyes tracking Keeva's movements, then she asked to practice with Keeva. Zeke made to leave then as Keeva smiled her thanks, his eyes darting to Scarlett before he went to the far side of the room and lay down on the mat, working through his own frustration in the form of sit-ups.

Keeva shook her head and returned her eyes to Scarlett with a grin. "I'll get you some pepper spray to carry around in your bag. That shit burns your eyes like you stuffed jalapenos in them. Don't leave the building without it."

Scarlett nodded, blinking her eyes before she said, "I know that apartment is a no-go, but I'm making good money now—we could try and get a place together again. Are we planning on staying here forever, Keeva?"

"That is an answer that I think I would like to hear myself."

Keeva spun round to see Malakai leaning against the doorframe. His gorgeous chocolate eyes were tired, but other than that, he looked absolutely fine. Keeva resisted the urge to run into his arms and kiss him, suddenly feeling a little self-conscious. Scarlett nudged her as she walked away, pausing to have a quiet word with Malakai before she left. Zeke, too, made himself scarce as Malakai came into the room.

Silence stretched out between them as Malakai went over and switched off the stereo before coming to stand in front of her. She felt like there were all these things she wanted to say to him but couldn't find the right words to say what she was feeling.

"You're okay?"

OH, hello, Captain Obvious. Smooth, Keeva. Very smooth.

Malakai's lips quirked, and Keeva cursed herself for not remembering that Malakai seemed to be able to read her mind. She wet her lips; his eyes immediately followed the movement as Malakai's smile deepened.

"I heard what happened to Angus and after."

Keeva shrugged, kicking the mat with her foot. "Seems like we've both been through the wars. Never a dull moment, right?"

He studied her for a minute, then simply said, "You have a terrible singing voice."

Oh, by the Gods, he had heard her singing to him. Her freckled face heated as Malakai strode forward and cupped her cheek. "I heard your voice every day. I smelled your scent, and all I wanted to do was awaken and hold you in my arms. When your body is immobile, your mind has a lot to consider, and I spent a lot of time, Keeva Cross, thinking about you."

"Kai …"

"I thought of your smile, of how I wanted to learn every freckle that adorned your body. I want to know what makes you smile, what makes you cry, and see inside your soul. I want to wake beside you every night and feel you against me at every dawn."

Malakai leaned in and pressed his lips to hers, Keeva letting out a sigh as he pulled back, his face determined. "I want to share my secrets with you. I want to have someone beside me on this journey of life and death who challenges me, who is my equal or perhaps my better. I had not realized how much I lived in the darkness until you crashed into my life, and I find I cannot let go of the sunshine."

Keeva's heart was cracking open with every word he spoke. He spoke as if she was the light when she considered herself a part of the dark. His words indicated he might feel for her what she felt for him, and she stared at him in disbelief.

Malakai leaned in and pressed his lips to her throat, her pulse jumping the moment his cool lips grazed her flesh. "In case you need me to say the words, I'm in love with you, Keeva. Stay with me. Stay here with me. Be mine, and let me be yours."

Keeva thought back to the moment when she had slipped inside Sicarius Security to kill Malakai, just a short few weeks ago, had felt the connection there and then. Malakai was so much more than Primus of vampires. He was a good man who loved his family and would die to protect them. He had shown her that he would not try to cage her; he wanted her for who she was.

Her lips tugged into a smile. "I love you too, Kai. I realised it the moment I thought I would lose you. I never had a family until Scarlett, so I'm not sure how well I can adjust to being part of one. But I'm willing to try. I just want to be with you."

Malakai kissed her then as Keeva locked her arms around his neck. Malakai took them to the mat as Keeva laughed, hooking her leg around the back of his knee. Her vampire kissed her with a hunger that melted her bones, and as Keeva whispered in his ear for him to make love to her, the moment their bodies were joined, Keeva knew, held in Malakai's arms, she had finally found a place to call home.

CHAPTER TWENTY

Malakai

MALAKAI HAD SPENT TWO BLISSFUL DAYS AND NIGHTS IN BED with Keeva, getting to know her, learning every curve of her body, feeling her, then finding out that he loved the way she said his name when she came. He had not known happiness could be like this. As his flame-haired banshee snored softly in his arms, Malakai had an epiphany that he had tried to fill the hole in his life with work and making sure his family was okay.

He had not contemplated that he himself had not been okay.

Perhaps he was what the humans called a workaholic. His lifetime had been consumed with making enough money and amassing power so that they were set for life. And he was proud of his accomplishments and that of the rest of his Kiss. But after the decades he had spent using work to supplement the fact that he was lonely, now that he had Keeva, he knew what he had been missing.

As if she sensed his frame of mind, Keeva snuggled into his side, splaying her fingers over the place where his heart beat. Her lower half was already thrown over his thigh, his hands resting on her hip and the curve of her ass. He liked that she could not seem to get enough of touching him, tasting him and he of her.

Last night, he had indulged in his fantasy of having her up against the glass, her breasts flattened against the cool pane as he held his arm around her waist and slid in and out of her from behind, her palms on the glass, her emerald-coloured eyes wide and holding his gaze in the reflection as he felt himself near release, then sank his fangs into her throat as he emptied himself inside her, still thrusting.

Keeva had screamed his name as she shuddered in pleasure, the sound like music to his ears as Keeva melted against him.

However, he was not the only one who had indulged in secret fantasies.

Keeva stirred against him. Her sex riding his thigh had him considering cancelling the meeting that was scheduled for right about now. If he was late, no doubt one of his family would march right on up and drag him from his bed. He supposed he was lucky that they left him alone for two days.

Malakai dropped a kiss to Keeva's cheek, shifting so that she lay on the pillow. She slipped her hands under her cheek as he slipped on his boxers and jeans, and Keeva's eyes fluttered open. She yawned, sitting up to rub her eyes, and the sheet fell off her, exposing her pale skin and mouth-watering breasts.

"Do you want me to come?"

Malakai lifted his brows with a devilish smile that had Keeva throwing a pillow at him as she rolled her eyes. "Not what I meant, Cavanagh. Take your mind out of the gutter."

"I found myself thinking of making you scream my name quite often. I think I will have accomplished my goal once you shatter some glass."

Keeva had told him about the night she had killed Angus, shattering the glass in his office, and Dylan had also found the hairline fracture in the Honda he had loaned her. Malakai was trying very hard to see if those incidents were a one-off or if Keeva had finally found her scream.

Leaning in to kiss her lips, he let himself lick at her bottom lip until she opened for him and kissed him back and then some. He reluctantly pulled back from Death's kiss and reached for a T-shirt. Pulling it on over his head, he looked at Keeva and said, "Stay and rest. Come join us if you get bored. I expect there to be shouting, so I may need you to protect me."

Keeva rewarded his jest with a husky laugh. "El Diablo does not need Death to protect him. Is it really bad if I admit I'm turned on at the prospect of seeing you in action? I mean, I can just picture you in your favourite Armani suit, kicking ass and taking names."

It was Malakai's time to laugh as he left Keeva with another kiss and headed down to meet with his family. He stepped into the living space, pausing to take in the sight before him. Dylan was trying to grab food from the platters Jazz was setting out, with his sister smacking Dylan's hand with every attempt. Zeke was pouring coffee, an amused expression on his face as he watched the sibling's fight.

They all seemed happy enough, and that only added to Malakai's own feelings of content.

Dylan spotted him lurking, beckoned him over as they took their seats around the table. Jazz sank down in the chair beside him and reached out to squeeze his hand. "Happiness looks good on you, brother."

"It would seem, Jazz, that the vision of Death's kiss was not a curse but a blessing. She … she … completes me."

Dylan clasped him on the shoulder with a grin. "Less of the soppy shit, Kai. It's making me feel like sitting down and watching some of Jazz's romcoms. Herself and Scarlett have taken over the TV, watching some shit about *27 Dresses* or *Made of Honor.*"

Everyone laughed, even Zeke, who poured Malakai a cup of coffee and slid it toward him. Malakai sipped his coffee as his siblings traded barbs with one another. It made Malakai think of another family member who had died, the brother they refused to talk about because his death had almost broken them all. But as Malakai basked in his own happiness, it was hard not to think of Dante.

"Thinking of the past won't do you any good, Kai. Let Dante rest in peace. No need resurrecting old ghosts when you are sickeningly happy."

Of course Dylan would know where his thoughts had gone, and of course his brother was right; there was nothing he could do for Dante now. Malakai set his mug on the table and cleared his throat.

"I'm taking an extended leave of absence from the company."

You could hear a pin drop at Malakai's statement, for no one knew what to say or whether or not he was yanking their chains. Dylan rolled his eyes and sat back in the chair. "No, you're not. Stop messing about, Kai. You would never cope with not working, and the company cannot afford to lose you."

"The company had managed quite well while I was recovering. From all accounts, you all survived without me when you had to. I have spent an eternity looking after others. The company is strong; you all are strong and capable. I find that I need to take this time to recharge."

Dylan shook his head. "No. No fucking way. I'm not okay with this. Kai, you are the company. None of us can do what you do in a day. Do you expect me to sit down in a suit and negotiate contract terms?"

Malakai sipped his coffee again, reaching for a biscuit as he let Dylan calm down before he said, "No, Dylan. You will be in charge of the day-to-day running of Sicarius with help from Isolde and Roman, who has proved himself and then some. You can still manage the assassin contracts or delegate. That choice is up to you. Jazz will manage Dante's like she has always done, and because her workload will be more than usual, she can hire someone to help or ask Roman to help. I'm pretty sure that man never sleeps."

Setting down his mug, he prepared for a fight as he lifted his eyes to Zeke. "Zeke will take over the reins from me on a temporary basis. All of the information I get when negotiating contracts and the likes, I get from Zeke. He knows the business as well as I do, even more so."

"You cannot ask me to do this, Kai. You cannot."

Malakai reclined in his chair, folding his arms across his chest. "You all are equal partners in this business we run. I have led you for decades, and I ask you to allow me some free time to be happy. I have not once taken a holiday or a day off since we sat around that campfire and decided we should become assassins to make money."

"I am not the right person to be the face of the company, Malakai. Look at me!"

Zeke's words were panicked, like someone who suffered from agoraphobia and was being dragged outside. "You can. It is time that you came out from behind the library doors, Ezekiel, and truly lived. I am leaving for a month on vacation, so you all will just have to suck it up and deal."

Malakai bit back a smile as he sipped his coffee again and then said, "And should you need assistance, Zeke, stepping into my role also means you inherit my secret weapon."

"And what is that?" Zeke asked, his tone strained as if he already knew what Malakai was going to say.

"Why, Scarlett, of course. That woman is a *godsend.*"

Zeke grunted as Jazz barked out a laugh. The doors to the elevator opened as Keeva came in wearing leggings and one of Malakai's T-shirts, carrying a box in her hands. Walking straight over to Malakai, she pressed a kiss to his cheek and set the box down.

"Sorry to interrupt, but Izzy dropped this off, and I get a weird vibe from it so didn't want it in the room."

Malakai smiled as Dylan asked, "Izzy?"

"Isolde. She hates me, so I call her Izzy. I'm trying to figure out what she is so maybe if I make her mad enough, she'll hulk out and then I'll know."

Malakai snagged her around the waist, pulled her closer so that she was sitting on his leg. Dylan jested that he was going to start calling her Izzy now as well and told Zeke to do it too. Zeke shook his head and said, "I do not start fights unless I intend to win."

Malakai blocked out their chatter, setting his hand on top of the box to see if he got the same vibe as Keeva, but he felt nothing. The box was rectangular, white in colour and wrapped up in a red bow. His name was embossed on the front of the box, and as Malakai went to untie the bow, Keeva set her hand on top of his and said, "Wait. Let me."

Her fingers quickly unwrapped the bow, and then she lifted the lid, her eyes narrowing as she reached in and took out a solid gold stake. His banshee leaned in, sniffed the stake, her nose crinkling as she said, "That smells like death."

Malakai reached out to take it and Keeva snatched it away from him. "Are you insane, Cavanagh? You just recovered from a near fatal dose of gold and you want to go fondle the stake."

Malakai grinned as he squeezed her hip. "I'm dating you. I must like courting danger."

His banshee rolled her eyes as she turned the stake over in her hands with a frown. "It's got all your names etched in the hilt of it. My names on it too. Guess that means I'm officially part of the family now it's etched in death. I'm touched."

Malakai was worried. He had to be, because what this stake represented was a declaration of war. He had no doubt that it was a vampire who had issued this edict, no doubt in his mind that it was an old vampire, because this was how it was done when there had been a disagreement between two rival Kiss. It was customary to send the leader of your opposing Kiss a golden stake as a statement of intent.

This ninja assassin, as Keeva had taken to calling him, was

indeed old school, and Malakai could not think of who could be introducing the old laws in order to court chaos within the Inferna.

Keeva tilted the stake and squinted to see the other writing that had been carved along the length of the stake. She held it out to Malakai, careful to keep it away from touching any part of him.

"I'm afraid my Latin is mostly made up of swear words and the odd phrase. What does it say?"

Malakai studied the phrase for a moment before he explained. "It is an old proverb that is loosely translated as, 'Vengeance is slow but stern.'"

Keeva snorted, shaking her head. "This Vindicta dude is seriously a drama queen. It's like he's challenging you to a duel or some shit. I mean, does he realize this place is a fortress?"

Giving her a warm smile as Keeva tossed the stake into the box and closed it, Malakai remarked, "You managed to get in."

Keeva flashed the table a cheeky grin of smugness. "I did. Aren't you glad?"

"If you two are going to be making lovey-dovey eyes at one another, then I'm going to go get blind drunk before I have to act responsibly. I take it you two are not leaving tonight?"

Malakai pressed his lips into a firm line as he regarded Dylan. "I've chartered a plane for Saturday night, so get whatever you need out of your system. But you will be careful."

Dylan gave him a salute as he pushed his chair back, striding around to ruffle Keeva's hair much like he would do with Jazz, before he left them to their conversation. It was ingrained in Malakai's DNA to worry about his family, and he was worried about Dylan and how he would deal with the responsibility while he was away. Of course, Malakai kept the fact he was terrified of leaving when Zeke was skating on thin ice to himself, but he lifted his gaze to Jasmine, who had been uncharacteristically quiet.

"Jazz? Have you any thoughts?"

His sister flicked her blond hair off her face with a shrug. She reached out and touched his hand, her eyes glossing over as they whitened and she said, "Vengeance comes for the cries of the innocent. Faith is tested as destiny beckons war and conflict is doused with flames."

Blinking rapidly, her eyes came slowly back to her royal blue colour as she removed her hand and reached for the glass of water that Zeke had gotten up to get her while she was locked in the vision. She sipped on the water after offering a smile of thanks to Zeke.

"I can stay, Jazz. If you think I need to."

Jasmine reached out and gave his hand a squeeze. "Nothing will happen while you are gone, big brother. In fact, I think you need to go. The world will not end in the month you'll be gone. And you guys will only be a phone call away if anything changes. Maybe this Vindicta will ease off if you and Keeva are wandering around Scandinavia."

Keeva's eyes widened as she smacked Malakai on the chest. "Scandinavia?"

"You have always wanted to see the northern lights. And I have long since wished to return to the place where my father's people came from."

Keeva kissed him quickly, rushing off to go and fill Scarlett in on their plans. He watched her go as Zeke excused himself, his shoulders slumped as if he considered the fact that Malakai was leaving for even such a short time as a fate worse than death. Before Zeke locked himself in the room, Malakai got to his feet and went to the other vampire.

Setting his palms on Zeke's shoulders, Malakai held his gaze as he offered Zeke some words of reassurance. "I have faith in you, Ezekiel. You will look after the family in my absence. It is time to reconcile your past and your future and decide if you wish to torment yourself for eternity. Speaking as someone who has tasted happiness, it is even more addictive than the most delicious of blood."

Zeke grunted in response and left Malakai where he stood. Malakai turned back to Jasmine, who merely shook her head with a shrug. "He will adapt. We all will. I think we don't realize how much we depend on you, Kai. This past week has been exhausting. I don't know how you do it. But you and Keeva deserve this. Go and be happy and remember that under the northern lights, with your banshee by your side, would be the most romantic place to propose."

His sister smiled as he rubbed his temple, wondering why he ever thought of keeping that secret from her. He didn't probe her to know if Keeva would say yes—that, he prayed to the old gods and the new. But he wanted to put a ring on Keeva's finger so that everyone knew that she was his and damn anyone who came for her.

Jasmine excused herself then, leaving Malakai to clean up the mess on the table that his family had left behind. He did so with a smile on his face, rinsing the dishes as his banshee came back from Scarlett's room. She wrapped her arms around Malakai from behind, resting her cheek against his spine.

"Are we really going to see the northern lights?"

"Would I lie to you?" he said in a teasing tone as Keeva hugged him tighter.

"Scarlett told me about something she read in a romance novel about using snow in certain places can be super erotic. She's loaning me the book for the plane."

Malakai turned around with a growl, his hands on her hips as he lowered his lips to her ear, tugging the lobe before he murmured into her ear. "I've said it before and I'll say it again: Scarlett Russell is a godsend."

Keeva threw back her head and laughed before Malakai

captured her mouth with his, letting her know how much he loved her with his hands, his tongue, his teeth, as Keeva embraced the sensuous part of her nature, one that she had long buried, and Malakai wondered how, in all that was holy, he got so damn lucky.

CHAPTER TWENTY-ONE

Keeva

DANTE'S WAS ABSOLUTELY PACKED TONIGHT. AS JASMINE WORKED her magic on the decks, the throngs of people gyrated and moved in time with the music. The dance track wasn't usually Keeva's sort of jam, but even she was tapping her toes along to the music. Movement out of the corner of her eye called her forward as she slipped around the human bartender to take a drinks order.

When Malakai was in a tizzy because Dylan had been MIA for three nights, Keeva had offered to work his shift behind the bar. When Malakai made as if to argue, Keeva had held up her hand and said, if she was to become part of the family, she had to pull her weight, and if that meant working the bar, then so be it.

She was not afraid of hard graft, and so Malakai had no choice but to let her.

He'd come along to the bar tonight, watching from the VIP section with Scarlett and Zeke as they ran through the final few bits before Keeva and Malakai left on their holiday the next evening. Scarlett had been shocked when Malakai asked her to work with Zeke while they were gone, but her bestie had been all professional courtesy since then, and it was already fraying on Zeke's nerves.

The thought made Keeva smile and almost wish she would be around to see what happened next.

Handing the reveller two bottles of beer, she took the cash and went off to serve some other thirsty dancers. Roman strode through the floor, checking on things as Keeva whistled and tossed him a bottle of water, the shifter grabbing the water with ease. He nodded his thanks and then went back to work.

Scarlett got up from the table above. Keeva watched as she waved Malakai off and then began to descend the stairs, heading for Keeva. The music changed, and Keeva bit back a laugh as Jazz played Demob Happy's track "Succubus." Scarlett cast an annoyed glance over her shoulder at Jasmine, who just smirked as she danced away to her heart's content in her little DJ domain.

Scarlett sauntered over as Keeva hoisted herself up on the bar to lean over to Scarlett as she gave an order. Keeva pressed her lips to the succubus's cheek before she slipped off the bar and got two beers and a gin and tonic for Scarlett. She offered to carry the tray, to which Scarlett shook her head, sauntering away from the bar as eyes turned to watch her walk up the stairs.

Zeke was waiting at the top of the stairs to take the tray from Scarlett, and that made Keeva smile, even if she was a little worried about leaving Scarlett here without her. As much as Malakai was the one who looked after everyone, Keeva was the one who looked after Scarlett. It had been just the two of them for decades, and now Keeva felt a little guilty for leaving her.

When Keeva had mentioned her fears to Scarlett, her best friend had hugged her, telling her that she would be fine and that Keeva had finally found her wings and maybe it was time for her to find hers too. There was a resolve in her friend's voice that Keeva had not heard before, and it made her wonder—if she had not been set on the collision course that changed their lives, would Keeva be sat in her apartment now with Scarlett, eating her weight in ice cream and chocolate instead of embarking on an adventure with the man she loved?

The man in question leaned over the railing, his eyes

finding hers as a slow, sexy smile curved his lips. Someone called her name, asking her to go and get some mixers, so Keeva had to drag her eyes from Malakai.

Keeva hoisted herself up on the bar and landed on her feet easily as she strode down the corridor and opened the door leading down to the basement, where the barrels and bottles were kept. Keeva heard a grunt as she descended the stairs, was about to chew someone out for going into a restricted area, when Keeva rounded the corner and got a view of Dylan's bare ass as he fucked some human up against the wall.

Peering over his shoulder, the vampire winked as he fisted the girl's dark hair in his hands, jerking her head back as he pounded into her before he growled and sank his fangs into her throat. Keeva grabbed a few mixers and then got the hell out of there before she learned way more about Dylan than she ever wanted to.

Setting the mixers on the counter, she held up her hand to indicate that she needed five minutes, then darted up the stairs towards Malakai. He was still leaning against the rail as Scarlett and Zeke went over papers. Keeva mimicked his pose, leaning into his shoulder as she said, "I found Dylan."

Malakai turned his head toward her, and she lifted her hand to brush her knuckles along the stubble caressing his mouth and jaw. He lifted his brow in question as Keeva motioned with her head toward the cellar. "He's in the cellar. I got a fine ole view of his ass. I made my getaway before I got a look at anything interesting."

Malakai chuckled, leaning into her, resting his head on hers as they simply stood there, in each other's company, neither of them needing to say a word. Keeva checked her watch to see her five minutes were up, sighing as she straightened, ready to hit the stairs when Malakai rested a hand on the crook of her elbow to halt her, his eyes looking down to the dance floor.

Keeva froze at the sight of Roman leading Ivan through the crowd, the new leader of the Scream dressed in a simple pair of black jeans and a button-down shirt. Her heart pounded in her chest as panic flared and her hands began to tremble. Malakai placed a hand on the small of her back, trying to reassure her that she was safe, as he lifted his gaze to his office in a silent order to Roman.

Roman led Ivan up the stairs as Keeva dragged her heels, not wanting to find out what Ivan wanted. Her limbs moved of their own accord; her breathing was quick as her pulse raced. Roman stood outside the door as he inclined his head, the shifter opening the door and stepping aside so Malakai could head in.

"Malakai, good to see you again." Ivan's tone was pleasant, but Keeva wondered if he had changed his mind over her killing Angus and wanted to extend her sentence. Ivan had told her he had not approved of Angus leaving her in the dark for those two years, but now Ivan was in charge. Had he reverted to old habits?

Keeva would kill every single banshee in Ireland if it meant she would not be thrown back into the darkness. She hesitated outside for a minute until she heard Malakai ask what brought Ivan to Dante's this night.

"I have come on official banshee business, Malakai. I would speak with Keeva, if she does not mind."

Keeva rolled back her shoulders and crossed the threshold. Ivan turned and offered her a smile in greeting. The other banshee stepped forward as if to embrace her, Keeva holding up her hand at the exact moment that Malakai growled low in his throat. Ivan glanced from Keeva to Malakai, a smile tugging his lips as he inclined his head.

"What can *we* do for you, Ivan?" Keeva asked, putting extra emphasis on the word *we* so Ivan would know that she and Malakai came as a package deal.

Ivan indicated the seats in Malakai's office. "May we sit?"

Ivan lowered himself into one of the chairs as Keeva strode over to the one closest to Malakai and sat down. Malakai rested a hand on her shoulder as Keeva folded her hands in her lap and said, "Being formal doesn't suit you, Ivan. Either spit it out or leave us in peace."

Ivan crossed his right leg over his knee and rested his hands on his knee as he leaned forward. "Keeva Cross, on behalf of the Banshee Scream of Ireland, we absolve you of all guilt regarding the deaths of both Angus McFergus and Clodagh McFergus. The sentence imposed on you in regard to Ms. McFergus's death has been quashed, and no further actions shall be taken."

The breath left her lungs in a whoosh of sound as Keeva let loose a shuddering breath at hearing the words that she had longed to hear since the day Clodagh had died. She was free. She was actually finally free.

She glanced up at Malakai. Her vampire grinned at her, his love in his eyes as Keeva turned back to Ivan and she cleared her throat. "Thank you."

Ivan bowed his head as he regarded Keeva. "We have issued the council with notice of the vacation of your sentence and your free status. It is also noted that your kin offer their profuse apologies for the manner in which you were treated by our former leader. We have issued the council with notice to compensate you for the trauma you suffered and also for the work you did, where you received no pay during this time."

"I don't want your money, Ivan."

Ivan uncrossed and crossed his legs once again. "The money is yours, Keeva. Do with it as you wish. It is a small amount in comparison to what you suffered. You must also be made aware that Clodagh had amassed a small fortune herself before she died, her will only coming to light once we went through Angus's paperwork. She left everything to you,

Keeva, and Angus did not disclose it to any of us or we would have put it in trust for you."

Keeva shook her head as if she didn't believe his words. "I'm not sure what to say."

Ivan dusted off his pants and stood, handing her a card with an account number on it. "There is the bank account we deposited both the compensation and the money that Angus had kept from you. With interest over the decades, it will keep you comfortable for a while.

"How much is in this?" Keeva asked as she held up the card, lifting her gaze to Ivan's.

"About a quarter of a million, give or take a few euros." At Keeva's sharp intake of breath, Ivan turned to Malakai. "I believe you have a wise accountant who will steer her right on investments?"

"He hasn't seen me wrong thus far."

"Good." Ivan held out his hand, shaking Malakai's firmly. "I shall see you at the council meeting next month." Ivan looked back at me and then at Malakai. "Take care of her. She was always special, and we did not deserve her."

"I do not deserve her either, but I will spend my life trying to prove to myself that I do."

Keeva got to her feet and held out her own hand to Ivan. "Thank you," she repeated as Ivan's hand slipped into hers. A silent tear slipped down her cheek, and Ivan brushed it away with his thumb.

"As long as I am leader of the banshees, Keeva, you will always be welcome. Should you ever need aid, I am but a phone call away."

Ivan was gone then as Keeva's legs gave out and the tears cascaded freely down her cheeks. Malakai caught her, lifting her so that she could bury her face in his shoulder, and held her as she cried for the friend she had lost, cried for the freedom she had gained and thanked God for the life she would have.

Malakai set her down on the desk, swept her hair away and kissed her tear-stained face. "Hey, no more tears. This is the fresh start for us. It makes it even more special now that you are officially free."

Keeva huffed out a laugh. "You're just a big softy, aren't you, Kai?"

"Shh … that could ruin my reputation. El Diablo cannot be soft."

Keeva vaguely heard Roman close the door, shutting them inside as Keeva held up the card. "What the hell am I gonna do with a quarter of a million euros, Kai?"

"Anything you want, Keeva. It's your money. Spend it, burn it, invest it in whatever. Talk to Zeke when we get back. That man might give me grey hairs, but he is a genius with money."

Keeva tucked the card into her back pocket as she released a sigh. "I never expected to be free, Kai. I never expected my life would turn out like this. I didn't know it was possible to feel this happy. What if it's an illusion? What if, just when things are finally going my way, it all goes to shit?

Malakai nudged her chin up to look into her eyes. "I have travelled the world over a dozen times not knowing what I was searching for. Until I met you. I found the other part of my soul when I first kissed you. I can tell you I love you every minute of the day if it convinces you that this, us, is meant to be.

"Jazz had a vision of you where she warned me to beware the kiss of death, and while you did not kill me, your kiss brought me back to life. Though my heart did beat, I did not truly feel it until I met you."

Keeva made to answer when the door burst open and Jazz looked panicked. "Dylan is drunk and won't listen to reason. You know he doesn't listen to me. Oh my God, are you guys back from holidays yet?"

Keeva laughed as Jazz swept like a hurricane from the

room. Malakai brushed his lips over hers, resting his forehead on hers as he said, "One last drama before we run away."

Taking her hand, Malakai hurried down the stairs before they headed back up to the VIP area. Jazz was back at the DJ booth, glaring at Dylan, who was dancing like an idiot, his eyes glazed over. Malakai let go of Keeva's hand to lean in to him. Dylan rolled his eyes, gave Kai a gentle shove, and then he grabbed Keeva and twirled her around.

"Dance with me, Keeva!"

Keeva let him whirl her around for a few minutes before she slipped from his grasp, earning a frown from the vampire. Keeva went to Malakai, quirked her head toward Dylan. "What's up with him?"

Malakai leaned down so that his words were whispered into her ear. "You know Dylan can feel emotions, but when he wants to, he can let himself be overcome with the feelings of others. So now, he is as drunk as everyone in the room. It's not the first time."

Keeva laughed as Malakai tried to give a nonchalant shrug of his shoulders, even though Keeva could see him itching to go and control the situation. She nudged him with her elbow.

"You won't be able to rest until you make sure he's okay. Go, or you'll spend the entire trip checking in with him, and I have plans for you, Malakai Cavanagh."

Malakai moved stealthily away from her. He threw an arm around Dylan's shoulder and ran his knuckles over Dylan's skull. Dylan laughed, ducking out of his grasp and playfully shoving Malakai. The brothers jostled each other as Keeva rolled her eyes but had the biggest smile on her face.

Scarlett came to stand beside her, linking her arm in hers. "You look so happy."

"I am. Ivan just told me I was free for reals and gave me a hell of a lot of money."

Scarlett jumped up and down, clapping her hands. "Oh

my God, Keeva, you're finally free. Officially. This is so exciting."

Keeva knew her friend was genuinely happy for her, so Keeva turned to face her. "You absolutely sure that you will be okay with the hulk?"

Scarlett rolled her eyes and gently smacked her. "I'll be fine. He's a big teddy bear, really."

Keeva ignored the blush that crept up Scarlett's face as she flashed her a sceptical look. "I do not think there is another person in the world who would describe Ezekiel Collins as a teddy bear."

Dylan seemed to have calmed himself down, was now sitting in beside the aforementioned teddy bear, and the two of them were engaged in a conversation about some sport.

Malakai wrapped his arms around her as she spent a little time chatting to Scarlett, content to simply stand beside her, until he whispered in her ear and asked if she was ready to go. She gave Scarlett a massive hug as Malakai went to say goodbye to his family in case they had already left for the plane by the time they woke.

Before Keeva let go of Scarlett, she held her friend's face in her hands and let a serious expression fill her face. "Scarlett Russell, I am going to miss the hell out of you. Promise me if you get the chance, you'll let the teddy bear break your headboard."

"Keeva!" Scarlett exclaimed as her face flamed, and Keeva darted away with a grin as she left Scarlett standing there dumbfounded. Malakai raised his brow in question, and when Keeva told him what she had said, Malakai convulsed laughing, the expression lighting up his entire face.

Man, she really had it bad.

They didn't get much sleep that day, for various reasons, and it wasn't long before Keeva was sitting beside Malakai in a small little plane, her legs bouncing in excitement as they took off on the start of their holiday together, her fingers entwined in Malakai's as Keeva stared out the window to soak in all of the wonderment because she didn't want to miss a thing.

They had spent three weeks of adventure traveling round Denmark, Norway and Sweden, the snow falling thick and fast as they travelled. Malakai lavished her with time and attention, until one day, when he seemed distracted and kept looking at his phone.

Keeva wondered if he had enough of her then, if he was bored of travelling and wanted to return home. Even when he surprised her with a gorgeous candlelight dinner on the deck of their cabin, Keeva was starting to worry something was wrong.

"I was thinking, Kai, maybe we should head home. I know its hard being away from everything so we can go, if you want."

Keeva clamped her mouth shut, her eyes drifting to the northern lights above her as she wondered if now that the danger was past if Malakai was bored of her.

"Keeva."

For a minute, Keeva didn't turn at the sound of her name on his lips, his tone even but then she glanced to where Malakai has been sitting to see that he was not there.

Instead, he was down on one knee, a diamond the size of a small island in his hand.

"The past three weeks have been amazing and have confirmed to me that I want to spent the rest of my life with you. I was not expecting you, Keeva Cross but now that I have found you, I never want to let you go. I want you as part of our family, my family. Will you marry me?"

For a moment, Keeva was rooted to the spot before she launched off the chair and into his arms, knocking him to the ground as he chuckled, her kiss the only answer he needed to know that she would indeed marry him.

Vindicta

STANDING on the rooftop across from Sicarius Security, Vindicta let the tails of his hooded cloak billow out as he tried to get a glimpse of the vampires as they entered the building. He could make out the bulky frame of Ezekiel, the cocky gait of Dylan as he walked backwards, and Jasmine, who all but skipped toward the building, the werewolf and the succubus trailing after the vampires.

Malakai had indeed built his impenetrable fortress to guard his princes and princess. His work was indeed something to marvel at, however, all good things could come to an end, and the end was almost upon them.

"Sir."

Vindicta did not even spare his assassin a glance as he lifted his hand, motioning for her to speak.

"Malakai left the country this night with the banshee. I believe he intends to be away for some time. He has left the others in charge."

He never expected Malakai to simply walk away and leave his kin for the taking. These were not unseasoned warriors, and though Malakai treated them like children, he had seen first-hand how vicious and fierce they could be.

His little pet trailed beside him; her blue hair swept in the wind, revealing the pointed curve of her heritage, her soft footfalls the only sound in the moonlight.

"What would you have me do, sir?"

He ran his eyes along the building, motioning for her to nock her bow, which she did without question, letting the arrow glide through the air. He stepped back off the ledge and moved away from the building but could not stop himself from glancing toward where the succubus screamed as Dylan went to his knees.

"What would you have me do now?"

Always eager to please. He simply shook his head. "Nothing. Let

*them think that the danger has passed. Malakai must have consid-
ered my declaration was not serious enough if he could swan off to
another country. Let them be comfortable. Let them lower their
guard."*

"And what will we do then, sir?"

*Even though she could not see it under the mask of his clothing,
he smiled a sinister smile, making a clear statement. "We kill them.
We kill them all."*

*The city would bathe in blood, and he would be the one to
spill it.*

Vengeance would be his.

*The Sicarius Security series
continues with*

LEAP OF FAITH

SICARIUS SECURITY BOOK 2

SUSAN HARRIS

sicarius
security

PLAYLISTS

Malakai

1. Futuristic - Epiphany (feat. NF
2. Harry Styles - Watermelon Sugar
3. Pulled Apart by Horses - The Big What If
4. Falling in Reverse - Popular Monster
5. Crobot – Gasoline
6. DIAMANTE – Iris
7. Palaye Royale – Anxiety
8. YUNGBLUD - strawberry lipstick
9. Justin Timberlake - What Goes Around.../...Comes Around (Interlude
10. Bush - The Kingdom
11. Architects - Royal Beggars
12. Bring Me the Horizon – Doomed
13. Marilyn Manson - If I Was Your Vampire
14. HIM - Vampire Heart
15. I Am Ghost - Pretty People Never Lie, Vampires Really Never Die
16. HIM - When Love and Death Embrace
17. Kill Hannah - Lips Like Morphine
18. Queens of the Stone Age - The Vampyre of Time and Memory
19. The Wombats - Tokyo (Vampires & Wolves)
20. Arctic Monkeys - Perhaps Vampires Is A Bit Strong But...
21. Jaymes Young - What Is Love
22. Skillet – Comatose
23. Post Malone – Otherside

24. Creeper - Be My End
25. Don Diablo – Bad
26. Anavae – Human
27. Caught A Ghost - Can't Let Go
28. Three Days Grace - Somebody That I Used to Know
29. Moby - Extreme Ways
30. Fink - Looking Too Closely
31. Jarryd James - Do You Remember
32. Ozzy Osbourne - Straight to Hell
33. Madalen Duke - Born Alone Die Alone
34. Everything Everything - Violent Sun
35. Paper Route - Wish
36. Two Door Cinema Club - Are We Ready? (Wreck)
37. Nothing but Thieves - Real Love Song - Alternative Version
38. Chase & Status - All Goes Wrong
39. Neoni - Bloodstream
40. Foals - Inhaler - Tom Vek's Wheezemix
41. Mike Shinoda - About You (feat. blackbear)
42. Mike Shinoda - Running from My Shadow (feat. grandson)
43. blackbear - lil bit
44. Normandie - Jericho
45. Chris Cornell – Patience
46. grandson – Darkside
47. Hugo - 99 Problems
48. Damien Rice - 9 Crimes
49. The Hipster Orchestra - Seven Nation Army
50. Korn - The Devil Went Down to Georgia

Keeva

1. The Hunna - I Wanna Know
2. Juice WRLD - Life's A Mess (feat. Halsey)
3. Foals - White Onions
4. Highly Suspect – Canals
5. Slaves - Talk to a Friend
6. From Ashes to New – Panic
7. The Violent - Fly on the Wall
8. grandson – Identity
9. blackbear - i feel bad
10. Fitz and The Tantrums - I Just Wanna Shine
11. Ozzy Osbourne - No More Tears
12. Pennywise - Fuck Authority
13. Frank Carter & The Rattlesnakes – Fire
14. WARGASM (UK) - Spit.
15. Bring Me the Horizon - Parasite Eve
16. Bring Me the Horizon - Can You Feel My Heart
17. Fall Out Boy - A Little Less Sixteen Candles, A Little More "Touch Me"
18. I Am Ghost - So, I Guess This Is Goodbye
19. Peter Gundry - Bury My Heart
20. Yelawolf - Pop the Trunk
21. My Chemical Romance - I'm Not Okay (I Promise)
22. The Seige - Run for Your Life
23. Panic! At the Disco - Don't Threaten Me with a Good Time
24. Billie Eilish - when the party's over
25. Wicked Crew - I'm Not That Girl
26. Doja Cat - Boss Bitch
27. Ellie Goulding - Worry About Me (feat. blackbear)
28. All Time Low - Monsters (feat. blackbear)
29. Anavae - Afraid (In Isolation)
30. N.E.R.D - She Wants to Move
31. Paramore - Ignorance - Acoustic

32. Bring Me the Horizon - Fuck (feat. Josh Franceschi)
33. Billie Eilish - my future
34. grandson - Riptide
35. Foals - On the Luna
36. Sam Fender - That Sound
37. Bea Miller - it's not u it's me
38. Marmozets - Play
39. Wrabel - Bloodstain
40. Folly Rae – Sniper
41. Rihanna – Consideration
42. Halsey - Graveyard
43. Tommee Profitt - Who's Gonna Stop Me
44. You Me at Six – MAKEMEFEELALIVE
45. Phlotilla - Going Down Fighting
46. Pearl Jam - Jeremy
47. Nirvana - Smells Like Teen Spirit
48. Disclosure - Watch Your Step
49. Nothing but Thieves – Unperson
50. Annie Murphy - A Little Bit Alexis (From Schitt's Creek)

ACKNOWLEDGMENTS

My parents,
Thank you for all that you do for me. I love you guys very much.

LJ and Taylor,
I love you both to infinity and beyond!

Melanie Newton,
My soul sister. Thank you for your never-ending support and friendship. Your drive and determination is infectious, and you make me want to also strive to do more…even if you make me fact check weird stuff in books that no one else would pick up on!

Ritchie Connor from Primal Ink Tattoo,
Thank you so much for designing the logos for Sicarius Security and Dante's!
I've proudly worn your art on my skin for years and now, readers get to see those skills with the artwork you created.
An amazing artist, person, and friend.
Thank you so so much!

Emily Newton for fact checking my Latin! You are gonna change the world one day soon, and I can't wait to see you do it!

To Melanie's Musers Fam- You guys are the best and such a supportive bunch!

Thank you to all the readers,
whether this is your first book by me or you've been with me
for years! I only get to do this because of you and I am
eternally grateful to each and every one of you who took a
chance on this Irish author.

*And finally, none of this would be possible without an amazing
team supporting me!*

Many thanks to my amazing team:

Publishing House: CTP Publishing
Cover design: Marya Heidel
Interior Formating: Gem Promotions
Editor: Chris Kridler
Proofs: Ashley Brilinski

ABOUT THE AUTHOR

Susan Harris is a writer from Cork, Ireland and when she's not torturing her readers with heart-wrenching plot twists or killer cliffhangers, she's probably getting some new book related ink, binging her latest TV or music obsession, or with her nose in a book.

Susan LOVES connecting with her fans!
www.susanharrisauthor.com

www.ingramcontent.com/pod-product-compliance
Lightning Source LLC
Chambersburg PA
CBHW022204170626
46807CB00005B/2345